We can judge the heart of a man
by his treatment of animals.

—Immanuel Kant
German Philosopher
1724 - 1804

# Hiss, Whine & Start Over

Jane Caryl Mahlow, DVM

Cuppa Press

Bartlett, Texas USA

Hiss, Whine & Start Over

Copyright © 2006 by Jane Caryl Mahlow

Inquiries should be addressed to
Cuppa Press
17181 FM 487, Bartlett, Texas 76511
www.hisswhine.com

First Printing 2006

Cataloging in Publication Data
Mahlow, Jane Caryl
Hiss, Whine & Start Over/Jane Caryl Mahlow—1st  ed Cuppa Press
p.      cm.
ISBN-13:  978-0-9776456-1-9
ISBN-10:  0-9776456-1-4
1. Animal shelters—Fiction. 2. Animal Welfare—Fiction. I. Title.
PS 3601 H7838      813.54 Ma      2006920767

Grateful acknowledgement is made to the following:

Excerpt from "The River" by Anthony de Mello from *Wellsprings:A Book of Spritual Exercises* Copyright © 1984 by Doubleday & Company, Inc. Originally Published in India by Gujarat Sahitya Prakash. Reprinted by permission of Doubleday & Company, Inc.
The American Humane Association for the reference to their T-shirt "Who says neutered dogs have no balls?"
The Texas Humane Legislation Network for the reference to their T-shirt "Texas. It's their state too"

Printed in the Unites States of America
At Morgan Printing in Austin, Texas

## Dedication

This book is dedicated to the men and women who have made a difference in the way humanity treats the creatures with whom it shares this planet.

## Notes to the reader

Enjoy this fictional story. It is based on values and principles, not real people or circumstances.

Any mention of name brands does not serve as an endorsement.

This book is sold on the understanding that neither the author nor the publisher are providing legal, managerial, or other professional advice.

# PART I

Men have forgotten this truth, but you must not forget it. You become responsible, forever, for what you have tamed.

from Antoine de Saint-Exupéry's
*The Little Prince*

# Part I

# Prologue

W as there anything better than a tummy rub? Doubtful. Unless it was going for a walk and chasing smells in the neighbors' yards. But that rarely happened anymore. Percy seldom ventured further than the backyard. Which was all right with him. Just getting out of the house was a treat. Especially on days like today when the sun defrosted his bones.

When Mrs. Bethke's toe finished scratching his belly, Percy flopped onto his side and rested his muzzle on her shoe. His ear twitched away a fly that had been fooled into thinking it was still summer.

Life was good. Sure, it was slower than it used to be. Lickety-split dashes across the yard and flying leaps onto the couch—those were all things of the past. But some things never changed, like sneaking a catnap under the pecan tree. While Mrs. Bethke sat on the glider, muffled noises coming from her slack mouth, Percy stretched out on the sweet-scented grass beneath her.

Today's naptime ended as it always did with Mrs. Bethke pushing herself off the seat, her knees creaking in synchrony with the joints of the wooden glider. Percy rolled upright, ears at full alert. His tongue swiped his nose while he looked expectantly at her. She delivered the much-awaited line.

"Ready for your frankfurter?"

There had been a time during the far distant past when the promise of a wiener triggered circus dog tricks. But not any more. Nowadays, his routine was to pause at the bottom of the back porch and lift his eyes to hers. Built like an overstuffed hotdog himself, he sometimes had trouble maneuvering the three steps, particularly when his joints were stiff. With unvarying predictability, Mrs. Bethke slowly bowed her back. While her knobby fingers clutched the railing, her other hand cupped the underside of his chest to give his stubby legs a boost. Together, they took the stairs one halting step at a time.

"My little Persimmon, just a hair bigger than a breadbox," Mrs. Bethke liked to say about him.

That was another thing that was timeless—how good Mrs. Bethke made him feel.

### # # #

But the dependable orderliness disappeared the day Mrs. Bethke fell to the floor. Amidst a big commotion, two people whisked her away on a stretcher. Into the house moved a person considerably larger than Mrs. Bethke and with a much gruffer voice. A plastic doghouse was placed under the pecan tree. Percy's neck felt the unfamiliar weight of a chain. In a complete break with anything he had ever known, he was left outside, not only all day but all night as well.

Once a day, kibble was dumped in Percy's bowl. He used the opportunity to nuzzle the person's hand. Maybe he'd get a pat on the head or, better yet, taken inside the house. But time and again, Percy was pushed aside until he stopped trying.

A blast of winter slapped autumn out of its way. Percy's bucket of water turned into a solid block of ice. For two days, he curled into a ball in the corner of the doghouse and plumped out his wiry hair, but he couldn't get warm. The relentless ache deep inside his joints made sleep impossible.

When the cold snap ended, Percy peered from the opening of the doghouse, his chin on his paws, his gaze fixed in perplexed loneliness on the back door. Certainly she would appear, gripping the railing as she eased down the steps one by one. But the door remained closed and the porch empty.

*W* *ho says neutered dogs have no balls?*

*W* Something about the words across Darrell's chest just didn't fit in with the spirit of Christmas Day.

Let's face facts. The problem wasn't the brash words above the picture of a militant, double-muscled pit bull. Actually, the T-shirt's message to neuter pets was both clever and admirable.

The real problem was that, effective twenty-four hours ago, Carly was in charge of the Humane Society, whether she wanted to be or not. So if any employee counseling were needed, the odious task would fall squarely in her lap.

Her stomach roiled at the thought of having to reprimand Darrell. Or any employee for that matter. Should she pull Darrell aside and explain that although the T-shirt's words might sound right at home in a hockey rink, they were unsuitable for a place of business? Naw. She shooed away the idea like a cow's tail whisked away pesky flies. If and when he wore the T-shirt on a day the shelter was open to the public, then a little one-on-one talk would be in order.

Carly, Darrell, and Penny were the three employees who signed up for December 25th pooper-scooper duty. Carly volunteered because, well, why not? Her parents were still living on the farm in Iowa. Her ex-husband was still—as far as she knew—living with Jocelyn. Her cats were still curled up in front of last night's Yule log. Besides, she'd taken care of patients and boarders for eight Christmas mornings at her former job at Doc Griffin's veterinary hospital. It just didn't seem like Christmas without soupy turkey and giblets spilling from a pull-top can and bright eyes looking for a scratch under the chin.

Speaking of scratches under the chin, Carly detoured to run #15 before starting her Christmas cleaning, feeding, watering, and walking.

Hailey
Female. 2 years old
Great with kids, cats, & other dogs

Carly went in the run and squatted next to the large dog. "How's my pretty girl today?"

Truth be told, Hailey wasn't all that pretty. The russet and black dog was undoubtedly nothing more than the upshot of a chance encounter between two long bloodlines of commonplace mutts.

"Guess what," Carly told the dog. "I got an early Christmas present yesterday. A big promotion!"

Hailey cocked her head attentively and waited for more.

Carly leaned closer and whispered, "Don't tell anyone, but I'm as scared as a beetle in a chicken yard, as my dad likes to say."

She removed a brush from her pocket and coursed the bristles through the dog's thick hair. Hailey's eyes half closed, and Carly could tell their chick chat had taken a back seat to the delectable tingles of the brush. So Carly's recap of yesterday's events was confined to her own head, just like the previous twenty-five replays.

Hugh, the boss at the Zhirnov Springs Humane Society, had called her into his office to inform her that he would be taking an extended leave of absence. Hugh was sixty-something and normally had the kindly face and quiet deportment of a golden retriever. But yesterday he looked ninety-something and at the end of his rope. Wedged between the trenches of age, worry, and exhaustion was a patch of silver that had eluded his razor.

Small wonder Hugh was sagging with fatigue. His wife had a stroke a couple weeks ago, and he was running ragged between work and the hospital. Now that his wife was coming home, she needed someone with her 24/7. Plus Hugh's son and daughter-in-law were counting on him for help with their young daughter while they grappled with their son's newly diagnosed leukemia.

Carly almost fell off the orange, hand-me-down cafeteria chair when Hugh proposed she fill his shoes while he was on leave. A slew of thoughts leapfrogged over one another. What flight of fancy was this man on? Didn't he realize she had neither the knowledge nor the skills to do the job? When Hugh's finger had gone down the list of employees, why in the world had it stopped beside her name?

Carly did a high-speed assessment of the strengths and weaknesses of her nine coworkers and came up with weaknesses weighing in on the heavy side. None had the qualifications to run the place. They were all worker bees, drudges like herself.

Drudge. What an image that conjured up—her at age sixty-five, stooped-backed from thirty-three years of scrubbing dirty litter boxes. Thirty-three. The exact number of years she already stumbled through life. What would it be like to be an old maid living hand-to-mouth in a dilapidated house plastered with "Condemned" signs?

Unless she made some changes, that's exactly where she was headed. Eddie was no longer around to make her financial ends meet. She was barely scraping by from one skimpy paycheck to the next. Squirreling away money for retirement was a pipedream. Not a single day passed that she didn't yearn for a good-paying job, but so far, her wishy-washy wants had gotten her nowhere. Which was hardly surprising. Her vision of the future was so blurry, she didn't have a clue where she was going.

When Carly responded to Hugh's proposal with nothing but a mute, saucer-eyed stare, he informed her that her salary would be increased by half while she was acting in his stead. And he dropped more glad tidings— the Humane Society would foot the bill for her cell phone.

On the outside, she sat stock-still like a pointer waiting to be released from the stay command. But inside, her thoughts whirled like a West Texas dust devil.

Interim Executive Director. She could already picture the words on her resume. Next, her mind's eye penciled the temporary raise into her checkbook. Then she considered how being the queen bee would put her in a position to make a real difference for the animals, an inner ache she'd had since she was a kid bringing home strays. All she had to do was say, "I'll do it." But instead, she responded with the humble reflexes that had been bred into her.

"But Hugh, I'm not qualified. I'm just an Animal Caretaker. And I've only worked here a year."

"You've been here longer than half the other staff."

True. Most shelter employees were quick to find other jobs that didn't involve stinky litter boxes and surly canine teeth. "But I really think you're barking up the wrong tr—"

Hugh interrupted her self-deprecation. "You've got what it takes to do a great job."

*You've got what it takes.* Wow! Talk about an ego boost.

Her parents had instilled in her that humility was the foundation of all other virtues. Her ex-husband, on the other hand, questioned the likelihood of the meek inheriting anything, especially the earth. As loath as she was to admit that Eddie was right about something, she ceded this point. She knew firsthand how the hobgoblins of self-doubt and fear of failure paved the way for self-defeat. Boy, did she know. So how could she pass up this opportunity? Not only could she accomplish something really worthwhile for the animals but she could also jumpstart her career.

So yesterday, while Santa was hitching up his reindeer, Carly took over the reigns of the Zhirnov Springs Humane Society.

Carly gave Hailey a body-length stroke of the brush. "I don't care what Hugh thinks." Her hand holding the brush fell limp to her lap. "I just don't think I've got what it takes."

Hailey opened her eyes and angled her head at Carly.

"I know, I know. I worry too much." Carly resumed brushing the dog. "It's a great chance for me to start over. Just like you need a chance to start over." Carly ran the bristles through the black hair that formed a necklace on Hailey. "Don't worry. Somebody will give you a good home real soon. I promise. Listen, I gotta go. I may be the Executive Director, but right now I have cages to clean. See you tomorrow."

What Carly didn't disclose to Hailey was that dogs like her were hard to place in homes She lacked the cuteness of a puppy. She in no way resembled a purebred. She was too big for an apartment and bordered on being too large for a backyard. And her thick, medium-length hair shed like crazy.

Like most of the employees, Carly made certain she was emotionally landlocked while she was on the job. Otherwise, the endless stream of animals and their tragic tales would tear her to pieces. But every once in a while, one of the animals would worm its way into her heart. This run-of-the-mill mongrel, with her docile eyes and eagerness to please, was one of those unintended few.

As Carly walked down the aisle between the double rows of yapping, jumping dogs, she glanced back at run #15. Hailey's gaze was locked on Carly. Her tail coursed back and forth in quiet expectation.

Carly set her jaw. Hugh would be on leave six months, give or take a month or two in either direction. During that time, come hell or high water, she was going to make a difference for the animals that found themselves in this place. Not that Hugh wasn't doing a great job. But there was so much more that could be done to improve the 1-in-4 odds that an animal leaving the shelter would go to a new home rather than the landfill.

And in those moments when she wasn't leading the shelter to new heights of accomplishment, she'd deal with Darrell's No-Balls T-shirt.

Just as Carly was about to exert a little elbow grease on some dirty cages, a gust of wind blew pint-sized Penny through the back door of the kennel.

"Hey, man! Cool hair!" Penny funneled her hands so Darrell could hear her over the barking dogs, the clang of the stainless steel bowls, and the reverberating bong of rambunctious feet bouncing off chainlink.

Darrell bent his knees, seemingly so his hand could reach the top of his head. His palm skimmed the spiky tips. He had sheared off his ponytail in favor of a Mohawk. Dyed a Kris Kringle red, it was as festive as the stripe on a candy cane. "Seasonally awesome, huh?"

"Is it ever! Have some cookies to go with it." Penny extended a tin of green wreaths, her Christmas ornament earrings swinging with good cheer.

"Cool." Darrell clamped his incisors on the cookie. Frowning, he withdrew the wreath, held it up to the fluorescent light, and squinted at it. He thunked it against the cement block wall. A light bulb clicked on inside his nearly scalped noggin. "Awh, Penelope, you hoodwinked me again."

Penny gave her famous smile—dimpled cheeks with freckles scattered like cupcake sprinkles and white teeth that reached from dangling earring to dangling earring. "Third year in a row. I thought you'd have learned by now!" Baking Christmas biscuits for the shelter dogs was an annual tradition with her.

Penny volunteered for Christmas duty because at twenty-two, she was bereft of spouse, boyfriend, and mortgage. Her time, energy, and money were channeled toward helping those who couldn't help themselves. In addition to her work at the Humane Society, she was on the board of directors for the local wildlife rescue group. At one time or another, her apartment had served as a hospice for baby or injured bunnies, raccoons, opossums, armadillos, and a dozen different species of birds.

Carly couldn't come up with a reason why Darrell volunteered for Christmas duty. It certainly wasn't because of overtime holiday pay. The Humane Society paid the same wages 365 days a year. Carly suspected that the uniqueness of the date had merely slipped past Darrell and, since this was his regular workday, he came to the shelter as usual. Darrell seemed like a throwback to the early 1970s, but he wasn't old enough to have been a flower child. His age was an enigma. He had the naiveté of a child, the gauzy goatee of a teenager, and the heavy-lidded eyes of a thirty-year-old who'd downed too many magic mushrooms.

The three workers fanned out to separate parts of the shelter. Carly tackled the cat ward. Penny cleaned the puppy cages, doling out her dog biscuits as she went. Darrell plugged in a decades-old boombox and hosed out the dog runs, pushing the squeegee toward the floor drain in loose-jointed rhythm with "Rocking Around the Christmas Tree," à la heavy metal.

For the next couple of hours, Carly was treated to selections of what Darrell called "alternative holiday music." An acoustic rumba version of "O Tannenbaum." "Here Comes Santa Claus" performed on a South American woodpipe. And a choral ensemble that, unless Carly's ears were deceiving her, sounded like "A Buck Naked Christmas."

Over her shoulder, Carly hoisted a red- and white-striped plastic bag filled with soiled newspaper, used kitty litter, and dirty paper towels. She weaved her way through the mountainous holiday donations of dog food and kitty litter to the rear door, where she tossed the sack into the dumpster. It landed on a pile of other trash bags, all of which also had red diagonal stripes. The composite picture had the look of herringbone gone awry.

The candy cane bags were a well-meaning gesture by the wealthiest member of the volunteer Board of Directors, Sophia Zhirnov. Carly thought the eccentric matron was the penultimate example of having more time and money than sense. Here was the perfect case in point. In a firm belief that a cheerful holiday decor would boost not only employee morale but adoptions as well, Sophia Zhirnov had scoured the Internet until she found white bags with red stripes. She purchased several dozen cartons at her own expense, asserting that the bags added an unexpected seasonal atmosphere to the shelter's trashcans.

The problem was that the well-intentioned woman hadn't considered the indelicacy of candy cane sacks doubling as body bags. After an animal was euthanized, it was put in a trash sack and placed in the walk-in freezer. Sophia Zhirnov's generosity gave rise to a freezer stacked with scores of candy canes of various sizes and shapes. Some of the sacks were tiny, containing only a cat. Others bulged with dead chows and shepherds. The result was a grisly juxtaposition of festive body bags and dead animals.

Carly took one of the trash sacks to Hugh's office for her last remaining task of Christmas Day. She was greeted by a wild shriek.

The Panama Amazon parrot came into the shelter last spring as a cruelty case. It was one of forty-two parrots, parakeets, and finches seized from a man who avidly collected birds but rarely fed them. Hugh took a liking to the parrot and turned it into a sort of shelter mascot. The dark green bird was already answering to its new name when the vet informed Hugh that Mary Louise was a male.

Mary Louise's claim to fame was his penchant for singing tunes that dealt with sunshine. The parrot was particularly fond of time-honored favorites such as "You Are My Sunshine." Today, while Carly swept up his Christmas droppings, she was regaled with a spunky 1940s' classic.

♪ *Plenty of sunshine headed my way.*
*Zip a dee doo-dah, zip a dee ay.* ♪

Carly actually had a ulterior motive for coming to Hugh's office. She wanted to ponder a little interior decorating. Not an extreme makeover, mind you. Just some personal touches here and there to make the room less Minimalist Utilitarian.

She reached in the bottom desk drawer where she had already stashed a bag of comfort food. As she munched on some Cheetos, she contemplated her new surroundings. Her brass lamp would add a warm sparkle to that corner of the desk. And a throw rug between the desk and the two visitors' chairs might add a homey feel. On second thought, nothing would improve the looks of those orange chairs, both so old that the stippling in the molded plastic seats was rubbed smooth.

Let's see. Her landscape print by Dalhart Windberg would look good on the far wall. A photo of her husband would fit nicely on the bookshelf—if she had a husband. And that other wall would benefit from a framed college diploma—not that she had one of those either.

Three years ago, Carly found Eddie under the mistletoe warming his hand beneath the neighbor's sweater. Through a tearful holiday season, Carly listened to Eddie's apologetic tale about how, after a decade of marriage, he had fallen out of love with Carly and in love with Jocelyn, supposedly in that order. Eddie moved out, and Carly clung to the hope that he'd eventually come home with his tail between his legs. The following May, she was handed divorce papers.

She and Eddie Chevalier had met at the University of Iowa when she was a freshman and he was a junior. He had all the reckless, irrepressible fervor for life that her conservative upbringing had disallowed her. A quick thumbing of their respective high school yearbooks spoke volumes. In addition to the assorted photographs of him on the football field, wrestling mat, and tennis court, the golden boy was the star attraction in the shots of the Student Council and the Drama Club. Beneath Carly's name was her curriculum vitae: National Honor Society, 4-H Club, and Refreshment Booth Booster Club. While Eddie was stretching for the finish line, Carly was still sorting out the rules of the game.

It seemed only natural that she, lacking a clear-cut career plan, trade a murky future for a more vivid one with Eddie. So as a starry-eyed twenty-year-old, she dropped out of college and supported her new husband through law school.

Eddie obtained a position with Agri-Cuts, a Fortune 500 company headquartered in Minneapolis that produced frozen, refrigerated, and table-ready meats. No sooner was Eddie hired than the conglomerate sold off their animal production divisions. He was given the opportunity to continue his job with Pocahontas Farms smack dab in the middle of Texas.

Pocahontas Farms supplied state-of-the-art housing, feeding, and waste management systems to factory farmers who wanted to raise 100,000 newly hatched turkey poults into thirty-pound toms. Eddie's job was to write the contracts with the farmers, pursue litigation as needed, and keep the company out of hot water over issues like pollution of the aquifer and antibiotic residues in the meat. He grew to despise turkeys, going so far as to pelt the NBC peacock with dirty socks because it resembled a turkey in full strut. He refused to eat turkey, even on Thanksgiving and Christmas. Anything with the slightest flavor of the all-American bird—gravy, dressing, potpie, casserole, salad, soup, sandwich, a la king—was considered as toxic as Chernobyl's fall-out zone.

Carly's mind wandered to what and where the son-of-a-bitch was eating today. Was he visiting his parents in Iowa? Or were he and Jocelyn spending the holiday with her family, wherever that might be? Or were they at home, pulling the cork on a bottle of wine to have with their ham dinner?

"Don't be such a masochist!" Carly gave herself a tongue-lashing before addressing Mary Louise. "Do you want me to cover your cage or not? Whichever you prefer." After slipping the bird a raisin but receiving no discernible response except a fanned tailed and fluffed neck feathers, Carly left the cage uncovered.

Her eyes swept her new office one last time. She promised herself that from this room she'd launch her new career. At that rickety desk with its chipped Formica top, she'd toil and labor and surmount all obstacles in order to alter society's disregard for the animals it domesticated.

Back in the kennel, she found Darrell looping his arm around his Mohawk. A hand-knitted scarf with 1960s' peace symbols circled his neck like the coiled tail of a pug dog.

"So, Darrell, are you signed up to work New Year's Day with me?" Penny asked.

As he reached behind his head, Darrell lost his grip on the long end of his scarf. He tried to snatch it by circling about like a dog chasing its tail. "New Year's Day? Like the day after New Year's Eve?"

"What do you plan to do with your hair to welcome in the new year?" Penny asked him.

"Gold Glitter. Just a dusting on top." He stopped spinning and dropped his head forward to give her imagination full advantage of the top of his dome. "Tell me, too slick or what?"

"Slicker than snot on a door knob," Penny replied.

Darrell's eyes went big. "Now there's an expression I haven't heard in years!" He silently mouthed the words as if recommitting them to a memory that had somehow misplaced them during life's magic carpet ride.

He gave the end of his scarf a final, jaunty flip. "As they say in Hawaii, *Mele Kalikimaka!*"

"Merry Christmas to you, too!" the two women called as the scarf's fringe disappeared just before the door closed.

"Time to call it a day here, Penny," Carly said. "What do you have planned for the rest of the afternoon?"

"I thought I'd take Hailey to the nursing home."

"Today? It's Christmas."

Penny's glance at Carly insinuated *That's the point*, but she merely replied, "There's a lot of people with nowhere to go and no one to visit them."

Penny's soft response made Carly feel lower than a snake's belly.

A close second in Penny's heart to the animals were the elderly. On her own time, she took shelter dogs to the Legacy Care Center. The bed-ridden and wheelchair-bound residents loved Penny. She was as pretty, petite, and perky as a Mouseketeer. The seniors loved to love on her as much as they enjoyed hugging the dogs.

A pounding on the back door somehow permeated the barking that reverberated off the open rafters of the metal roof. Carly assumed it was some disgruntled dog owner whose animal had been impounded for running loose. People were forever showing up at odd hours to reclaim their pets.

While Penny answered the door, Carly made a final round of the kennel to make sure everything was in order. She heard an angry, masculine voice but couldn't make out the words over the animals' racket. She went to the rear of the kennel to get her denim jacket. She heard the man again. This time the words were loud and clear.

"What do you mean? I thought I was doing a good deed and you're telling me you're going to put the dog to sleep!"

Something akin to a cement slab fell on Carly's chest. The breath went out of her. Her throat locked down, and she couldn't get any air. She was having an anaphylactic reaction to Eddie's voice.

Carly flattened herself commando-style against the cement block wall as she strained to hear the words. Eddie was irate over what he perceived to be Penny's lack of empathy for a hurt animal and his own selflessness for rescuing the dog. Heart hammering, emotions galloping, Carly pieced the story together. Eddie found a stray dog with a broken leg and brought the animal to the shelter, dirtying his clothes and his Lexus in the process. He was livid because Penny—in compliance with the Humane Society's policy of full disclosure—told him if they couldn't find the dog's owner, it would be euthanized.

Carly knew she should step up to the plate and handle the situation. She could put an immediate stop to the rudeness and save Penny from further battering. Carly took long, deep breaths and waited for her pulse to slow, which didn't happen. Why, she lamented silently, couldn't Eddie have shown up on a regular workday when she was wearing not only makeup but something other than patched jeans and a ratty flannel shirt? Her tongue ran over her teeth, searching for Cheetos remnants. If only she had time to comb her auburn mop. And put on lipstick. And run away.

She rounded the corner and gave Eddie a cool nod. Beside him was a thin lab mix, standing on three legs and panting nervously. No collar. No tags.

Eddie's baby blues grew to the size of goose eggs. "Carly?"

"Hello, Eddie." She hoped the thumping of her jugular vein would slide past him unnoticed.

"What are you doing here?"

"I work here. Why don't you come to my office and we'll talk about this. Meanwhile, Penny will make the dog as comfortable as possible."

While she held the door open for him between the kennel and the hallway, she sucked in her middle-aged stomach and threw out her adolescent chest. My, my, she thought as he edged past her. Doesn't he still look good, all six feet of him. He was still fit and trim, from what little she could tell beneath the leather jacket. His hair was shorter and possibly a little thinner on top than the last time she had seen him twenty-six—no, twenty-seven—months ago.

She went around to her side of Hugh's desk, embarrassed to have nothing to offer him except orange cafeteria chairs. He crossed an ankle over the opposite thigh and intertwined his fingers around the raised knee. No wedding ring, she was quick to note. So, he and Jocelyn hadn't tied the knot.

"I'm surprised to see you here, Eddie."

"Same here." His tone was polite but still agitated from his encounter with hard-hearted Penny.

"I thought you lived in Megalopolis."

"I recently moved back to Zhirnov Springs. Some changes in my life." The slight flutter of his head indicated the changes were insignificant and not worth his time to discuss them.

Ah ha! He and Jocelyn have split. Carly told herself not to jump to conclusions. Besides, she couldn't care less who he shacked-up with.

"So you found a dog?"

"I can't believe you people can't fix his leg and find him a new home."

"We're not a vet clinic, Eddie," she said with more than a hint of sarcasm. Stop it, she told herself. Derision will accomplish nothing good. "We'll do our best to locate the owner. We really will. But please under-stand, we simply don't have the funds to treat sick and injured animals. As much as we'd like to, we just can't."

He looked around the cramped office that wasn't much bigger than an animal control truck. "You the top dog here?" At his own pun, his firm jaw line broadened into a grin.

The grin hadn't changed. It was the same one she had found so irre-sistible. The one to which she had inevitably acquiesced, no matter what the disagreement.

"For the time being. The Executive Director is on extended leave. How about you?" Reams of questions went through her mind, but she asked only one. "Are you still with Pocahontas?"

"No, I couldn't take it any more. A couple of months ago, I opened my own practice in Zhirnov Springs. Completely remodeled one of those old buildings downtown." He pulled a business card from his wallet and slid it across the desk. "Fourteen-foot ceilings. Original beaded tongue-and-groove wainscoting. The kind of stuff you'd love. Maybe you'll stop by sometime?"

She ignored the business card and the half-proffered invitation. "So you left those poor turkeys without legal representation?"

"And not a minute too soon. I was having fantasies about Newcastle disease wiping out every one of the nasty suckers within 500 miles."

Mary Louise began dancing in circles, parrot body language for *I want some attention!* Carly sent a telepathic plea to the bird—this was not the time for sunshine music.

Eddie looked around the room again. "I knew you liked animals, but I never figured you'd work at a dog pound."

"Animal shelter."

"Oh, yeah, I guess this place isn't run by the city."

"Even if it were, the proper term is 'animal shelter.' Listen, I'm sorry we can't do more for that poor dog. I really am. It breaks our hearts, believe me."

"Yeah. I guess you guys do as much as you can. I probably shouldn't have been so tough on that girl."

"So if we can't find the dog's owner, maybe you'd like a new pooch to go with your new house and your new job?" She pulled her lips back, hoping it looked like a smile.

He acknowledged her attempt with a smile of his own. "Oh, no. I already have a dog."

"Oh?"

"Yeah, a Border collie."

"You *bought* a Border collie?" Irritation crept up her spine as she thought about how animal shelters euthanized thousands of good mixed breed dogs like Hailey. And what does Eddie do? Buys a purebred. What right did a French-Dutch-Swede have being persnickety about owning a single-ethnic pedigreed dog?

"I just sorta ended up with it."

Ahhh. Jocelyn left the dog with him when she vacated the picture.

He stared at his thumb pulsating like a piston against his knee. He broke the silence by asking about their cat. "You still have Yuri? How's my old fella doing?"

"Just fine. I added a second cat. Chamomile. Camey for short."

"Is that right?" He obviously didn't find "Chamomile" to be nearly as spirited a name as "Comrade Yuri Andreyevich Zhivago." "How's the old house? Still nailed together?"

"Pretty much. Needs a new roof. Plus I noticed a couple of the floor boards on the porch are rotten."

"Rotten boards? Haven't you kept it painted?"

"That's *exactly* what I was getting ready to do when I noticed the boards." Against her will, three years of bitterness squeaked out.

His eyes narrowed into question marks. "Hey, I didn't mean anything by the comment. I was just asking."

"And I'm just telling you that—"

"I'm sure you're keeping the place in good shape."

"Would you let me finish my own sentences for a change?"

He fell silent, the look in his eyes one of edgy tolerance.

"I'm just telling you," she enunciated each syllable, "that I'm doing the best I can."

He shifted his jaw to one side in thought. "Carly, listen. I'm really sorry things worked out the way they did for us. I really am. I wish...." His hand grasped his knee as he leaned slightly forward. "I wish things hadn't ended on such a sour note."

She acknowledged his words with a nod.

His eyebrows rose. "Maybe I could come over sometime and fix those boards for you?"

She strove for poker-faced-but-hospitable. "Sure. That would be really thoughtful of you."

"Say, you never came across my old coin collection, did you? I can't find it."

She shook her head.

"If you don't mind, maybe when I fix those boards, I could go through those boxes in the attic. Those coins have to be there."

"I've gone through all those boxes, but you're welcome to look."

The room was silent except for Mary Louise's footfalls as he strutted up and down his perch. Eddie lowered his leg so both feet were on the floor. Carly took it as a sign the reunion had reached its conclusion.

She stood, thrilled to beat him to the punch for once in their lives. "I don't mean to be rude, but I need to give Penny a hand in the kennel."

He rose to his feet. "Yeah, I need to get going. After dinner, I'm headed to the lake. Waterskiing."

"Waterskiing? On Christmas?" Her little finger dug in her ear like she was dredging out a word-muffling wad of wax.

"That's what's nice about Texas. The temperature's supposed to reach sixty today. With a wetsuit, no problem. You need to try it sometime."

Carly's jaw tightened. Wasn't that just like him to tell her what she needed to do?

"I took some great video last month of me skiing at sunset. The water was as smooth as a skating rink." His arm swept the horizon. "The sun was melting into the trees. Phenomenal!"

While Carly walked him to the lobby, she pondered how one takes a picture of oneself skiing?

After completing the admission form, she unlocked the main entrance. Using the horizontal metal bar, she held the glass door ajar for him to slip past her. He paused and looked down at her extended arm. He grasped the bar and drew the door closed. Her arm fell as limp as a rag doll's.

"How are you really, Carly? Is everything going all right for you?"

"Yeah. Everything's fine." He wanted more. He wanted her to open up and tell him what was really happening in her life. But she couldn't do it. She didn't have the emotional strength to let him into her world while at the same time keep him at a safe distance.

His eyes traveled her face. "Look, I know I don't deserve forgiveness. But I'd like to think that someday we might be friends again. You shared an important decade of my life. No matter how long I live, you'll always be a part of me."

Damn him, she thought. He always knew the right words to weasel into anyone's good graces.

"I hope you know that I'm here for you if you ever need anything." Eddie's eyes almost pleaded with her to believe him.

She lightened the conversation with, "Well, there's those boards on the porch…."

"Consider it done. I'll give you a call." He let himself out.

Back in Hugh's office, she closed the door and sagged against it. Talk about a blast from the past. He was still drop-dead handsome. Even more so as a mature man than when he had been young and raffish. And he still had that magnetic pull that his life offered more excitement, more rewards, than her own.

She mulled over their conversation. *You'll always be a part of me.* Skip that part. It was nothing more than empty, ingratiating words.

*Completely remodeled one of those old buildings downtown.* How totally in character for him. No strip center box for top-of-the-line Eddie.

*A Border collie.* She supposed she could forgive him for owning a purebred dog. Probably Jocelyn bought the dog, then turned her back on it when it was no longer convenient. As shallow people are prone to do.

So his latest sport was waterskiing. Oh, yeah. She could picture it. A waterfall of spray fanned out behind the slalom ski as Eddie's elbow skimmed the water on a hairpin turn.

The unsolicited image broadened. *Water smooth as a skating rink. Sun melting into the trees.* Uninvited though the image was, she took it a step further. The boat at anchor. The rhythmical lap of the waves. She and Eddie.... She quickly dropped the curtain on the scene.

Oh, Eddie, you are so dangerous.

Having that man in your life was like being a kid and soaring to perilous heights on a swing. You craved and feared that moment of weightlessness at the peak of the arc when your stomach rose to your throat and you knew the big rush was eminent. And while you were still breathless from the ride, you'd feel Eddie's hands push you again. This time harder. Higher. Faster.

*Maybe I could come over sometime.* What would she do if and when he did? Welcome him into the house they had shared? Forgive his trespasses and maybe he'd forgive hers?

Why was she falling victim to these conflicting emotions? She had been all set to hate him the rest of her life, and now look what happened over a span of twenty minutes. Why did that slithery, two-timing, wife-cheating piece-of-puke have such an effect on her?

♪ *Come rain or come shine.* ♪

She flung the blanket over Mary Louise's cage.

**4**

Carly tossed her purse on the couch. The air was still redolent with last night's cedar logs and bayberry potpourri. The cats hadn't moved from the hearthrug. Santa hadn't shown up to fill the lone stocking on the mantel.

She pulled the band from her ponytail and stabbed her fingers through the coils. It wasn't bad enough she had to endure the frizzies every rainy, foggy, or even damp day. Each morning, while the dog runs were being hosed down, the kennel became a drippy cloud that sprung her hair into orbit. For the rest of the day, she looked like an Angora goat with a bad perm.

She tapped the button on the answering machine.

"Hi, honey! It's Mom and Dad. Called to wish you Merry Christmas. Guess you're still at work. We'll try later."

Delete.

"Hey. It's Annalisa. Just wanted to remind you to stop by this afternoon."

Carly had promised her friend that she'd come over for a sliver of pecan pie and a piece, probably two, of fudge while Kaye and Crosby crooned their way through a white Christmas inside a high definition TV. Annalisa was married and opened her home to those less fortunate. Stopping by for a little holiday cheer throughout the day were widowers, grandmas whose loved ones lived half-way around the world, and college kids who couldn't get home for Christmas. And childless divorcées like Carly.

"Remember Walt from down the street?" Annalisa continued, cheerful as a chickadee. "Wanted to warn you he'll be here. He keeps circling like a buzzard—asking about you. See ya."

Delete.

Yes, Carly remembered Walt. A marshmallow of a man whose delight in life was fantasizing about trips to exotic places and then detailing his armchair travels to anyone who would listen. Carly's eyes wandered wistfully to the chenille afghan and the half-completed jigsaw puzzle. Wouldn't her gray flannel PJs feel great right about now? Maybe she'd just skip Annalisa's and stay home. No, she couldn't do that. She couldn't allow herself to become another Penny, who, as far as Carly knew, had no life outside of her job and her charity work.

After a steamy shower, she slipped on straight-out-of-the-package socks. New socks had that cushioned whisper-softness that caressed all the ticklish, fleshy, calloused, bony parts of the foot. The fleecy weave tempted her to put her feet up for a few minutes before she crunched the springy fibers into a pair of shoes and the downy nap got slicked down with toe jam.

She poured a self-pampering cup of chamomile tea. Camey opened one aquamarine eye and promptly closed it. Yuri displayed slightly more ambition by unfolding his legs and tail. Once all four feet were under him, he bowed his back like the St. Louis Arch and stretched fifteen hours of sleep out of his body. He made a dignified leap onto the windowsill to verbally threaten the lone cardinal that was pecking at sunflower seeds in the birdfeeder.

The cats' names, although lacking in tradition, were far from short in significance. Chamomile was as mellow and serene as Carly's favorite tea. Yuri Andreyevich Zhivago was named after the lead in her and Eddie's favorite movie. The video that tugged at their heartstrings. The love song that provided the background when he asked her to marry him.

She scooped up Chamomile, who was as flaccid as a well-used feather pillow, and eased into an overstuffed armchair. Her head dropped against her grandmother's crocheted doily. From under the awning of half-closed eyes, she looked at the satisfying clutter of her living room. Eddie let her keep most of the furniture. However, she made him take the bed. She couldn't bear to sleep on the mattress that bore the vestiges of a decade of tangled limbs and lives.

She and Eddie bought the mothballed house when they moved to Texas nine years ago. With dogged determination, they scrimped and saved. The mortgage was almost paid off when Eddie moved out. Thank goodness she got the house free and clear in the divorce settlement. Otherwise, there was no way she could afford to live on her income from the Humane Society.

Her eyes settled on the empty space next to the red and green Rudolph stocking. Her mother knitted the *Carly* and *Eddie* stockings when they became engaged. Although Eddie played the role of the dutiful husband

and joined in the Shannon clan holiday traditions, Carly sensed he cast a disparaging eye on the big kitchen table of mismatched china, the frayed throw rugs that offered feeble insulation against the cold wood floors, and the ceaseless parade of good cheer from her extended family.

Carly loved the beauty of the countryside when it was painted white, but Eddie was more at ease in the gray slush of the city. They spent their second Christmas at the Chevaliers' English Tudor where ankle-deep carpet stretched from baseboard to baseboard and a coat of arms—of all things—looked down on the heirloom dining table. After the five-course dinner, Eddie took ownership of the deep, brass-studded wing chair. While he flicked the remote to check the scores of the various bowl games, Carly was left to carry on a lethargic conversation with his mother.

After moving to Texas, they avoided the headaches of holiday travel by observing Christmas with Eddie's coworkers who were also displaced Yankees. Eddie agreed to commute forty minutes to Megalopolis so they could live in Zhirnov Springs, which a decade ago, boasted a hometown atmosphere. They purchased the two-bedroom, one-bath house in a neighborhood full of gnarled, hundred-year-old live oaks and neighbors who had lived there even longer. Although the longleaf pine floorboards were warped and closet space was nonexistent, Carly adored the old house and couldn't wait for the end of her workday at the vet clinic to come home to it and Eddie. Their plan had been to stay in the bungalow a few years, cash in the equity, and build a four-bedroom house wrapped with Texas limestone. They'd start their family in their bedroom inside the French doors off the upstairs balcony. They were finalizing the blueprints when Eddie found the mistletoe and Jocelyn's breasts simply too enticing.

Carly slid her thumb around the rim of her cup. All those young promises made. They were as dead as the candy-caned animals in the freezer.

She had done everything by the book. Put Eddie through law school. Kept her 150,000-mile Mazda running. Lived off coupons. Built up their savings. Waited to have children until they could afford them. Obliged Eddie's every wish.

And here she was—living alone, without an education, working at a job that barely paid her bills, and wondering why her house was as quiet as a tomb instead of alive with the shrieks of a child tearing into Christmas presents. That's what she got for following the rules.

All the rules except one.

No! She forbid her mind to hop down that bunny trail of self-blame again.

A door burst open and a screech filled the room. She wondered why she keep that noisy cuckoo clock? Nobody had cuckoo clocks anymore. She needed to a) have a garage sale, b) stop rehashing wilted dreams that should have been laid to rest three years ago, and c) make a phone call.

"Hi, Mom! Sorry I missed you earlier."

Her mother informed her that central Iowa was enjoying a white Christmas. Did Carly receive her package of homemade peanut brittle? Too bad it didn't turn out as good as usual, but it tasted okay, didn't it? Yes, they loved the Double Gooey Caramel Pecan Pralines she sent them.

"I was just leafing through the Burpee catalogue when you called. I think I'll try their Beefsteak Hybrid tomato this year. Although I hate to abandon Big Boy—it's always such a faithful producer. Here's your dad. He wants to say hello."

"Merry Christmas, Carly-girl!" her father greeted her with the nick-name he used since the days she was wrapped in a receiving blanket. His conversation didn't dwell on transitory holiday topics but leapt to more germane issues. In six short sentences, Carly found out that the government had reimbursed them for spraying for corn borers last summer and that the county had, at long last, blacktopped the old gravel Kerry Dairy Road. His voice deep with nostalgia, he told her that he had torn down the old farrowing pens. "Wasn't no point in keeping them. Can't make no money in hogs, not now that the big corporations have taken over."

When her mother got back on the line, Carly described her new, temporary position at work. Marge gushed her congratulations as though never in her wildest dreams had she expected such a lofty accomplishment from her lackluster middle child. Her volume faded as she held the phone away to share the prodigious news with her husband.

When her mother returned to the mouthpiece, she moved right along to the local gossip. Junior Swenson, Carly's old boyfriend, had bought another farm. "He's farming over 700 acres now. Maybe you should come home and give him another looksee."

Carly recoiled from the jab to her ribs. Why did Marge Shannon, the icon of motherhood, a dead ringer for June Cleaver, insist on inflicting those painful stabs? What was her motive this time?

Was her mother once again prodding with her dull paring knife—saying that in the nine years Carly had been in Texas, she'd never once been home for Christmas?

Or was she wielding the knife that had just sliced the turkey, trying to carve a new life for her daughter by coaxing her to start over in Iowa and perhaps she'd have better luck than she had with Eddie Chevalier?

Or was it her mother's sharp, clean-edged stainless steel knife—the one that was forged out of principles and moral values? The one that periodically ripped through the neatly tied ribbon that concealed it had been Carly's moment of impetuosity with Junior Swenson four years ago that had put the first gash in her marriage.

"I hope to get home this summer. Promise. Give my love to everyone."

M idway between Christmas and New Year's, Hugh stopped by the office with Alan Drake, the Chairman of the Humane Society's Board of Directors. Together, they charted Carly's first steps as interim Executive Director.

They felt her new job duties would keep her so busy, she should cancel her humane education visits to the second grade classrooms. Plus she should assign another employee to take over her orientations for new Humane Society volunteers.

Carly shifted in her chair. Find someone to take over the orientations? Like who?

Hugh told her that the Board of Directors met the last Tuesday of every other month at Alan's law office. Carly's attendance was required to answer any questions that might arise. Prior to the February meeting, the Board expected to have in their hands the annual summary—the number of animals sheltered, euthanized, adopted, and reclaimed by their owners, broken down by dogs, cats, and others. They also wanted a run-down on the sources of income—government contracts, fees, donations. Sophia Zhirnov, of candy cane trash bag fame, specifically requested that charts accompany the numbers. And not just any charts. She wanted "vibrant colors that shouted their message."

Carly decided not to tell Hugh that the sum total of her computer skills was basic word processing, e-mail, and Internet shopping.

Without pausing for breath, Hugh said she'd have to give his scheduled presentation on the Humane Society to the Zhirnov Springs Newcomers Club.

She thought it best not to mention that she was such a scaredy-cat about public speaking, she threw up during her high school speech class.

The final topic was the vacant Operations Manager position. After four years at the Humane Society, the previous Operations Manager, Amy Jo Pearson, cratered with severe burnout and went running for the hills of New Mexico to work with the Pueblo Indians. Carly had known from the get-go that had an Operations Manager been onboard, Hugh would have chosen that person to fill his shoes instead of being forced to dredge the bottom of the barrel.

"With the shelter short-staffed, you need to get that Manager position filled," Hugh said. "Revise the job description as needed. Come up with some interview questions."

Carly cocked her head. Huh? Her hiring experience had always been on the applicant's side of the desk.

Hugh apparently noticed she was a little green around the gills because he said, "Just call me, Carly, if you run into any problems. I'm only a phone call away." He spoke like he was comforting a dog dumped on the side of the road.

"Tell you what," the Board Chairman chipped in, stroking his salt-and-pepper moustache. "I'll stop by after the first of the year to see how you're doing. In the meantime, take a few days to organize your priorities, write down your questions, get your ducks in a row, so to speak." This coming from a man whose last name was Drake.

On January 2, Carly clicked opened the graphics software and puckered her brow at the mumbo jumbo on her monitor. Stymied, she abandoned the graphics program and tabbed over to the spreadsheet program. The blank page looked like a 400-pane mullion window. Carly's left hand dropped from the keyboard to her lap. Her right hand slipped to the comfort of the Cheetos drawer.

She yanked back the offending limb. Eddie's words, *I'll give you a call*, had sent her into serious diet mode. Of course, his casual phrase didn't necessarily mean he would call. "I'll give you a call" were words a person—especially a person like Eddie—tossed about as a common pleasantry, much like "How ya doin'?" and "Have a good day." And even if he did call her, she wasn't sure what her reaction would be. And if he didn't call, which wouldn't be a surprise, sooner or later she'd run into him now that he had moved back to Zhirnov Springs. And when she did, she wanted to look as slinky as a Siamese.

Instead of Cheetos, she nibbled some fat-free Very Berry yogurt. *Nibble.* Yeah, right, she smirked. The term was, at best, an imperfect synonym for sliding a congealed dairy product down one's throat without furnishing the teeth so much as a glancing sideswipe.

She looked down at the expanse of belly pouching over and below her waistband. The few pounds she had gained over the past decade hadn't come anywhere close to turning her into Shamu, but why had every ounce settled around her middle? All of her clothes were too tight, but she couldn't afford a new wardrobe. She had made a vow to herself to stash away her expanded but transitory paycheck for the new roof she had already put off far too long.

She was so tired of pinching pennies. She'd been doing it the whole of her adult life. And she was so very good at it—heck, she'd had twenty years of practice as a kid before entering the adult marathon. Not that she needed a Donald Trump lifestyle. But wouldn't it be nice to have the luxury of splurging just once in a while?

She had to, simply *had to*, do well in this temporary position so she could move on to a respectable career and a decent paycheck. She could no longer afford to trot down the path of least resistance, as 20/20 hindsight clearly showed was her modus operandi. When Eddie came into her life, she tied her future to his coattails. When Doc Griffin retired, she took the first available job and ended up at the Humane Society.

But things were about to change. She'd been handed the opportunity to prove she was worth something, and she wasn't going to screw it up.

She turned back to the computer monitor, grimaced at the gobbledygook, then dropped her eyes back to the Cheetos drawer. Good gosh, Carly-girl, she scolded herself. Where was her self-discipline? Girl? Why did she call herself girl? She was crossing over the line into middle age. She needed to act like a grown woman.

She tossed the Cheetos bag into the trash, then shook her head. Not good enough. The temptation needed to be irretrievable. She snatched the bag and dumped the orange squiggles atop the discarded papers and wet tea bag at the bottom of the wastebasket lined with peppermint stripes.

She scraped her spoon around the bottom of the Very Berry carton but couldn't grab hold of those final dregs of yogurt wedged in the seam. She wondered whether her tongue would reach the bottom.

With a flick of her hand, the carton joined the Cheetos.

Enough monkeying around. Time to get to work. Surely she could learn a new bit of software. She was smart enough to be a college graduate—even if she wasn't one.

She pushed her tailbone against the back of the chair and sat ramrod straight. The chair's beleaguered springs squealed, sparking a high C from Mary Louise. ♫ *Blue skies smiling at me.* ♫

Darrell popped his head in the door. The Lucille Ball-red of his Mohawk had faded to magenta. "Hey, sunshine bird, you're off-key."

Mary Louise was undeterred. ♫ *Never saw the sun shining so bright.* ♫

Darrell ambled into the small office. Carly gulped. Oh, no. He was wearing the No-Balls T-shirt.

She opted for the coward's way out by killing two birds—the cryptic computer programs and the T-shirt skirmish—with a little chirpy conversation. "Nothing like having Willie Nelson right in your office!"

"Actually, Willie was one of the last to perform that tune," Darrell said. "That's an Irving Berlin number, first done by Ben Selvin in the late twenties."

Carly missed a beat before saying, "Ben Selvin. Interesting."

"Of course, in the forties it was done by Frank Sinatra, Bing Crosby, Count Basie, and Benny Goodman. And then Jim Reeves in the sixties."

Mouth slack, Carly shifted her weight onto one hip, like a tuckered-out puppy. "I had no idea."

Darrell told Mary Louise, "You ought to try a little Gershwin." He rhapsodized as he backed out the door, "Old man sunshine, listen you. Never tell me dreams come true...."

Carly shrugged her shoulders, at a loss as to purpose of Darrell's visit. She was also stupefied by the amount of musical trivia that occupied the airy spaces of his down-filled brain.

The T-shirt reappeared. Darrell slapped his forehead.

"Forget something?" she asked.

"Like, what a nincompoop. Two things. First, Hailey got adopted."

"Great!"

"Second, Ruby and Juan Pablo are having another of their little tiffs."

"Have they come to blows yet?"

"*Nyet.*"

For some obscure reason, two of the Humane Society's best employees couldn't get along. From the first day they worked together, they were like gasoline and matches, despite their similarity in age—late-twenties—and stalwart dedication to animal welfare.

Ruby Wesolowski was as thick of neck and torso as a cross between an overfed Welsh corgi and a beer keg. Makeup never touched her face. The moment her dishwater blonde hair skimmed the upper curve of her ear, she made tracks for a $7.99 haircut. Brusque and feisty, she barreled through the shelter the same way she barreled through life, like the proverbial bull in a china cabinet.

Juan Pablo Ramos's job was to investigate allegations of animal abuse, instruct guilty but ignorant owners on proper animal care, and use cruelty laws to his advantage when education didn't solve the problem. Juan Pablo was perfect for the job—his tender heart was disguised by the hard flesh and raw determination of a street fighter, complete with a broken nose that had healed off-center. Feet planted apart, jaw set at an obdurate angle, he bore a striking resemblance to a bullmastiff, minus the wrinkles.

Seldom was an animal owner dimwitted enough to try to out-bully the cruelty investigator. Most men were shamefacedly intimated by Juan Pablo's indomitable body. Steroid-pumped weight lifters gazed with envy at his rippling abs and pecs.

It was the lucky guys, however, who found themselves between the sheets with him.

Carly arrived in the kennel to find Ruby with her knees braced and both arms extended as she clutched a hose nozzle like it was a .357 Magnum. A pressurized jet of water blasted the euthanasia room's metal door, held partially open by someone behind it.

"Come on out, you chicken shit!" Ruby's alto rose above the animals' clamor.

"All right, what's going on?" Compared to Ruby's bellow, Carly's voice had the force of a teacup poodle's.

Ruby continued to fire her water bazooka at the door.

Carly shouted louder. "I said, what's going on?"

Still no break in the action.

Carly wrenched the nozzle from the vice of Ruby's grip and released the trigger. "What is going on!"

Ruby's eyes were a storm of indignation. "He's in another one of his snits."

"*He's* in one of *his* snits? What do you call *this*?" Carly shook the hose at Ruby. "Come with me." She inclined her head toward the euthanasia room. At the same moment, a dripping wet giant emerged from his hunkered position behind the door and crept in the opposite direction.

"And you too," Carly directed Juan Pablo.

As Carly stepped into the little room, her eyes veered to a corner that, until today, had been buttermilk yellow. Now it radiated a sea-green fluorescence. On the counter, big glumps of gelatinous paste bulged out like viscous bubble gum in a bottle of blue-green tidal water. Where had the lava lamp come from?

She drew her attention back to how to handle the situation at hand. She folded her arms across her chest and did her best to look perturbed and authoritative. Perturbed was a piece of cake; authoritative was next to impossible. "Do you want to tell me about it?"

"He's on my case again." Ruby jerked her double chin at Juan Pablo.

Her nemesis was leaning with his tush against the table and his hands curled around the metal edge beside his hips. His drenched T-shirt molded to his chest while his black jeans hugged the sinews of his legs down to the casually crossed ankles of his leather combat boots. His perfect Y could have just leapt from the movie screen. Carly kept her eyes on his face and away from the scenic vista.

Juan Pablo's voice was as smooth as hot cocoa. "If I told her once, I've told her a million times. She'll never find inner peace until she accepts who she is and comes out into the sunshine."

Ruby snorted. "Into the *sunshine*? Well, *Mary Louise*, as I've said before, I don't need you telling me what to do! In fact, I oughta rip that tongue right out of your mouth." In a John Wayne put-up-your-dukes action, Ruby took a step toward Juan Pablo, who towered a foot above her.

Juan Pablo lowered his head toward his advancing adversary and shook his wet, raven hair. Water flew like batter from the beaters of an electric mixer, halting Ruby's blitz. Her scarlet face grew more brilliant until it looked ready to burst into flames.

Carly's arms went out from her sides like a referee in a boxing match. "That's enough." Her mind scrambled for what to say next. "Juan Pablo, Ruby's sexual orientation is none of your concern."

Juan Pablo remained unfrazzled by Ruby's beaming told-you-so smirk. "It is my concern if she comes to work in a big huff, hurling food bowls and slamming cage doors. All because she spent a night full of disillusionment and self-denial."

Ruby lambasted him with a contemptuous look that would rival any chow's.

The seams of Juan Pablo's shirt strained against his shoulders as he folded his massive forearms across the expanse of his chest. His tone was one of a concerned parent. "Ruby, sweet pea, stop deluding yourself that you're something you're not. A bird migrates. A bee seeks out nectar. They just do what they're supposed to do, what's been choreographed for them. And you should do what you're supposed to do, pumpkin."

Ruby seethed at Juan Pablo's persistent use of sappy pet names. She routinely carried a nylon leash draped across the back of her collar like a doctor carried a stethoscope. She yanked the leash from her neck and lashed its looped end on the floor next to Juan Pablo's boot. "This is the last time you're going to tell me how to live my life!"

Unintimidated by her whip, Juan Pablo thrust forth an index finger. "There you go again. Full of pent-up frustration."

"Okay, Juan Pablo, we've heard your message before," Carly said.

"We don't want to hear it again. Ever. And you, Ruby, I'm surprised you didn't blast the paint right off the door. Your retaliation seems rather excessive."

The dueling eyes drifted around the room.

"How much respect can the other employees have for you when you brawl like a couple of hooligans?"

"Hooligans?" Both contenders swiveled their amused gaze toward her.

Carly could have kicked herself for such a weak choice of words. "You know what I mean. Now promise me you'll behave yourselves."

Juan Pablo's finger made an X over his bulging pecs. Ruby muttered some half-hearted commitment, although by the look of her snarled lips, she intended to take a bite out of him the first chance she got.

"Good. Now will someone please tell me who brought in that lava lamp."

"Who else?" Ruby and Juan Pablo said in unison.

"But why?"

"Because he's Darrell," Ruby said.

As Carly passed down the hallway leading from the kennel to her office, Penny's conversation with a woman at the front counter filtered through the doorway. "I'm terribly sorry, but we don't have any kittens right now. However—"

"What do you mean you don't have any kittens? I was given a Christmas gift certificate for a cat. See. It says 'Zhirnov Springs Humane Society' right here."

"We have lots of cats available for adoption," Penny explained, "but no kittens. Mother Nature made cats to have their litters in the spring and summer when the weather is kinder. A lot of people want kittens at Christmastime, but there simply aren't any. However—"

"You know, I don't have to get one here. I can get one from the—"

"The newspaper doesn't have any either," Penny interjected, having heard countless variations of the newspaper threat when something at the Humane Society wasn't to the customer's liking.

"Well! What do you suggest I do?"

Carly yanked the phone message from the clip beside her office door. *Call Eddie Chevalier.* Below was his office number.

Carly was certain he had called to set up a time to repair those boards. Her trembling fingers misdialed the first time. While she waited for his receptionist to track him down, she toyed with the idea of fixing lunch or supper while he was at her house. He always liked her fajitas. Maybe some guacamole. A couple of Tecate beers with a squeeze of lime.

"Hey there!" He sounded glad to hear from her.

"Sorry I missed your call earlier."

"Me too. I was hoping to come over Sunday to look for my coin collection and see what that porch needs."

"Sunday would be fine."

"But just a few minutes ago, a buddy of mine called with tickets to the Sabercats's game on Sunday. So maybe another time?"

"Oh. Okay." She targeted her tone midway between cordial and nonchalant. "When would be good for you?"

"My schedule's kinda crazy right now. Let me get back with you."

"Oh. Okay." Shit!

After strangling out a pleasant good-bye, she cradled her forehead in her hands and cursed Ruby and Juan Pablo's childish behavior for making her miss Eddie's phone call. Not to mention, she was pretty sure she hadn't handled their silly fight with Executive Director-panache. And where had the word "hooligans" sprung from? And then asking the two of them to promise to behave themselves. Why didn't she simply ask them to cross-their-hearts-and-hope-to-die?

Why hadn't she stood her ground with Hugh and insisted she wasn't qualified for the job? She didn't know a thing about supervising employees. And she didn't have a clue how to turn a spreadsheet into Technicolor pie charts and finally into a budget. And to cancel her visits to the second graders—she couldn't think of a greater travesty.

Humane education was the cornerstone for a more compassionate tomorrow. Second graders caught the drift of her sketches of fifty dogs and cats and only five houses. They comprehended, better than their parents, when she explained that for every one person born in the United States, six puppies and kittens are born. They understood that a good owner made sure his pet received food and water, shelter, plenty of love, and veterinary care, including spaying or neutering. Unless the next generation was taught to behave more responsibly than their parents, animals would continue to multiply exponentially. The ultimate outcome would be an escalating parade of excess animals streaming into animal shelters, requiring even more tax dollars be squandered on a preventable problem.

She wondered who she could pawn the New Volunteer Orientations onto. She'd like to ask Juan Pablo to do it, but he already had a ton of overtime hours that he'd probably never recoup. Carly went down the list of employees, and Penny's name floated to the top. The problem with Penny was that she unintentionally misrepresented reality. Through her

Kewpie doll eyes, Penny viewed the world as an expanded edition of *Charlotte's Web*, founded on principles of self-sacrifice, loyalty, team effort, and survival of the weak. On the flip side, she was personable, articulate, and enthusiastic. Bottom line—Penny was the pick of the limited litter.

Speaking of whom, the pixie poked her head in the doorway. "The woman at the front counter wants to speak to the supervisor."

"What does she want me to do?" Carly protested. "Give birth to a litter of kittens?"

Penny shrugged. "I guess she thinks a humane society should be like a fruitcake factory and gear up for holiday sales."

"Tell her I'll be there in a minute."

Penny's head was replaced by Darrell's. "What do you want to do about the walk-in freezer? It's heebie-jeebies are getting worse."

"Hasn't Joe Becker been by yet?"

Joe was a Humane Society volunteer who earned his living as a refrigeration technician. Hugh had been badgering him for weeks to take a look at the rattling, hiccuping compressor. Time and again Joe assured Hugh he'd stop by, but he always got waylaid. In concept, volunteers sounded like a panacea, but even the best intentioned ones all too often either couldn't or didn't uphold their end of the bargain.

"No Joe. If that freezer conks out, we'll be waist-deep in doo-doo, man." Darrell pinched his nose to stave off the stench of decaying carcasses.

"I'll call someone to come look at it." While her right hand fished about for a bottle of aspirin in the desk's top drawer, her left hand reached into the bottom drawer for the phone book. "Oh, Darrell?"

"Yeah?"

"About your T-shirt?"

"Yeah."

"Well, I don't think it's appropriate for the shelter. I mean, I like it just fine and all. It's a clever way to get the message across about neutering. But I'm not sure about the public. They might take offense. You know what I mean? So, I'd appreciate it if you wouldn't wear it to work."

"Ummm. Okay. I see where you're coming from. That's cool."

If Carly hadn't spent the past week dreading this discussion, chewing over the details until it reached altercation-level, she would have simply been grateful that Darrell was agreeable to her suggestion. End of discussion. But she had prematurely put on her boxing gloves with Darrell and was geared up to use them. She was also ticked off that she had to cancel the second graders, peeved at Joe Becker's failure to keep his promise, fed up with unreasonable customers, and resentful that she missed

Eddie's call because of Ruby's conniption fit. So rather than stopping right then and there, she plunged ahead. "And that lava lamp."

"Yeah?"

"It's gotta go."

"Gotta go?"

"I just don't think it belongs in the euthanasia room." She was quick to add, "Or anywhere else in the shelter." She groped toward the back of the drawer. *Where's that damn aspirin?*

"Huh?"

*What didn't he understand?* "Please take the lava lamp home."

Darrell's fingers raked his goatee. "Take the lava lamp home?"

She nodded.

He looked as confused and crestfallen as a puppy who was just spanked for piddling on the floor. "You don't like it?"

"It's not that I don't like it—"

"What don't you like about it?"

"I like the lamp. I just don't like it in the shelter."

"What if everybody else likes it?"

"It's got to go." She aligned the childproof cap and poured a couple of headache-squelchers into her palm.

"Excuse me." Penny's head appeared beside Darrell's. "Sophia Zhirnov is on the phone for you."

"Put her through."

"But the kitten woman is waiting for you."

"I'll be right there."

When Carly looked back at Darrell, his face was smeared with the hurt of betrayal. "Right," was all he said as he backed out the doorway.

An employee named Monica replaced Darrell. "Someone just brought in an injured snapping turtle they found. It needs to be euthanized. Any suggestions on how to do that?"

"Euthanize a turtle?"

One look at Carly's blank expression was all Monica needed to seek her answer elsewhere.

The phone trilled.

"Ms. Shannon? This is Sophia Zhirnov. I understand you'll be working closely with the Board of Directors. Why don't I stop by sometime and bring you up to speed on where I feel our financial problems lie. Would this afternoon be all right?"

"This afternoon?"

"Plus I'd like to discuss the Groundhog Day decorations with you.

And while I have you on the phone, whose idea was that larval lamp?"

*Larval lamp?* Carly thought it best to let the misnomer slide. "I was just discussing it—"

"Such a clever inspiration! It brightens that bleak, windowless room of death. A yin-yang type of effect."

As she hung up the phone, Carly contemplated how she could gracefully rescind her directive to Darrell. Nothing like eating a little crow for a mid-morning snack. She tossed the aspirins to the back of her throat and cast covetous eyes on the orange squiggles in the bottom of the trash can.

She picked up the phone message to return Eddie's call and started to tear it to shreds when she realized a second message was stuck to the back of it.

> Reporter from the Courier wants to know why the Humane Society isn't doing something about the stray cat problem at the high school. He's on a short deadline. Call ASAP.

The message had been taken over an hour ago.

Maybe it was time to move back home to Iowa—rebuild her father's farrowing pens, spray for corn borers, check out what Junior Swenson was up to nowadays....

**6**

"That's enough, you faggot!" Ruby screamed like a banshee in the employee break room that was the size of a postage stamp.

Carly had been the interim director for two months when she was faced with another of Ruby and Juan Pablo's tiffs. She was starting to feel like a kindergarten teacher.

"Ruby! If you want to continue being employed at this shelter, you will not call your coworkers, or anyone else for that matter, derogatory names!"

Ruby's nostrils flared like a bull being tormented by a matador's cap. "Then why's it all right for him to say whatever he wants?" Ruby reached across the microwave to shove the tip of her finger between the unyielding hills of Juan Pablo's chest. Her stocky finger curled back like an Oscar Meyer wiener. "I told you to butt out of my business! Clean out your ears! I'm. Not. Gay."

"Ruby. Sweetum." Juan Pablo placed his hand over his heart and settled his voice into a mellow baritone. "'This above all: to thine own self be true.'"

"Shove your Shakespeare up your ass."

Juan Pablo cocked his head as he entertained the possibility. "Could be fun except—"

"Take your gutter-filth somewhere else, you slimeball!" Ruby latched onto a tin of pepper sitting on the microwave and poofed a blast in Juan Pablo's face.

Juan Pablo lapsed into a paroxysm of sneezing. Remaining cool as a cucumber, he wheezed, "Don't you hear yourself, dumplin-cakes? You're deceiving yourself just so you can live up to the expectations of others."

Carly interrupted with, "This is an inappropriate discussion for the workplace. Put the pepper down, Ruby."

Ruby plunked the tin on top of the microwave. The curl on her lip would make any junkyard dog envious.

"I'm just sharing my personal experience." Sneeze. "It was only after I extracted myself from the influence of people and beliefs outside myself," sneeze, "that I was able to drop the social mask and be truly content." Sneeze. "You have the same need for approval now that I had then."

"That's it! I'm not going to let you ruffle my feathers any more." In direct opposition to her words, Ruby rolled up a copy of the *Zhirnov Springs Courier* that had been left lying on the old kitchen table. She raised it like a club.

"Ruby, put the paper down," Carly said.

As Ruby chucked the paper back onto the table, her eyes latched onto the fire extinguisher on the wall.

"Don't even think about it," Carly warned.

"I don't tell you these things to ruffle your feathers, honey-bun. I say them in hopes you'll find peace with yourself." Juan Pablo rested his elbow on the microwave and dropped his chin onto the heel of his palm. "Surrender to *el destino*. Accept yourself as the Infinite Organizing Intelligence intended you to be."

The tips of Carly's fingers rapped her temple. "I don't understand you two. You're about the best employees we have, yet you can't behave yourselves. What kind of example are you for your coworkers? Huh? Tell me that! Especially you, Ruby, considering your new position."

Ruby, in competition with five other applicants, had been successful in her bid for Operations Manager. Although Ruby was pleased with her accomplishment, Carly was the one whose buttons were bursting with pride. Her maiden voyage of advertising for, interviewing, and selecting an employee had gone pretty smoothly, if she might say so herself. Ruby was an honest, dedicated workhorse who played by the rules. Now if Carly could only temper Ruby's short fuse.

Monica, who was working at the front desk that afternoon, stuck her head in the break room to hand Carly a phone message and announce that her visiting Brownie troop was waiting in the lobby.

With the voice of absolutely no experience, Carly concluded her admonition with, "If you two engage in any more of this misbehavior, I'll have no alternative except to document it in your personnel record." The threat left a bad taste in her mouth, but what choice did she have? She had tried the nice approach in the past without success. She'd had enough of this nonsense.

As she walked down the hallway, she read the telephone message. *Call Eddie Chevalier.* Carly was split right down the middle. The Brownies were waiting for her. But she *so* wanted to return Eddie's call. *Now.*

But her brain asked her heart, Why? Why would she interrupt her life to run to the phone and call Eddie? She hadn't heard hide nor hair from him for eight weeks. Let him wait.

In the lobby, she found herself surrounded by a swarming mass of brown vests, sashes, skirts, shorts, skorts, and pants. She shook the hand of the only mother she saw. That was unusual. They typically came in packs of two or three to keep their charges in line.

"Hello. I'm Carly Shannon. I'll be giving the tour."

"Hi!" said the elfin blonde who looked maybe old enough to vote. She gushed her appreciation for Carly's contribution of time. "And this is my co-leader, Charlie VanCleave."

Carly turned to the man she had assumed was another customer. A male Brownie leader. Interesting.

"More of a helper than a co-leader." Charlie extended one hand, his other resting on the shoulder of a Brownie, presumably his daughter.

Carly shook his hand and nodded hello. "Charlie."

"Carly."

"Charlie," she repeated, and they both had a good chuckle about the Charlie-Carly business. She laughed a tad longer than was necessary, letting her eyes linger. A good looking man. Great smile. About her age. A Brownie leader. Who'd have thought?

As Carly shepherded the group into the hallway, she glanced at her watch. She needed to leave the shelter at 4:30 to go to her first meeting of the Pet Expo Committee. The Expo was an annual Humane Society fund-raiser and public awareness event. The meeting was back to back with tonight's Board of Directors meeting—also her first. She had a total of forty minutes to give the tour, answer the kiddos' questions, and get them out the door. She hated that the most valuable part of her day— instilling humane principles in the next generation—was given the least amount of her harried time.

Inside the kennel, she encountered Penny. Her fawn-like eyes were moist. Penny paid a price for her deep compassion. Any sad event associated with animal—euthanasia, a cruelty case—would switch her from buoyant to despondent in the blink of an eye. Carly thought the nano-second mood swings seemed neither natural nor healthy.

Penny leaned close, her pink dolphin earrings skimming her collarbone. "It's Hailey. She's back," she whispered.

"What!"

"Digging. The new owners said they couldn't put up with it."

"Crap!" Carly mouthed.

"Carly, I need to talk to you about something."

"Sure, but I can't right now."

"Later?"

Carly nodded at the same time she said, "Okay, girls, let's go this way first and see the kitties. They're in a room by themselves so they don't get frightened by the barking dogs."

After the cat ward, the storage room, the grooming area, and the tiny medical room, Carly herded the brown-clad half-pints past the euthanasia room. For children this young, Carly bypassed the euthanasia room and the freezer. However, some kid invariably brought up that he or she had heard that the Humane Society killed dogs and cats, which opened up a thorough discussion of the importance of spaying and neutering.

"The dogs and cats in this room are under observation for rabies. That means they bit someone and have to be watched for ten days to make sure they don't have rabies. Because if an animal has rabies, what happens to the person that was bitten?"

One Brownie made a slicing motion across her neck.

"That's right. The person gets rabies and dies. That's why it's so very important that you take your dog or cat to the veterinarian to get it a rabies vaccination."

Fifteen little heads nodded that a rabies vaccination was a good thing.

After a hasty discussion about how to avoid dog bites, Carly took the girls to their last stop—the dog kennels. She asked Penny to get a dog or two for the Brownies to pet. While they were occupied, she snuck away to find Hailey.

"Oh, girl, why are you back?" Carly crouched beside the dog, who wagged her tail in apology. As Carly smoothed the fur on the dog's head, Hailey curled her tail under her and sat like a lady. "A digger. I knew you had to have a flaw. Let's hope it's not a fatal one."

Carly ached at the look in Hailey's eyes. In them was the questioning bewilderment of how a horrible twist of fate had once again brought her to the shelter. Carly had a lump in her throat bigger than Dallas. She reached around Hailey's neck and drew the dog to her.

Something caught the corner of her eye. She wasn't alone. Charlie the Brownie leader was on the other side of the gate.

"Oh, hi." She rose and casually brushed the hair off her skirt. "We'll do the best we can for you," she told Hailey as she ran her hand along the dog's muzzle. Hailey stood up and swayed her tail like a metronome.

"Seems like a nice dog," the Brownie leader said while they walked back toward the second graders.

"She's a very nice dog. But we had a hard time finding a home for her the first time she was here. Her new owners brought her back because they couldn't put up with her digging. Chances are slim we'll be able to place her again."

"Why is that?" Behind his glasses, his soft gray eyes seemed genuinely curious.

"Sixty pounds is a lot of dog to keep in the house, so she'll probably be relegated to the backyard."

"Where she'll dig." He glanced back over his shoulder at Hailey. "I think she's a pretty dog."

"So do I, in a plain-Jane sort of way. But most people want powder puff lap dogs." Carly bit her lower lip. "I hate to do this, but would you mind if I cut out on the Brownies? I'm running behind schedule. Penny will answer any questions they have."

"No, I don't mind at all."

"I'm really sorry to have to do this, but I've simply run out of time."

"I understand. Thank you for the tour. The girls got a lot out of it." He extended his hand.

She placed her hand in his. "You're welcome."

"Good-bye, Carly."

"Charlie."

"Carly."

They laughed again about their nursery rhyme names. Not only was he nice looking, he was just plain nice. And married. Of course. All the good ones were taken.

She race-walked to her office to squeeze in the call to Eddie before heading to the committee meeting. His secretary told her he had already left for the day. Damn!

"Please tell him Carly Shannon returned his call."

As she grabbed her briefcase, she remembered Penny had asked to talk with her. It would have to wait until another time.

7

Carly looked down the impossibly long and grimly imposing table in Alan Drake's law office. Not a single blemish marred the harsh gleam of its boards. The high-backed burgundy chairs surrounded the conference table like a conclave of thrones.

Where did the sole employee sit during a Humane Society Board of Directors meeting? Maybe she'd just stand over here in the corner until everyone was seated and take whatever was left.

Carly sniffed the air. Two incongruent scents battled for control of the room—Chanel No. 5 and Lady Stetson.

Alan Drake took his seat at the head of the table and indicated Carly take the empty chair beside him. A third scent was added to the air when he popped a potent breath mint in his mouth.

Alan introduced Carly, and she smiled at the twin colonnades of dour faces lining the table. When she leaned back, air swooshed from the supple leather cushion. This chair was heaven compared to the one at her desk. Hugh's relic would no longer raise or lower, its vinyl armrests were in tatters, and the imprint of Hugh's heinie was sculpted into the frayed cushion. Carly figured not a single person in this room would tolerate Hugh's tumbledown chair for even one day.

The minutes from the last meeting were approved, followed by the treasurer's report. The ensuing discussion—a minor change to the by-laws, possible names to fill the vacant Board position, liability insurance for the Board members—was gibberish to Carly. Which was fine. It meant nothing was expected of her.

Under the table, she kicked off her pumps to let her feet breath. Her toes worked into the deep pile carpet. It wouldn't be long and she'd be peeling off those pantyhose.

The treasurer brought up the age-old problem of the disparity between income and expenses.

Sophia Zhirnov responded with, "As commanding as the color red is, it's not what I'd like to see on our balance sheet."

Carly assumed that Sophia was kept on the Board out of deference to her financial generosity. Her husband's great-grandfather had emigrated from Russia during the 1880s and settled in the area that would bear his name. Generations of Zhirnovs prospered on the fertile prairies, branching from cotton farming into merchandizing, real estate, and commodity speculation. Following her husband's death due to forty years of vodka consumption, Sophia threw herself into her dual passions of animals and the town's cultural heritage.

Carly thought Sophia's heart was in the right place, but her head seemed stuck inside a sample paint color brochure. She saw everything in terms of color—the trash bags (seasonal), her hair (steely blue), the acrylic on her fingernails (several degrees brighter than the molten tip of a soldering iron).

Of all the colors, Sophia was most comfortable with green. She married into green, amassed more green, and spent green freely. She, better than any other Board member, understood what money could accomplish.

Sophia waved a piece of paper splashed with coloring book blue, green, red, and yellow. In her effort to reduce copying costs, Carly had squished all the pie charts onto one sheet. The result bore an amazing likeness to tiddlywinks.

Sophia loved the charts' colors, but she abhorred the message. "If everyone would please look at the chart of last year's income. That's the third one from the right on the bottom row. Note the city contract. Zhirnov Springs is paying us a mere pittance. Because we're handling a societal problem, we're essentially footing the bill for the taxpayers—particularly the irresponsible ones who let their animals run loose and breed like rats."

Unlike the majority of other humane societies and SPCAs, which were non-profit organizations that survived solely on donations, the Zhirnov Springs Humane Society had an additional source of income. It contracted with the City of Zhirnov Springs to house lost animals.

Zhirnov Springs was no longer the small town that had lured Carly a decade ago. Its 45,000 residents composed a bedroom community for the exploding metroplex of Megalopolis. All the town's services—its parks, street maintenance, library, municipal court, police and fire protection— were struggling to keep up with the escalating demands of its citizens. The City's animal control program, which had been bestowed with the more palatable name of Animal Services, was no exception. The animal control officers of the Zhirnov Springs Police Department had a hard enough time patrolling the streets 24/7 without assuming the additional 365-day-a-year responsibilities of housing, adopting, reuniting lost pets with their owners, euthanizing, and quarantining for rabies observation. So several years ago, the Humane Society stepped up to the plate—for a fee.

The dividing line between the City and the Humane Society was the building's door. Zhirnov Springs's animal control officers handled everything in the field—loose dogs, road kill, citations for failure to vaccinate against rabies, and enforcement of the ban on poultry and livestock within the city limits. The Humane Society took charge of the animal once it passed over its threshold. The sole exception to the demarcation between the City and the Humane Society was cruelty investigation. Citing budget constraints, the City refused to enforce the state's cruelty laws, so the Humane Society, as a facet of its altruistic mission, hired Juan Pablo to do the job.

Alan's conference room lit up like lightening, charged by Sophia's comments about the little non-profit organization picking up the tab for what was technically the City of Zhirnov Springs's responsibility.

"We need to stop pussy-footing around!" The declaration was made by a man named Reinhardt, a pasty-faced retiree whose stomach rested on his knees. "We can't afford to suck hind teat any longer!"

"That's right!" Reinhardt's backer was a very blonde woman whose face would have benefited from a more liberal use of sunscreen over the years. She was wrapped in a western suede jacket with fringe across the front yoke and down each sleeve. Strings of turquoise beads dangled from silver baubles like pasties over her nipples. "Either the City pays its fair share or we'll sever the contract!" Her hand sliced through the air.

Ahh, Carly thought. That's who was marinated in Lady Stetson.

Sophia lowered her chin to look over her turquoise reading glasses. "What we need to know is how our income compares with the population growth."

"I can compare this year's figures side-by-side with last year's figures," the treasurer volunteered.

"That's peachy, but we need more than that," Sophia said. "We need a comparison of how Zhirnov Springs's population has grown versus our contract with the City. With inflation factored into the equation. And we'll need to know how many animals we handle for the City now versus when we first entered the contract."

"You want seven years worth of numbers?" The treasurer's eyes were wide with trepidation.

Alan gave a minty sigh. "That's a tall order but a point well made. We need to step back and take a broad view of this organization's finances."

"Let's hold on a minute, Alan." The treasurer's forehead furrowed like a Shar-Pei's. "Please remember, I *am* a CPA and we're in the middle tax season. My free time is limited."

Sophia continued with her wants, oblivious to the demands the workplace imposed on most Americans. "And it's not just Zhirnov Springs. The County isn't paying a dime for the animals we take in from outside the city limits. Please include a graph of the County's growth over the past decade." Sophia removed her reading glasses, folded them with a meticulousness that rivaled Felix Unger's, and laid them atop her stack of papers. "The next thing we need to discuss is fund-raising. We've had an unparalleled opportunity fall in our laps—"

Alan cut her off. "That's further down on the agenda."

Sophia pulled in her own reins. "Of course. But we should discuss fund-raising in general. The Board needs to buckle down and find ways to increase revenue."

"The Board?" questioned pasty-faced Reinhardt. "What about the staff? Shouldn't they be doing exactly that?"

"The staff?" Sophia was aghast. "The staff have their hands full running the shelter. Oh, no. The staff's role in raising revenue is minimal. Unless you think we should hire a full-time Director of Development." Sophia's steely gaze matched her hair.

"What about her?" Reinhardt pointed to Carly.

Carly bolted upright. "Me?" Her paper-thin voice sounded like it belonged to a fifth-grader asked to stay after school to help the teacher.

"Yes, you. Raising money is part of the Executive Director's job."

"Only partially," Alan explained. "Ms. Shannon serves as an ex officio member of the planning committees of all our fund-raisers. And she speaks to community groups to cultivate goodwill. Plus she's expected to operate the shelter in a fiscally responsible manner. But it's not her responsibility to raise the revenue required to run this organization."

As Carly's eyes wandered from blank face to blank face, a distressing revelation smacked her in the forehead. Most of the people around this table didn't even know what the Executive Director's job was!

"I agree with Hugh," said a woman whose aquamarine eyes were as fetching as Camey's but were set above a beak that rivaled Mary Louise's. "I used to work for a nonprofit center for abused women. The Board constantly shirked their responsibility to ensure that the financial needs of the organization were met."

That sparked a discussion about possible fund-raisers—garage sales, candy sales, bake sales, tamale sales. Sophia halted the brainstorming by pointing the earpiece of her glasses at each Board member in turn. "This nickel-dime stuff has its place, but let's face it. Real money comes from planned giving. Wills. Bequeaths. High-dollar donations we can use to start an endowment fund."

Her fellow Board members had no argument but were unclear how to initiate a planned giving campaign.

"We could start with an article in our newsletter," suggested the woman with the aquamarine eyes.

Dottie Newman, the editor of *Paw Prints*, agreed to include an article.

"Speaking of our newsletter, I have an idea that might be useful." Carly forced the words out of her mouth. Ten heads turned toward her. She looked to Alan. "Is this the appropriate time to bring it up?"

Alan could do nothing but nod. His tongue, unfurling like a New Year's Eve blowout noisemaker, was capturing a mint from between his thumb and forefinger.

Carly wished she had Sophia's turquoise glasses so she could take them off, giving her hands something to do besides shake. "I read that we can save money by publishing the newsletter quarterly instead of monthly. And cutting it from twelve pages down to eight."

Dottie Newman was quick to defend her turf. "Of course we can save money by publishing a smaller newsletter less often. But what about the money the newsletter generates?"

"But it's not the newsletter per se that brings in donations," said the aquamarine woman. "It's the organization's good works. And those can be articulated just as well in eight pages as in twelve."

Carly continued, "I also read that a newsletter can sometimes be more effective at raising money if it's in the hands of a professional company who publishes newsletters and brochures full-time."

"What!" Dottie squawked, a homicidal look in her eyes. "Hire someone to do what's currently being done for free?"

"No one is saying *Paw Prints* isn't good the way it is, Dottie," Alan stroked her injured ego. "You do a crackerjack job."

Dottie folded her arms over her flat bosom. "I should think so. I've been putting together our church bulletin for thirteen years."

"But Carly's point is that a professional company knows the tricks of the trade to get our message across. And one of our key messages is that this organization can't survive without donations." Carly's defender was once again the aquamarine woman.

"But won't the amount the company charges to produce the newsletter offset any extra money generated?" the treasurer asked.

Following a few more discussion points, Carly was told to check out two or three companies, their prices, their client referrals, and whether any of them actively pursued paid advertising.

After having the newsletter ripped from her, Dottie Newman reclaimed her prestige as deftly as a cat that accidentally rolled off the bed. "If I might voice a concern I have."

"Certainly," the chairman said.

"I'm unclear exactly who we have running our shelter. I mean, I don't know a thing about Carly Shannon, her experience, her qualifications." Puckers radiated from Dottie's pinched mouth like folds around a drawn purse string.

"You're right. I should have done a more thorough job of introducing Carly," Alan said. "Carly, would you do the Board a favor and fill us in on your background."

He wanted her to talk about herself? She licked her lips. "Well, I—"

Dottie cut the biography short. "It's not that I'm not interested in her background. I just feel that if Hugh's replacement is going to serve for goodness-knows-how-long, then we need to be certain we have the right person. We should get the qualifications of several candidates before we make a selection." Dottie's *Paw Prints* wounds were clearly deeper than simply a nose knocked out of whack.

A battering ram slammed into Carly's stomach as she watched her brief career as interim Executive Director come to an abrupt end.

"Be that as it may," Sophia said, "no one would apply for a job that ends in less than six months. Besides, we don't want to change horses in midstream."

Once Carly was deemed adequate to handle the job on a short-term basis, Alan glanced at the wall clock. "Any further discussion on fund-raising?"

Carly raised her hand. "I have another suggestion." Who would she tick off with this one? "I was thinking about a Web site for the shelter."

"Web site?" pasty-face Reinhardt asked. "What the dickens for?"

"If you search the Internet, you'll see that most shelters have Web sites. They list their hours, location, fees, pictures of the animals."

"Now you're talking, little lady!" It was the evening's first contribution from a man named Sonny Parmer. Sonny was a crusty old rancher who looked like he just came in from the back-forty—a two-day growth of beard, scuffed boots worn down at the heels, a denim shirt stained with an assortment of greens and browns. Not only was Sonny an unlikely candidate for the board of directors of a humane society, he was also the last person who would be suspected of being a closet cyber geek.

Sonny's tongue scuttled the toothpick from one corner of his mouth to the other. "Businesses that aren't on the Web are as dead as last year's cornstalks. That's a ripsnorter of an idea you have there, missy."

"Picture it!" Sunbaked Lady Stetson said. "The home page can include the "Pick-of-the-Litter" animal that's up for adoption. And a button to click for pictures of the other adoptable animals. We could call it 'Homeward Bound'!"

Her suggestion stimulated the group's creative juices.

"Or 'Recycled Pets'!"

"Or 'Looking for Love'!"

"We can put the newsletter on the Web to save postage," Alan said.

Carly thought she heard a hiss come from Dottie's direction.

"Do you know how to set up a Web site, Carly?" the aquamarine woman asked.

"N-n-no."

"Hell and tarnation, she don't need to!" Sonny said. "There's plenty of companies that design and maintain Web sites. Just like there's companies that publish newsletters."

Dottie recrossed her arms. Her eyes were as threatening as a hungry shark's.

"But companies will charge money," the treasurer said.

Sonny screwed up his craggy, weather-worn features and looked at the treasurer as though she were a two-headed calf. "I don't give a fart if it costs money. Without a good Web site, we'll lose money. And adoptions. By the truckload."

The group nodded their agreement.

"The question is how to pay for it. Carly, check out our options and give a report to the Ways and Means Committee. We'll leave the decision to them. Let's move on to the last agenda item." Alan nodded for Sophia to proceed.

"As I mentioned earlier, an unparalleled opportunity has dropped into our laps. A well-known artist—a very well-known artist—has agreed to auction one of her original paintings. The proceeds are entirely ours to keep. I thought we could hold the auction in conjunction with a gala at the Country Club. Who wants to serve on the committee with me?" Sophia's smile was broad, having grown even broader over the years by the nips and tucks made by her cosmetic surgeon.

"Hold your horses!" Reinhardt's well-fed cheeks blossomed with color. "We haven't even voted on this yet. Who's the artist?"

"That's the best part!" Sophia leaned forward. Her penciled eyebrows jerked up and down twice. She scrutinized the corners of the room for eavesdroppers. Content that the suspense had built long enough, she whispered, "A.A. Malakov."

Several people exclaimed, "You know A.A. Malakov?"

"Who the Sam Hill blazes is A.A. Malakov?" The poorly phrased question came from Reinhardt.

Sophia's acrylic nails tapped the tabletop. "She happens to be one of the most accomplished young impressionist painters in this country. Her works have been exhibited in New York and Miami and are in private collections throughout the world. Her first book is about to be published— a collection of her prints. She also happens to be my goddaughter."

"What do you mean, a gala?" Lady Stetson asked.

"Well, a gala. Gowns. Black-tie. Sit-down dinner." Sophia's blue-veined hand poked at the lacquered hair at her temple. "Certainly you've been to a gala before."

"No, I can't say that I have," Lady Stetson said.

"We've never had a fancy shindig," Sonny said. "How much would tickets be?"

Sophia waved her hand airily, her Chanel No. 5 fusing with Lady Stetson and Alan's spearmint breath into a potentially lethal amalgam. "Oh, let's say $250 a person. Four hundred a couple."

"What? In Zhirnov Springs?" the room sputtered.

"Why ever not?" Sophia's taut, surgery-enhanced cheeks tightened as though her name had been taken in vain.

"People won't pay that price in this neck of the woods," Reinhardt said.

"Hogwash!" Sophia's thumb and forefinger seized the half-moon lens of her glasses and lowered them until the earpiece rested against her lower lip. Her narrowed eyes targeted her challenger. "This isn't Podunk U.S.A. anymore. We're on the outskirts of one of the fastest growing metropolitan areas in the country, full of wealthy Yankee refugees and millionaire baby-boomer retirees and Me Generation go-getters."

After ten minutes of discussion, a motion was passed to proceed with the gala, scheduled for June. Tickets were priced at $150. Two Board members agreed to serve on Sophia's committee.

"Make sure this hoity-toity party includes a complimentary 'whine' tasting." Reinhardt gave a phlegmy guffaw.

In response to Alan's, "If there's no new business…" Sophia jumped in with, "But I have more."

The men stopped shuffling their papers. The women put down their purses.

"Here's the second part of the equation." Sophia gloated like she was about to pull a rabbit out of a hat. She explained that A.A. Malakov had agreed to paint a mural on the west exterior wall of the shelter. "South-of-the-border colors—the kind that will turn drivers' heads. Watermelon red, juicy orange, kiwi green. And she'll unveil a sketch of the mural at the gala."

The group concurred that the wall, which faced a side street and was composed of gray concrete blocks, could use revamping. Its windows, which were essential for ventilation in the kennel, had been kept small and placed high under the eaves to prevent break-ins and break-outs. The gunmetal gray and the high, narrow windows made the building look exactly like what it was—a prison where cats and dogs were confined, then executed.

"Good. I'm glad you're all in agreement because A.A. will be flying in from New York later this week to look at the wall. That settled, I'd like to call your attention to an upcoming holiday, International Dog Biscuit Appreciation Day."

Reinhardt's palm slapped the table. "I move we adjourn the meeting."

At least four voices seconded the motion.

**8**

Have you heard from the Advocates yet?"

Carly was being given a personalized tour of the huge Megalopolis Animal Control Department by its director, Bob Hicks. After the Board of Director's meeting, Alan suggested Carly call Bob and introduce herself. Bob immediately invited her for an insider's tour of his facility. He turned out to be a pleasant man in his fifties whose bearing implied he'd been around long enough to know all the ropes.

"Heard from whom?" Carly asked.

"The Animal Advocates of Central Texas."

She shook her head as she and Bob walked toward the dog runs.

"You'd better batten down your hatches. They're zealots, excuse me, I mean, a grassroots organization that, until now, has focused its enmity on the biggest target—Megalopolis. They're unhappy about damned near everything. Conditions in the shelter. The hours we're open. The number of animals we euthanize."

Carly interrupted. "How many animals *does* your facility euthanize?"

"About twenty-five thousand a year."

She tried not to wince.

"You'll get to know the Advocates up close and personal because they're expanding their efforts into neighboring towns. I heard they're planning some protest demonstrations."

"To protest that we kill too many animals? Don't we already know that?"

Bob laughed. "That we do. That we certainly do. But the Advocates, fanatical though they may be, might actually be accomplishing some good. They've managed to capture the politicians' collective ear. Thanks to the Advocates's ranting and raving, Prairieland recently changed some of its ordinances, including eliminating their licensing program."

"Eliminate license tags for dogs? That sounds like a bad thing."

"Why do you say that?"

Oh-oh. Why did she say that? Simply because years of dogma left her with the unquestioning belief that licensing was part of an effective animal control program.

"Who is it that obeys the law and buys license tags?" Bob asked. "The people who let their animals run loose and fornicate in broad daylight on our city streets?"

Carly liked Bob's dry sense of humor. "Good point. The conscientious pet owners buy the tags while the negligent owners simply blow it off."

"Exactly. Responsible people always foot the bill for the irresponsible ones."

In a flash of inspiration, Carly said, "But licensing generates revenue for animal control."

"Does it? Do you honestly think that a $5 or $10 fee covers the tag, administrative cost of the paperwork, data entry, etc, etc?"

"Umm, probably not."

"Not to mention, I don't know of a single city that funnels the licensing revenue back into animal control. The few thousand dollars generated through licensing invariably goes into the city's General Revenue fund and shrinks to a meaningless drop in the bucket."

Carly's brow puckered. There had to be a valid reason to license dogs. "But it *is* a good way to locate the owner of stray animals."

"Don't rabies tags do the same thing, plus meet a public health need?"

"I guess I never really thought about the whys and wherefores of licensing."

"Most people haven't. Don't misunderstand. I'm not saying licensing is inherently bad or inherently good. But don't be surprised if you see it fall by the wayside in favor of breeding permits."

"Breeding permits?"

"That was another one of Prairieland's ordinance changes. Forty bucks if you want your dog or cat to have a litter. Prairieland also made it illegal for the newspaper to accept a want-ad to sell or give away a puppy or kitten without a permit number. There's a $200 fine if you're caught red-handed with a litter and no permit."

"Prairieland residents must be screaming."

"They are. But the Advocates convinced the City Council that the citizenry shouldn't have to pay taxes for animal control to put a Band-Aid on the problem created by those people who allow puppies and kittens to come into this overcrowded world."

"But the breeders must have fought it tooth and nail."

"They certainly did. They came back with their typical argument that it's the mongrels that wind up homeless. But you know yourself that's not true. Twenty percent of the dogs that come through this shelter appear to be purebreds. Multiply 20% by the twenty or thirty million animals that go through the shelters in this state, and that's a sizable chunk of change for Joe Taxpayer to pay."

Bob stopped walking. With alarming directness, he looked her square in the eye. "I've been in this business twenty-five long years. I've come to realize that, as a profession, we can't cling to our old ways. Not if we're going to make a noticeable dent in mankind's disregard for the animals it domesticated. Animal overpopulation and abuse are multifaceted societal problems—problems that will require an entire spectrum of non-lethal preventive strategies. We can't continue to blindly and reflexively spout our timeworn tenets of spay, neuter, license, and euthanize."

While Carly considered his words, Bob continued the tour, zigzagging through various buildings erected over the course of several decades. The facility covered two acres and housed 35,000 animals a year. As they wandered through the endless maze of dog runs and cat cages, Carly noted that Megalopolis's kennels were in no better condition than her own. Urine, humidity, teeth, and claws wrecked havoc on metal, paint, and wood. And, Bob explained, just like all the other government-run animal control programs, his facility was at the rock bottom of the budget priorities.

There were those words again. City council. Budget. They had such ominous connotations. Alan had made it politely but unmistakably clear she was expected to take a lead role with the City contract, and she felt as inadequate as a steer surrounded by cows in heat. She was ignorant of governmental affairs, zoning out whenever the political reporter came on the news. When Eddie left, she cancelled the newspaper subscription.

In the stray dog ward, Bob paused to answer a question from a man looking for his missing pet. To avoid eavesdropping, Carly wandered down the aisle of dogs. A bouncing Benji look-alike. A tan mutt with scabs of mange over his bony hips. A shaggy dog with his muzzle thrust through the chainlink, its eyes beseeching Carly as she walked by. A dog whose face was peppered with the gray of old age, its chin lying despondently between its outstretched paws.

Her feet grew leaden as she walked past one gate to the next gate and to the one after that. At the end of the three-day holding period, the majority of these animals would be promptly euthanized. Then they'd be carted to the incinerator to be reduced to ash.

She felt weighed down with the enormity of the problem. How would shelters and humane organizations ever, *ever*, change society's insidious disregard for its so-called companion animals? She felt like a tiny swallow meeting a gale head-on. She could flap her wings until she was exhausted and still not make any headway.

She looked from one face to another. Too many luminous eyes were focused on her. Something deep inside of her began to hurt. These were sentient beings, not inanimate possessions to be discarded at will. They felt pain and confusion and hunger. And contentment and happiness. She squeezed her eyes shut against the immeasurable death and suffering and fear. It was all so completely needless.

What was happening to her? This reaction was so unusual. She loved animals, but at her own shelter, she rarely was swept away by the endless flood of animals. When she walked through the Zhirnov Springs kennels, her roving eyes checked for cleanliness, safety, and efficiency. Were any hoses lying on the floor? How long had the bulb been burnt out? How many employees called in sick? But at someone else's shelter, she didn't have those responsibilities. Her attention was tuned to the loneliness, the hopelessness, the senselessness.

The morose feeling in her chest brought back memories of her first months working at the Humane Society. In those days, she empathized with the caged animals. She believed she understood what the animals were feeling. They wanted to explain to someone how wonderful and filled with love they were. But no one seemed to care or understand. Their round eyes looked for comfort but found only hard, cold concrete. Meanwhile, the minutes ticked away until their time was up.

She paused and looked at what she had initially mistaken to be an empty run. But lying in the far corner was a black puppy about four months old. Its tummy was round and tight with worms.

Carly stooped and put her fingers through the chain link gate. The pup flattened its ears against its head and wedged further into the corner.

Carly crouched low and whistled softly. "Come here, boy. Come on."

But the dog merely cowered lower.

"Come on. Be a brave puppy."

The pup's whole body quivered as it averted it face, its eyes shooting furtive glances at Carly.

God! A puppy that age should be playful and trusting and craving attention. What kind of hell has it been through that it lives in cringing fear? What has society done to man's supposed best friend?

Hot tears burned her eyes. She pressed the knuckles of her fist against her lips. She couldn't cry! Not here. Not in front of Bob.

She fought to contain her feelings, but the tears spilled. She hurried to the end of the aisle where a stainless steel contraption automatically fed cleaning solution into the water hose. While pretending to inspect the apparatus, she wiped away the salty wetness.

"Sorry for the interruption," Bob said as he rejoined her.

"No problem. I just appreciate you spending this much time with me." She prayed red eyes didn't betray her.

"Don't mention it. This is such a frustrating, migraine-generating business, all of us have to give whatever support we can to each other."

They finished their hour-long tour in the employee break room. Bob got a soft drink from the refrigerator and offered her one.

As he popped the top on his drink, he pointed his elbow toward a platter on the countertop. "Have a seat. Help yourself to a cinnamon roll. Every once in a while, I stop at the Sin-A-Many Shop on my way to work and buy some for the staff."

"Thanks but I'd better pass." As she sat down, she gave her saddle-bags a pinch, then safely secured her hands beneath her thighs.

Bob backtracked to their earlier discussion. "Talking about new solutions for old problems—at our place, we've examined the reasons why people surrender their pets. Sure, there's the usual 'Had litter. Can't find homes,' and 'Divorce. Can't keep,' and the classic, 'White hair on my dark couch.' But a lot of owners hate to part with the animal; they're simply at their wits' end. Chewing. Barking. Digging. Won't use the litter box. Basic run-of-the-mill pet behavior problems. I plan to ask for money in next year's budget to hire a pet behaviorist."

"Does the City usually give you the money you ask for?"

"Rarely. But I might be able to convince them this time by saying the program will save money in the long run. If we can teach owners how to properly train their pets in the first place, or help owners work through behavior problems, the shelter will take in fewer owner-surrendered animals. I'm going to call it 'Pet Parenting Class.' Plus the behaviorist will put tips on our Web site."

Carly shifted. Web site. It was another one of those terms demanding her reluctant attention. It was a perfect example of the old be-careful-of-what-you-want syndrome.

"Of course, it all hinges on my boss agreeing with my request and including it in the budget he forwards to the City Manager. Then the Council has to approve the budget. After that, the fiscal department has to properly apportion the money, which is always a perilous procedure." Bob intoned the mind-dulling hoops he'd have to jump through.

"And then I have to write a justification for a new position.

"And it gets lost so I resubmit it.

"And Human Resources finally approves it.

"And the position gets posted, but no one applies for the job because the pay is so low.

"So I appeal to Human Resources and the Budget Department to increase the salary.

"And I repost the position.

"And interview the applicants.

"I slice someone's office in half to make room for an additional person.

"So, just as I'm at the point of bringing the behaviorist on board, the City imposes a hiring freeze." Bob's voice was winded. "By that time, today's problem puppies that are peeing on the floor will be geriatrics leaking urine on the carpet."

Carly threw her head back and laughed. Her eyes landed on the three remaining cinnamon rolls. So irresistibly tempting. The aroma of yeast. The soft dough passing over her lips. The white icing caressing the roof of her mouth. The syrupy pecans releasing their nutty piquancy.

Stop right there! Better to picture herself in the produce aisle at the Sup-R-Val-U. There, in front of the Golden Delicious apples, her cart bumps into Eddie's. She apologizes. His eyes appraise her top to bottom. He wonders what he ever saw in Jocelyn.

"You may not realize it, but you're fortunate to be part of a small organization," Bob was saying as she swung her attention back to the moment at hand. "As a small agency, I'm sure you wish you had the resources that an organization our size has. But at least you have room to maneuver and make the changes you want."

"I'm not making very many changes. Remember, I'm only temporary. In fact, when Hugh returns, I'll probably be looking for a job."

"Looking for a job? Can't you stay at Zhirnov Springs?"

"I guess I could go back to my old job as Animal Caretaker...." Her voice trailed off.

"Ah, I understand." He nodded knowingly. "If you return to your old job, you'll feel cubby-holed. Unchallenged. Underutilized."

"You got that right."

"Plus, I suspect you no longer have the same rapport you used to enjoy with your coworkers."

"Exactly! How did you know that?"

"The boss always feels segregated from his employees. It's part and parcel of the job."

Wow, he just scored a bull's eye. Ever since she took on Hugh's duties, Ruby and Juan Pablo were the only staff who continued to talk to her without stilted deference.

Wouldn't it be great to work for a guy like Bob, she thought as she looked at his compassionate eyes, wrinkles of experience, and down-to-earth demeanor. She felt like the animals in the shelter. She wanted to shout, Please take me! Give me a chance! I might not look like much, but I'll make a valuable addition.

Carly swallowed hard and pushed past her shyness. "I hope that pitch hitting for Hugh will serve as a springboard for a better job."

She held her breath, waiting for Bob to say that Megalopolis had just the spot for her with a sky's-the-limit salary and crème de la crème benefits. But he simply took a drink of his calorie-free, caffeine-free cola while he waited for her to continue. Apparently she hadn't wowed him enough for him to make even a paltry offer.

"I'd like to find a job that would allow me to grow professionally," she concluded lamely.

He was on the verge of responding when an employee poked his head into the break room. "The police have a lead on our latest asshole."

"Let's hope so," Bob responded. "I want to hear about it as soon as I'm through here."

After the young man went on his way, Bob explained. "We're trying to find the guy that used duck tape to muzzle a golden retriever and hog-tie its legs, then drowned it in the lake."

Carly's stomach flip-flopped. The cinnamon rolls suddenly looked as appealing as coils of spoiled bratwurst and the icing was as appetizing as the morning remains of a wet dream.

"I've taken up enough of your time. I can see you have other fish to fry. Again, thank you so much."

Bob told her to never hesitate to call if she needed anything.

As she crossed the lobby, Carly mulled over how much she could learn if she worked here. And wouldn't Bob be a great role model? Polite but not a push-over. Always ready with a razor-sharp response.

Darrell? Why was Darrell at the Megalopolis Animal Shelter?

The second he saw her, he took on the look of a cornered animal. He stashed what appeared to be a job application behind his back.

"Hi, Darrell! What's up?"

"Oh, I dunno. Nothing much. I'm on lunch hour. What's up with you?" He gave a pathetic version of a smile. Patches of color appeared on his cheeks that matched the magenta of his hair.

"Just got out of a meeting. I hear we've got some animal activists headed our way."

"Oh, you mean the Advocates."

"You've heard about them?"

"Yeah, man. We've been talking about them in the shelter."

"Oh? I haven't heard anyone talking about them."

His rocked heel-to-toe, his fingers fiddling with the zipper on a pocket of his cargo pants. "Right."

"Right what?"

"Right. You wouldn't."

"Wouldn't what?"

"Wouldn't hear anyone talk about them."

"What do you mean?"

"I mean, like, you're never in the kennel anymore. And you never come by the break room."

"That's true. I'm not in the kennel as much as I used to be. A time crunch, you know?"

"Yeah, I know." His normally sleepy eyes jitterbugged around the lobby, looking for an escape hatch to the wild blue yonder.

"Maybe you can fill me in sometime on what you've heard about the Advocates? Unless of course, you no longer work at Zhirnov Springs Humane Society?"

"Yeah, sure." More eye shifting. More rocking back and forth.

"Yeah, sure, what? You'll fill me in? Or yeah, sure, you still work there?"

"Yeah, sure, both." He brought the application from behind his back and rolled it into a tube.

Darrell wasn't the best communicator in the world, but this exchange of information was taking unproductiveness to a new level. As much as she'd like to play ostrich and stick her head in the ground, avoidance was never a long-term solution. "What's wrong?"

"What do you mean?"

"I mean you're as tightlipped as an oyster. Why do you want to leave our shelter?"

"It's nothing, man. I just want to work closer to home."

"But you live in Zhirnov Springs, not Megalopolis."

"I'm thinking of moving."

They looked at each other for an eternal three seconds.

"I've always been straight with you. Can't you do the same with me?"

He flopped back his head and looked at the ceiling. "It's hard."

"What's hard?"

"You make it hard."

"Make what hard?"

He brought his gaze back down to a horizontal plane. "Talking to you."

Her mouth dropped open. She always thought that for two people with nothing in common except their jobs, she and Darrell got along quite well.

"Look. You used to be fun. But for the last two months, you've been running around the shelter like a caffeinated Pomeranian."

Carly flinched.

"Hey, man, I don't mean to hurt your feelings."

"No, no, it's okay. I need to hear these things." Her insides cringed as she asked the next question. "Anything else I should know?"

"Well, you're all business. When you talk to us, you talk from up above."

"Anything else, other than being an ice queen?"

He fiddled with his earring as though he wasn't certain whether her response was sarcastic or serious. She wasn't certain herself.

She rapped his arm with her knuckles. "I appreciate your honesty. I know saying those things wasn't easy for you."

Darrell relaxed and stopped his rocking chair motion. "It's been a downer for everybody."

*A downer for everybody*? "I guess my duties demand so much of my time that I ignore you guys. And don't think I don't miss all of you." As she said this, it struck her how much she would miss Darrell if he were to find another job. His funky hair. His loosey-goosey shuffle. His trouble-free look of a Weimaraner asking *What? Me worry?*

"My time is stretched so thin, usually with things I don't enjoy, like meetings and panty hose." She swung a leg in front of her and wiggled her foot. At least that got a chuckle from him. "Sometimes I feel like a hamster going round and round in a little wheel. I'll try to slow down and be more like the Carly of old."

"And stop second-guessing everything we do?"

"Have I been doing that?"

Darrell's head moved up and down with such vigor his chin crashed against his collarbone. "And you might want to check on Penelope."

"Penny?"

"Yeah. I mean, like, she's getting loony tunes. Really scary. High one minute. Lower than whale turds the next."

"High? Like on something?"

"I don't know, man. Could be. She's turning into one weird chick. Laughing. Crying.  And she smells."

"Smells?"

"Like...." He put his nose in his armpit.

"Thanks for telling me. I'll talk to her. Is there anything *else* I'm doing wrong?"

"*Nyet.*" The shake of his head was as casual as if he were answering whether he wanted a salad with his chicken-fried steak. His discomfort was already as forgotten as last weekend's hangover.

"You have my word that I'll take what you said to heart. And I'll try to pull my head outta my butt." Good, she got another grin from him. "I hope you don't leave the Zhirnov Springs Humane Society. But if you decide to move on, please let me know as soon as possible. I was hoping you'd be the point man for the Pet Expo."

"Point man?"

"Yeah. You know how the Expo is so spread out with the Mutt Strut and the Frisbee Catching Contest at the park while the other events are going on at the shelter. I need someone in charge at the park while I stay at the shelter."

"Me?" His open palm rested on his T-shirt, directly atop the plethora of hoof, paw, and claw prints that surrounded the Lone Star flag. Below it was the caption, "It's their state too." The flag billowed as Darrell puffed out his chest like a banty rooster. "Me, Darrell?"

"Sure, you." Actually, she hadn't considered the possibility until this moment, but now that she said the words, it sounded like a good plan. "Let me know if you're interested. Otherwise I'll have to find someone else."

Darrell's head bobbed like a cork. "Yeah. Okay. Yeah. Sure. I'll let you know."

**9**

She continued to clutch the steering wheel long after she turned off the ignition. She dragged her eyes toward the kennel's back door. The conversation with Darrell left a pit in her stomach the size of West Texas. She was a downer for *everybody*? And a micromanager? And an ice queen? And a Pomeranian? The one and damn-near only thing she took pride in was her people skills, and here she was alienating everyone. When she started working at the Humane Society, she thought she'd be able to help animals. Now more than ever before, she was in a position to make a difference. Instead, she was running off good employees.

Not only was she depressed, she was tired. Her mile-long to-do list grew longer by the hour. How was she going to juggle everything? And what was this business about Penny? High on something? Body odor?

Carly squeezed her eyes closed so tightly, her lids resembled peach pits. She was the one who agreed to take this job, and she was the one who had to own up to the attendant responsibilities.

Carly shouted what she hoped was a chipper hello to Juan Pablo, whose head was under the hood of the Humane Society's dilapidated van. Next, she waved at a man turning the soil in the flower bed. Sophia Zhirnov thought March 1 signaled the blossoming of spring, so she had her personal gardener plant a rainbow of petunias plus a bank of pink oleanders. In the center of the bed stood a five-foot plywood rodent, a left-over from Groundhog Day.

Carly stopped to chat with three employees who were on break, huddled in a powwow outside the backdoor while they got their nicotine fix.

In the kennel, a momentary lull in the dogs' chorus revealed a faint *Baaahhh*. Carly searched until she found the source. Monica was on her haunches inside a dog run, holding two bottles. At the end of each was a baby goat.

"New arrivals?" Carly asked.

"Juan Pablo was checking out a complaint by a landlord that some renters moved out and left two dogs inside the house. The surprise was these two little guys in the backyard."

Carly had to strain to hear Monica over the barking dog in the run opposite the goats. The piercing yap ratcheted Carly's tension up another notch. She glared at the carefree, adolescent Australian heeler mix. The gray-and-black mottled dog was all legs and mouth and no brains as it bounced off the cement block walls of the run, stopping its maniacal rico-chets only to chase its tail like a whirling dervish. Carly glanced at the cage card.

> Sundance
> Female. 6 months old.
> I sometimes get carried away with my emotions.
> Need patient owner who will spend time training me.

She started to tell Monica that in the world view of goats, the docile little creatures saw themselves as food for canines. To them, the kennel was the equivalent of a house of horrors. But she held her tongue. *Second-guessing everything we do.* Suddenly it was crystal clear. She was overcom-pensating for her own insecurity on the major issues by thinking for other people on the smaller, straightforward matters.

Carly looked at the little imps suckling their bottles, oblivious to their rowdy neighbors. They were in rhapsodic comas except for the flicking of their upright tails. Carly vetoed her own inclination to suggest that they be placed in one of the larger cages in the quiet cat ward. Instead, she asked if Monica had named them yet.

"No, not yet."

Carly opened her mouth to recommend that Monica refrain from doing so. They were, after all, livestock and might very well end up not as pets but wrapped inside a tortilla.

"I'll let my daughters name them," Monica said.

"Your daughters?"

"Remember last month I told everybody that we bought twenty acres east of town with barns and a farmhouse?" Monica wrenched the empty bottles from the Hoover-like suction. The kids' foamy-white muzzles nudged Monica's pants for more goodies.

"No, I guess I wasn't around when you talked about it."

"Guess not."

Monica's simple "Guess not" cut into Carly. Was the remark merely an off-the-cuff response or was it a potshot? Darrell's complaints made Carly's hide feel so thin, her intuition was tainted with paranoia.

"So you plan to adopt these little guys?" Carly asked.

"I'll talk to my husband about it tonight."

"That's terrific! Your two girls will love them!"

The goats' tiny hooves hopscotched across the concrete floor as they tried to follow Monica out the gate. Carly was about to suggest that the goats would appreciate some straw bedding, but Monica beat her to it.

"Ruby said she'd swipe a bale of hay from her horses tonight."

"Ah, good thinking."

She realized she was once again second-guessing to the point of being meddlesome. If she'd just shut up, people were smart enough to figure things out for themselves. Sundance's cage card was the perfect example. Very clever yet it got a point across. Come to think of it, she saw a cage card last week in the cat ward that would tug at anyone's heartstrings.

> Alice
> 9 weeks old. Female
> When Alice's family moved, they put their litter in a dumpster.
> Alice was part of the litter.
> Won't you give her a fresh start?

She left the goats and glanced at the cage cards as she walked down the aisle of runs.

> Bingo
> 7 months old. Male
> There's no place like home. But how would Bingo know?
> He's never had one.

She walked past a run with three tumbling black pups.

> Black Widow          Queen of Spades          Darth Vader
> 9 weeks old.          9 weeks old.             9 weeks old.
> Female               Female                   Male

Penny's precise handwriting was unmistakable. Such dark names, even for coal-black dogs. Penny was usually as sunshiny as Mary Louise. Something unhealthy was going on. Knowing an unpleasant discussion awaited her, Carly asked where Penny was. She was directed to the euthanasia room.

"That's not a valid reason!" Penny snapped while Ruby lifted a blonde cocker spaniel onto the euthanasia table. The dog's toenails glanced off the stainless steel as she scrambled to get her legs under her. Her whole body panted as her eyes roved the unfamiliar room.

"The heck it isn't!" Ruby stuck out her bulldog chin as she picked up a syringe.

"The heck it is!" Penny put her hands on her hips. Her voice rose in pitch and volume. "This is a good dog. You're not giving her a chance!"

"I'd love to give her a chance, but it's hopeless!"

"This is bullshit!" Penny slapped the dog's rear end. "Sit down!"

The cocker whimpered and dropped to the table. She rolled over to submissively expose her belly.

Carly gasped. She had never seen Penny direct anger toward any living creature, human or animal.

"Ladies!" Carly's voice was hushed but firm. "This dog deserves to die without fear. It's the least we can do for her. What is going on here?"

Carly stroked the soft belly. Once the trembling stopped, Carly righted the dog. The cocker cowered her head. A puddle of urine crept out from under her tail. Carly held out the back of her hand for the animal to sniff, then smoothed the wavy trusses of her ears.

Penny's breath was jagged as her fawnlike eyes filled with predictable tears. Her sprinkling of freckles was soon awash. "I'm sorry, girl. I'm sorry I hit you. And I'm sorry I have to do this to you." She stroked the length of the dog's back before resting her forehead on the dog's neck.

"I don't want to do this either, you know, Penny," Ruby said. "But you and I both realize there's no point in trying to find her a home."

By now, Ruby's tone had softened, Penny was sobbing, and the look in the dog's eyes had diminished from terror to trepidation.

"What's the dog's story?" Carly asked.

"Submissive urination," Ruby said. "I tried to explain the problem to the owner when he brought her in, but he said she ruined the carpet and he was fed up."

Submissive urination occurred in timid dogs in response to anything they perceived to be a threat—a verbal reprimand, loud noises, unfamiliar people. Like this cocker's owner, most people didn't understand the root of the problem and, therefore, disciplined the dog for its failure to be housebroken. Such action further depressed the dog's already low level of confidence, which in turn aggravated the piddling problem. It was next to impossible to find someone to adopt such a dog and spend untold hours working with it when the behavior may or may not end up being corrected.

Bob's Pet Parenting Class came to Carly's mind. If only the owners had identified and fixed the problem when the cocker was a puppy, how very different the outcome might have been.

Carly weighed her options. "Penny and I will take care of this dog, Ruby." The strategy allowed the employees to see her doing some hands-on work again. Plus it would give her the opportunity to talk privately to Penny outside the intimidating environment of Hugh's office.

Ruby's eyebrows rose in bewilderment when Carly set down her purse and took the syringe from her.

"Why don't you get ready for Sophia's goddaughter?" Carly said. "She should be here soon." A.A. Malakov was visiting from New York, and Carly had volunteered Ruby to show her around the shelter.

Penny stroked the cocker while Carly inserted the needle into a half-pint vial of smoky blue solution—unaffectionately nicknamed "Blue Juice" by those who used it day in and day out.

Whispering "Good girl, sweet girl," Penny reached across the dog's shoulders. Her delicate thumb and forefinger made a tourniquet around the animal's forelimb just below her elbow. Carly rubbed the front of the leg with a moistened cotton ball. A taut vein appeared beneath the slicked-down hair. Carly threaded the needle into the blood vessel and pushed the plunger.

She barely finished the injection when the fear left the dog's eyes and her nervous panting stopped. Penny's soothing words were the last thing the cocker heard as her tense body relaxed and sank into the gentle arms. Penny laid the animal on its side. She tapped the surface of the dog's eye. The lids didn't blink. She cupped her hand around the breastbone until she was sure the heart had stopped. Less than two minutes passed from the moment the needle entered the vein until death claimed its victim.

Carly's throat constricted. It was never easy, no matter how many hundreds of times she did it.

And Carly knew Penny felt the strain even more acutely. The gentlest of all souls, Penny empathized with every animal and mourned each death. An animal shelter was a tough place to work. Day-after-day of deciding who should live and who should die and then carrying out the execution would have weighed heavy on George Patton.

Carly snapped open a plastic bag and watched Penny slide the flaccid animal into the sack. Penny's hair needed a good shampooing, but otherwise she appeared as clean as anyone who worked around animals all day. Carly sniffed. Nothing unusual. But Penny did look like she had lost some weight. Carly wondered how Bob Hicks would handle the situation.

"Before you take the bag to the freezer, I need to talk to you for a minute."

Penny's eyes were full of suspicion. "I suppose I'm in trouble for yelling at Ruby."

"No, but I am going to ask what's wrong that you're so short-tempered."

Penny knotted the open end of the trash sack before answering. "I'm just tired."

"Tired of…? Working here? Tired in general?"

Penny glanced around the small room. "Both."

Carly leaned her forearms on the table. "It's not like you to hit a dog, even on the rump."

Penny's gaze stopped leaping around the room and centered on the phosphoric glow of Darrell's lava lamp. Her forefinger hooked her hoop earring. "I'm just so sick of it!"

"Sick of…?"

"Death! I'm sick of it!" She yanked so hard on her earring, it seemed ready to pull through the flesh of her lobe.

Carly put a hand on Penny's wrist. "Careful. You'll hurt yourself."

Penny picked up the empty syringe and shook it at Carly. "You don't know! You don't remember! All you do is sit in your office. You don't have to give them the Blue Juice!" Penny reared back and pitched the syringe across the room. It bounced off the paper towel dispenser. An aluminum *ping* reverberated through the tiny room.

Carly recoiled, not only from the flying object but from the verbal attack. "That's not true. I'm only temporarily the director. I euthanized the first year I was here, and I'll euthanize after Hugh returns. And I still do it, when time allows." To prove her point, she rapped the back of her hand against the black bag lying between them.

Penny's face caved in and tears once again fell in earnest. "I know. It's not fair to say you don't do your part. But I'm just so tired of it. Just fucking tired of it!"

Carly's shoulders tightened further. When had Penny gravitated to the f-word?

"I'm fucking fed up with killing animals because owners won't spend the money to have their pets fixed but they'll drop a hundred bucks at a restaurant just like that!" Penny's fingers snapped beside her head.

"We all feel that way," Carly validated Penny's viewpoint. "We all want to strangle the mother who wants her kids to see 'the miracle of birth.' And who wouldn't want to rip the *cojones* out of every good ol' boy who refuses to have his dog castrated because 'It'll ruin him,' or 'Life ain't worth living if you ain't gettin' any'?"

The early twitch of a smile cropped up at the corner of Penny's mouth. She wiped her cheeks on her sleeve.

"Do you need time off?" Carly asked.

"How can I take time off? The spring kittens are already starting to come in. Do you know how many animals are on the list to be euthanized today? And Hailey's one of them." The last phrase sounded intentionally spiteful.

"Hailey?"

Penny nodded.

"Have we put her in the *Courier* as Pet-of-the-Week?"

"Ruby doesn't see any reason to try to adopt her out again."

Carly felt a familiar tingle in the upper part of her nose. Tears were on their way. She sucked air into her lungs. "Another good dog that doesn't deserve to die."

"See, I told you Ruby is being—"

"No! Don't blame Ruby. It's society's fault. We're just the ones who have to do the dirty work."

Penny hung her head, her stringy hair hiding her face.

Carly softened her voice. "It seems like you never take any time off. You know how vacation works—use it or lose it."

Penny dipped a shoulder and grunted that Carly was right.

"We all need days off to revitalize ourselves." Carly felt like an idiot as she preached the detached words of a personnel specialist. "In addition to your anger, I saw something else that tells me you need some time away from here."

"What?"

"Some of the names you've given the animals. Black Widow. Darth Vader. Whatever happened to upbeat names like Marmalade and Tiger Lilly and Tinkerbell? Not to mention, we have to be careful with names like Queen of Spades. Racial undertones, you know."

Penny twirled a lock of hair around her forefinger while she gathered her thoughts. "If it's okay with you and Ruby," she spat her supervisor's name, "I'll schedule some days off for later this month."

"That sounds good, but for now, how about if you throw some cold water on your face and replace Alberto at the front desk."

"And make Alberto euthanize all those animals?"

"Someone has to euthanize, but today, it's not going to be you."

Penny moved the strand of hair from her finger to her mouth and began chewing on it. She picked up the trash sack. She seemed void of either gratitude or bitterness over Carly's counseling. She didn't seem to have anything left inside her except acquiescence.

Carly continued her journey to her office and was only a half-dozen steps away from it when a familiar voice halted her in mid-stride.

"Oh, Ms. Shannon, I'm so glad you're back from your meeting."

Carly froze like a bird dog on point, her upper body reaching toward the phone message clipped to her doorjamb. She squinted to make sure she correctly deciphered the scribble. Yes! Eddie! Returning her call from earlier in the week.

She turned to see Sophia Zhirnov standing beside the break room door, waving a vase of roses, delphinium, and lilies. Not now, Sophia! Carly mumbled under her breath. I have a phone call to return!

Carly reluctantly retraced her steps down the hall and was greeted by Sophia's borzoi, Bullwinkle. Carly was secretly jealous of how the ninety-pound dog's expansive chest narrowed into a waspish waistline. Whenever the pooch visited the shelter, he expected a few obligatory pats from every employee he encountered. Carly indulged the dog this afternoon but gently pushed him away when he stuck his Roman nose in her crotch.

"Bullzy and I are just fiddling around while Ms. Wesolowski gives A.A. a tour of the shelter. They're brainstorming ideas for the wall mural." Sophia proceeded to remind Carly that Easter was just around the corner and shouldn't they order some pastel leashes. "Perhaps lavender?"

Carly missed a beat. Was this the same no-nonsense woman who laid down the financial law-of-survival at the Board meeting? Today she was back on her color wheel, once again off-kilter with the dizzying kaleidoscope of muted hues, pulsating pigments, tones and halftones.

"Pastels would be nice," Carly agreed. "But nylon leashes are almost indestructible, and we have a ton of the regular ol' blue ones."

"Oh, yes. Sort of a Chinese porcelain blue, aren't they?" Sophia's ketchup-red lips slid to one side as she pondered the dilemma of having too much of a good thing. "We always have pet rabbits in the shelter, don't we? I was thinking we could set up a couple of cages in the reception area in the spirit of the holiday."

"That idea has merit, but we have to keep in mind that we don't want people to adopt on impulse. And that's what happens when they see a cute, furry critter. When they get it home, they find out they weren't prepared for the animal or they lose interest in it within a week."

Sophia fingered the pearls at her neck. "Ah, I see. Then back in the shelter it comes."

One thing about Sophia, Carly thought, was that the woman was quick to catch on. Once someone took the time to explain a concept, it would affix itself in her astute mind as tightly as the caps on her front teeth. Now if only she doesn't come up with the idea of putting dyed baby chicks and ducklings in the lobby.

Ruby bulldozed into the room. A.A. followed with the fluidity of a feline, her eyes heavy with the languid look of a cat coming off a catnip high. A paisley skirt billowed around the artist's calves, topped with a white peasant blouse and a black fringed shawl. Trailing behind her was a waist-length ebony braid, glistening with rivulets of premature silver. Her Yankee-pale complexion was untainted with makeup. Evidently she felt paints and pigments belonged on a canvas and not on her skin.

"What do you think?" Sophia's arm circled her goddaughter's elbow.

"I can't tell you how inspired I am by Ruby's stories about the Humane Society!" The fluttering of A.A.'s hand was accompanied by the wind chime resonance of a dozen copper bangle bracelets. "She's a fountain of creativity!"

Carly's eyes narrowed to tight slits. Ruby Wesolowski? A fountain of creativity?

"Next we'll meet Mary Louise," Ruby giggled to A.A. "He told me he expects a place of honor on the mural." Like a demented hummingbird, Ruby buried her nose in Sophia's bouquet. "Great flowers, by the way."

Carly's ears and eyes must be deceiving her. What tittering teenager was masquerading as the crusty Operations Manager?

Carly turned to Sophia. "If you'll excuse me, I need to return some phone calls. Thank you for the flowers. The staff appreciates them."

"I also put a vase on the front counter."

Carly zeroed in on her phone message. Eddie *had* to be calling about fixing the porch. And looking for his coin collection. And...?

As she passed the door to the reception area, she glanced at Sophia's second vase of flowers.

For the fourth time since she entered the shelter, she was sidetracked. Standing at the counter were the Brownie leader and his daughter.

H ello again." She scanned her memory for his name. "Charlie."
"Carly."

"Charlie."

She turned her smile toward the second grader. "I have to admit I don't remember your name."

"Allison." Her voice was soft but not bashful.

"Back again so soon?" Carly asked.

"We're here to adopt a dog," Charlie said.

"Great! Penny will help you fill out the paperwork." Carly winked at Allison. "We have to make sure you'll be a responsible pet owner."

As she turned to leave, Penny caught her arm.

"They want to adopt Hailey." Penny's puffy eyes bugged-out like a Boston terrier's.

Carly's eyes grew just as large. Hailey? she mouthed mutely.

Was she still alive? Carly nonchalantly tucked her purse under the counter. "Tell you what," she said to Allison. "I'll get Hailey from the kennel so you can tell her the good news yourself."

As soon as Carly cleared Allison's line of vision, she raced like a bat out of hell for the kennel. Please, God, please let her still be alive. Please.

In front of run #8, she twisted an ankle. Damn whoever invented high heels!

Please be alive.

Past Black Widow, Queen of Spades, and Darth Vader. Past the goats. Past Sundance. Anxiety squeezed her chest.

Finally, #15.

Empty.

Shit!

She sprinted down the aisle of runs. Around the corner. There was Alberto—walking into the euthanasia room. Beside him was a russet dog.

"Alberto! Wait! She's adopted!"

As Carly took the leash, Hailey looked up with her usual patient, gentle expression, as if she had all the time in the world.

Alberto told Hailey she was one lucky dog and went in search of the next animal on the list.

Allison threw her arms wide open. Hailey sashayed into them and greeted her new friend with a moist kiss. Hailey sat down with the poise of a debutante, her feathery tail sweeping the floor. Penny's face glowed with innocent happiness. So did Carly's heart. She was smiling with the unabashed gaiety of a dachshund, but she couldn't help herself. What was happening right before her eyes was why she was in this business.

Now that Penny was assured that Hailey still walked on this earth, she tackled the adoption forms in earnest with Charlie.

Out of the corner of her eye, Carly saw Ruby in the hallway. She stepped away from the counter and motioned the Operations Manager into the vacant break room. Carly explained her rationale for moving Penny to the front desk for the rest of the day.

"Let's keep her away from euthanasia for the next couple of days. She needs a break."

"Don't we all?" Ruby retorted.

Carly occasionally wished she had selected someone from outside the Humane Society as the Operations Manager, someone who wouldn't treat her like the lame duck she was.

"I have to find A.A. and rescue her from Juan Pablo," Ruby said. "The last time I saw them, he was describing his job to her, calling himself 'the champion of those that can't defend themselves.'"

On her way to her office for the umpteenth time, Carly stopped by the front desk to retrieve her purse. Charlie had finished signing the adoption form. His hand pushed his glasses up the bridge of his nose.

Carly nodded to herself. Yep. There it was. Shiny gold. Nothing fancy. Just your basic I'm-off-limits wedding band.

"Thank you, Mr. VanCleave," Penny said. "We'll give you a call in a few days to make sure everything's working out with Hailey."

"That would be great." He gave Penny a killer smile.

Just as Carly was pulling out her purse from underneath the counter, Charlie asked, "May I speak to you for a minute?"

"Sure." The purse was shoved back onto the shelf. What in the world did he want to talk about? Did he have a son whose Boy Scout troop needed a shelter tour? She couldn't squeeze anything else into her over-stuffed schedule. Plus she needed to return a phone call. ASAP.

She glanced at her watch, hoping he'd pick up on the signal that she didn't have much time. "Tell you what. It's a beautiful day, and Hailey might appreciate the opportunity to water the grass. Why don't we step outside?"

As Carly went around to the front of the counter, she asked Allison if she knew how Hailey had come by her name. When Allison shook her head, Carly told her, "Because we found her as a stray in the middle of a real bad hailstorm."

"Ah, very clever," Charlie said as they stepped into the unseasonably warm sunlight. He told Allison, "Take Hailey Hailstorm for a little walk. Stay on the grass, away from the parking lot. And away from those flowers." He turned to Carly. "Cute prairie dog."

"It's a groundhog. Courtesy of one of our Board members, Sophia Zhirnov. She means well, but she overdoes it sometimes." Carly crossed her eyes.

"I see."

"By the way, I really admire you for being a Brownie leader."

The compliment slid off him like water off a Labrador retriever. "I'm an unofficial leader. I help out when I can, which isn't that often. Besides working full-time, I've foolishly overloaded myself with extracurricular activities."

"Such as?"

"I'm on the Zhirnov Springs City Council."

Carly wanted dig a hole and disappear into the freshly tilled earth next to the groundhog. She really excelled at making herself look stupid. Why didn't she read the newspaper or watch the news once in while? As Executive Director, it was her job to know who the key players were in her community.

She gave a laugh that sounded nervous even to her. "I guess that would keep a person busy."

"Which leads into what I wanted to talk to you about. It's my under-standing that your organization is funded through donations from the public plus a contract to house the animals the City picks up. Am I right?"

"You are. A lot of people think that we receive funding from some national humane society in-the-sky. But there is no such thing."

"And I suspect that like most nonprofit organizations, you barely scrape by month-to-month. Your employees are underpaid with very little in the way of benefits. Your computer technology needs upgrading. As does your facility in general. Am I on target?"

The conversation put Carly on guard. Why was a City Councilman questioning her about the Humane Society's finances? Was he suggesting the organization was fiscally irresponsible? Did he know the Board of Directors was insisting on a substantial increase in next year's contract? Did he plan to recommend to the Council that the City of Zhirnov Springs build its own shelter and not renew the contract?

When she didn't answer him, he tempered his words. "I happen to know some people who are active volunteers with the Humane Society. They've told me the organization would like to provide additional services, but it just doesn't have the money. And you're in good company. Every charitable group in this town has the same problem."

As the sun dappled his face through the naked elm branches, he looked above suspicion. But instinct told her to tread warily.

"Are you interested in getting more money from the City?" he asked.

"Sure."

"Mind if I offer you a suggestion?"

"Not at all. Please do."

"The City Council votes on next year's budget in September. Prior to that, they need to be convinced that the Humane Society is doing a good job, but if it had more money, it could do an even more spectacular job. That can be achieved by a four- or five-minute presentation at one of our meetings. Give the Council the facts—the types of services you provide for the citizens, how many animals you take care of, and how both the number of animals and the cost has escalated over the past couple of years."

"Give a presentation to the City Council?" She wanted to laugh. This man was out of his mind! Carly Shannon address the City Council? She almost peed her pants when she gave Hugh's talk to the Newcomers Club.

"It will be worth your while to call the City Secretary and get on the agenda," he said. "Hugh Sherman met with the City Manager in the past, but the whole Council needs to hear what you have to say. The strategy has worked for other organizations. It'll work for you."

"Sounds like good advice." She crossed her fingers and toes that Hugh would be back at work in time to the presentation.

"Carly!" Penny's head was sticking out the door. "There's an Eddie Chevalier on the phone for you. He says it's the second time he's called."

"Tell him I'll be right there." She turned to Charlie. "Sorry. I have to take this call. Thanks for the suggestion."

"Sure." He held out his hand—the one without the wedding ring.

She shook it. As she turned toward the shelter, she called to Hailey and her new owner. "Good luck, you two!"

Allison stopped her earnest conversation with Hailey long enough to wave a hearty good-bye.

Carly thought she felt Charlie's eyes follow her into the building. Or maybe it was just wishful thinking.

When she reached her office, she found Darrell cross-legged on the floor with Mary Louise on his shoulder. Darrell's index finger undulated like John Philip Sousa's as he tried to teach the bird "Let the Sunshine In" from the musical *Hair*.

"Leeet the sunshine in. Oooooo. Leeet the sunshine in," Darrell sang a cappella. "Come on, M.L., sing with me!"

Despite Darrell's coaching, Mary Louise seemed hesitant to cut loose, choosing instead to merely bob his head up and down in cadence with Darrell's finger.

"Excuse me, fellas. I have a phone call. Can we let the sunshine in a little later?"

Even though her words sounded flip, her heart was pounding as she closed the door behind Darrell. She hated that she allowed herself to have these reactions to Eddie. She fingercombed her hair before she picked up the receiver.

After a brief joke about playing phone tag, Eddie got straight to the point. "I'm going to Houston next Friday and Saturday to meet with an important client. The kind of client where you go to him; he doesn't come to you. I was wondering, would you look after my dog while I'm gone? I trust you with him more than I'd trust anyone else."

"Look after your dog?"

"He could either stay at your place, or you could come by my house."

"Next weekend is a little full to squeeze in dog-sitting."

"Sure, I understand. By the way, I haven't forgotten about the porch. I'll call you when I get back from Houston. Maybe we could get together for a drink sometime? Or maybe dinner? I'd like to hear how your parents are doing. You know, I always liked your family."

Carly's mouth contracted into a skeptical line. "Just give me a call whenever."

"Let me know if you change your mind about the dog."

"You have my word on that."

After they said good-bye, Carly's nervous tension sprang her from the chair. She strode over to the mirror she recently hung on the back of her door. Or rather, Hugh's door.

She nodded to her reflection. She handled that phone call rather well. Polite but reserved. Friendly but detached.

*I always liked your family.* Yeah, right.

*Look after my dog while I'm gone.* The audacity of that self-absorbed jerk! If he has such super-rich clients, why is he too cheap to pay a dog sitter?

*Important client in Houston.* How did Eddie manage to pull that off? Not that she was surprised. He always went for the gusto. And usually got it. If she and Eddie got back together, her financial woes would be a thing of the past.

*Maybe we could get together for a drink sometime.* She ran her hands over her hips. Getting thinner every minute. When he called, she'd be ready.

She placed a hand under each breast and questioned whether a Wonderbra would be worth the money. She moved closer to the mirror to examine today's onslaught of new lines. She'd definitely start using that facial masque she bought over a year ago and then tucked away in her bathroom cabinet.

She stepped back from the mirror and scowled as she remembered the Eddie-induced shards of pain followed by months and months of hollow ache. She wanted to beat her head against the wall. Why was she doing this to herself? Why was she setting herself up for more hurt?

# PART II

The question is not,
Can they reason?
Can they talk?
but, Can they suffer?

Jeremy Bentham
1748-1832

# Part II

# Prologue

B eyond the freshly mown football field and past the pile of cigarette butts where the high school boys smoked over lunch hour, a small gray tabby crouched in the damp shade under the equipment shed. Her stomach tightened with hunger. Last night's hunting had yielded little except a few crickets. She had even stayed out longer than usual after sunrise this morning, hoping to catch a feckless robin. But when she returned to her lair, her stomach was still empty.

Even after a full day's sleep, she didn't want to go back out into the world. She had recently weaned her kittens and was just now getting her strength back. Besides, her head felt heavy, and her thinking was cloudy. Scavenging a meal required more ambition than she had, but her stomach told her she had to eat.

The slender tabby crept from under the floor joists and sniffed the evening air. It smelled of impending rain and Texas mountain laurel blossoms. There were other scents. Car exhaust. The rank dumpster that, last night, had contained nothing edible. But she wasn't able to detect odors like she should. Her tongue flicked away the mucus from her nostrils. She poked her nose higher into the air. Yes, in the distance, a hint of something useful—rodent droppings.

She sat beside the shed and curled her tail around her paws. She could see three other felines, grooming their fur with demure refinement. Unseen behind those three were scores more. Never in her entire one-year of life had so many cats hung about her neighborhood. That's why the mice had become so few and far between. Too many predators.

She wandered to a discarded tire for a drink of brackish water. Her throat was raw. She knew she could probably find a downed bat to eat under the railroad viaduct, but she didn't have the energy to journey a half-dozen blocks. She headed toward the apartment complex. Sometimes there was a bowl of dry cat food outside the end apartment.

Screeching insults, a mockingbird made a kamikaze dive at the tabby. She reflexively dropped to the ground. The bird darted up, circled, paused in midair, and swooped again. Sparring matches with mocking-birds offered a pleasant diversion when she felt frisky. But not today.

She reached the end apartment to find the bowl empty. Calling on her combined senses of sight, hearing, and smell, she foraged for food around the building and parking lot. In the moisture-laden air, there was an unidentifiable but delectable scent.

The meaty aroma came from the sun-flecked shade under the Indian hawthorn. She crouched behind an air conditioner and surveyed the area. There was something new—a bowl containing a tempting brown mash. The details were obscured by a troublesome galvanized mesh.

A timid cat by nature, she bided her time. When the sun sank below the rooftops, her silent feet crept closer. She continued to keep watch, shivering not from cold or fear but from fever. Only when the dampness seeped from the night soil did she sneak up to the contraption.

Her puffed tail issued a subliminal threat to whatever dangers might be present. Her nose investigated the steel rods. There was only one way to reach the bowl. She put her head in the opening, her whiskers brushing the unyielding sides. Her sixth sense warned of peril, but hunger was a powerful motivator. She stepped toward the bowl.

The door sprung shut in a metallic explosion. A single, powerful thrust of her legs hurled her to the back of the trap. She flew face-first into the steel bars.

With heart-pounding fear, she pushed and clawed, but the steel rods wouldn't give. She rammed the place where the opening had been. Her front leg stretched through the metal lattice and clawed the air in futile desperation. She slunk to the rear of the trap and huddled in glazed paralysis. In the ruckus, the bowl had turned over, but she didn't touch the food.

Around midnight, a bone-soaking downpour began. The shrub gave no protection. She closed her eyes to keep out the rain. Her quivering muscles throbbed. So did her head as the pressure inside continued to build. When the shower stopped, her tongue worked to lift the water from her drenched fur, only to have the rain start again. It didn't quit until splotches of morning sunlight appeared under the branches of the Indian hawthorn.

Her wide eyes watched a pair of trousers coming toward her. She tried to make herself small and invisible. The person picked up the trap. The tabby fought to keep her balance as the cage pitched wildly while being carried to a truck. Suddenly all was darkness, followed by noise. Lots of it. And a sensation of motion. But everything was shrouded in black.

Sunlight appeared once again. She was carried into a building full of mysterious and terrifying smells. The odor of hundreds of cats. Dogs. Disinfectants. Insecticides. People. It was a sinister place.

The trap's opening was placed at the edge of a larger and even more menacing stainless steel cage. She hunkered down. A dowel poked through the metal bars and prodded her out of the trap. The cage door slammed shut. Its sharp clang reverberated in her flattened ears.

Her claws splayed as she tried to climb up the slippery sides. But the stainless steel offered no footholds. Confusion and exhaustion set in. She cowered behind the litter box, hiding from the harsh fluorescent lights. The whole world was full of smells and noise and fear.

Images cascaded through her mind—the broad expanse of the football field, the mischievous mockingbirds, and the bowl outside the apartment. The tabby ached to be home, her chilled body soaking up the sun.

She gave a violent sneeze. And again.

**11**

Summer dumped an early load of hot, heavy air, and Carly's feral tendrils refused to be captured beneath the gimme cap.

**Hi-Top Feed, Seed & Semen**
Dora, Iowa

The cap accompanied her to Texas and was forgotten about until it surfaced while she was scouring the attic for Eddie's coin collection. She had promised herself she wouldn't spend a minute of her time looking for his coins. But she caved in to the image of handing him the Jefferson nickels and Liberty half dollars, basking in his accolades over her adroit sleuthing and bighearted effort. However, her search yielded nothing. Almost nothing. She stumbled upon the yellowed floor plans of the house they had planned to build. She tossed the plans into the trash, only to later retrieve them—just in case she ever had a use for them.

Her fingers tented the front of her Humane Society T-shirt, fanning her chest and neck with soggy air. The Pet Expo was always held the last Saturday in April, meaning the Humane Society prepared for everything from a bone-chilling spring shower to temperatures in the nineties. This year, it was Okefenokee Swamp weather.

Carly squinted through the heat waves rising from the asphalt parking lot. It was barely 11:00 and the petting zoo's huge bronze turkeys were already panting, the miniature donkeys' heads were hanging, and the llamas looked churlish. Monica's two young goats were as capricious as armadillos as they took a siesta under a blue tarpaulin. Father Donahoe dragged a forefinger around the moist inside of his high white collar as he hurried through his Blessing for the Animals. Sergeant McAfee asked that his police dogs give only the morning demonstration of search and rescue; this afternoon would be too hot to unnecessarily put them through their paces. Sentry, the fire department's Dalmatian, couldn't stand on the blistering metal of the hook and ladder truck, so the stately civil servant sprawled on his belly in the shade beside the goats, his rear legs distended behind him and his tongue lolling. Even the vexing grackles, which normally filled the air with their cackling and caked the sidewalk with their droppings, were quietly hanging out in the elm tree, looking wilted. The snow cone stand was enjoying a booming business.

But Carly was trying to catch a glimpse of something else through the pavement's heat gyrations. Actually, two things. First, she wanted to scope out the half-dozen people with "Animal Advocates of Central Texas" emblazoned across the front and back of their T-shirts. Clustered like a flock of geese, the Advocates waddled first to the Blessing of the Animals before moving en mass to the petting zoo. They scrutinized the Humane Society sign and poked their toes in the chuckholes in the parking lot. They turned their attention to the building, sniffing around like they were about to lift their legs to mark their territory. A woman scribbled on a steno pad. Another Advocate kept a camcorder plastered to his eye.

Carly knew sooner or later she'd have to square her shoulders and introduce herself to them. She also knew sooner was probably better than later. Even the most fervent activist wouldn't hang around long in this drippy heat.

Carly's second item of interest was one of the Pet Expo's traditional fund-raisers—a dunking booth. Every year, high school teachers, city administrators, television newscasters, and other local, well-known faces were coerced into thirty-minute stints in the booth. Sticking out his tongue at his constituents at this very moment was one of Zhirnov Springs's esteemed officials—Charlie VanCleave.

Carly duly noted that Councilman VanCleave was already drenched, his sleeveless T-shirt and cut-off jeans molded pleasantly to his tight torso. His waist tapered agreeably, and the sinews of his neck stretched lean and taut to his collarbone.

Someone called out, "When are you guys gonna fix the streets? My car dropped into a pothole and I haven't seen it since!" A ball was launched. A resounding *Dong* was followed by *Kerplunk*, and Charlie dropped from sight. As he hauled himself up the ladder for the next round of ridicule, Carly couldn't help but notice the water streaming down his legs. Pretty darn good thighs for a Brownie leader.

She sauntered in the general direction of the dunking booth, thinking it wouldn't hurt to get a little closer look at one of her elected officials. The scorched pavement felt spongy under her sneakers. The funny thing was, her knees felt a little mushy as well.

Face facts, Carly-girl, she chided herself. Charlie VanCleave was an intelligent, pleasant, attractive man. An intelligent, pleasant, attractive, *married* man.

She watched from the rear of the spectators as he egged on the latest contestant. He put his thumbs in his ears and wagged his fingers beside his head. The sun had already kindled his cheeks and nose into a pink that matched Sophia's oleanders. Wet hair tumbling almost into his eyes gave him the look of an impish Scottish terrier. Carly bit the inside of her check to keep from smiling. There was no denying it—that man was downright cute.

Just as Alan Drake announced over the loudspeaker that the Cow Chip Pitching Contest was about to start, Charlie caught sight of her. A smile blazed across his face as he pulled a thumb from his ear and waved to her. She returned the gesture. At the same second, there was a *Dong*, and Charlie once again disappeared in a splash of water.

She heard, rather than saw, Darrell return from the Mutt Strut and the Fido Frisbee Catching Contest at the park. No way was that sputtering, ramshackle, rust bucket van going to last another year. She tossed aside the worry. It would be Hugh's problem when he returned.

Someone tapped her elbow. It was a freckle-faced girl, probably second or third grade.

Carly smiled. "Hi! Can I help you?"

"You visited my school last year." The voice was as soft as cat paws on fresh snow.

Bracing her hands against her knees, Carly bent over so she could hear. "Did I talk to your class about animals?"

The blonde head bobbed. "You told us to make sure our pets got their surgery."

"Yes, I did."

"I talked my mom into getting our cat spayed."

"You did? Good for you!"

"She was five years old."

"Your cat was five years old? You had her since she was a kitten?" Another nod.

"How many litters of kittens did she have before she was spayed?"

"Four."

Carly was bowled over. A seven-year-old talked her mother into spaying a cat that would have otherwise gone on having litters for the rest of her shortened life.

"You did a very wonderful thing."

"I used my allowance."

"You helped pay for the surgery?" Carly straightened and reached an arm around the girl's shoulders. Her voice choked as her heart rose to her throat. "You should be very proud of yourself. Your mom should be proud of you, too. Thank you so much for telling me."

She frequently wondered if her school talks did any good. Here was proof positive that they did. Somehow, she had to reinstitute the Humane Society's visits to the second graders. Pronto.

She bid the girl goodbye, turned, and ran headlong into a dripping wet Charlie VanCleave.

**12**

Charlie's head jerked back. His hair flung a spray of water. Carly reeled in reverse. Her hand flew up between them. Her fingertips ended up millimeters from where his soaked T-shirt clung to nipples still erect from his last dip in the cool water. Off-balance both mentally and physically, her impulse was to reach for his glistening bicep. She somehow managed to squash the reflex and, instead, regained her footing with some hootchy-kootchy moves.

Excuse me," he said. "Didn't mean to get you wet."

"Don't apologize. In fact, could you maybe shake like a spaniel and sprinkle some more water on me?" Her hand fanned her flushed face. "Everyone is insanely jealous of you taking those cool dips."

He gave her a high-wattage smile. "Right. I'm sure everyone would like to have objects and insults hurled at them. Of course, if my daughter has her way, this will be the last year you'll need that dunking booth."

"Huh?"

"Allison has big fund-raising schemes. Tomorrow afternoon, she and one of her friends plan to earn points for a Girl Scout badge by raising money for the Humane Society. A lemonade stand, to be exact."

A bead of water ran from the hair that flopped over his forehead, down the bridge between his eyes, and alongside his nose. She couldn't believe how strong the urge was to stroke away the trickle and smooth the Dennis-the-Menace locks back from his brow.

"A lemonade stand? How thoughtful of them!"

"So you'll take the $20 or so the girls will raise?"

"Oh, definitely. Let's see—twenty bucks. That should cover about twenty seconds of our air conditioning bill."

"And what about the City's money? Will you take that too?"

"The City's money?"

"Just a friendly reminder that if you want to impress the City Council with the Humane Society's civic good deeds, you need to be at the next Council meeting."

"The next Council meeting? But this is only April. I thought the budget wasn't decided until September."

"The Council finalizes the budget in September. The city staff are drawing up a draft as we speak. The Council will review and amend the draft at their June meeting. So, if the Humane Society wants to make a presentation to the Council, that leaves...." He raised an upward palm.

Carly's eyebrows slammed together. "May's meeting." Hugh had given no indication he was returning anytime soon.

"Right. May's meeting."

"So, how do I get on the agenda?"

"Call the City Secretary Monday morning. I think that's the deadline."

"City Secretary. Monday morning." Maybe through repetition she'd find the courage to actually commit the words to action.

"The Council will be glad to hear what you have to say. Seems like we receive more phone calls and complaints about animal control than anything else."

"Really? That surprises me."

"Now I know who to turn to for answers. And the other Councilmen would like to put a name with a face as well."

His reference to her face unnerved her. In all likelihood, her mascara was melting down her cheeks. And her hair undoubtedly looked like Medusa's snakes crawling out from underneath a seed-&-semen baseball cap. But most mortifying was what she saw as she self-consciously averted her eyes. Large rings of perspiration were growing from her sweltering armpits. She self-consciously pulled the brim of her hat down her forehead.

He dovetailed his index and middle finger onto the bill of her cap and gently lowered it further. "Dora, Iowa?"

Even though he hadn't physically touched her, electric pinpricks ran down her spine. "My hometown." She pushed the visor back into place.

"You're an Iowa farm girl?"

She tilted her head playfully. "You making fun?"

"No way." His mouth ebbed into a prankish grin.

"So this farm girl needs to talk to the City Secretary Monday morning, huh?"

"Right. My fellow Councilmen will be expecting to see you at the next meeting."

"Councilmen? Aren't there any women?"

He grinned. " 'scuse me. Council Members."

Her legs felt funny—kind of tingly and weaker than water. She wasn't sure if the sensation was due to angst over a presentation to the City Council, embarrassment about her drenched armpits, or butterflies from Charlie VanCleave's dusky eyes pouring over her face. His eyes were the kind of bottomless well that women loved to tumble into. Without a safety net.

That's what it was! She knew there was something different about him today. No glasses! This must be how he looked fresh out of the shower—no glasses, disheveled hair, a pair of shorts.

Carly was still studying the murky pools of his eyes when he said, "Feel free to come over tomorrow and sample the wares."

*Sample the wares*? Oh yeah. The lemonade. "I might have to stop by," she said. "I'll need a good, stiff drink. Tomorrow is Paint The Front Porch Day."

"Then you'll definitely need a drink. Besides, Hailey's been asking about you."

"I take it she's made herself at home?"

"The minute she walked through the front door. So you'll swing by?" He gave her his address on Jackson Street.

No way was she going to Charlie VanCleave's house. The thought of meeting Mrs. VanCleave—yuk! Besides, she was considering calling Eddie to see if he'd finally make good on his offer to replace those rotten boards.

She was saved from responding by Darrell's frantic motions for her to come to the building. "If you'll excuse me, I'm being summoned."

Charlie pointed a finger at her nose. "City Secretary. Monday morning."

She parroted, "City Secretary. Monday morning."

They nodded their goodbyes.

"Carly."

"Charlie."

Darrell held open the door as she entered the building. With a bandana tied around his head, he looked like he just jumped off a Harley rather than extracted himself from the ancient van. Once in the air conditioning, she made butterfly wings out of her arms to dry out her armpits.

"Hey! How did everything go at the park? Were there lots of Frisbee contestants? There weren't any injuries, were there?"

"Everything went just ducky. Here's the list of winners." He reached into the pocket of his camouflage shorts and handed her a damp piece of paper torn from a spiral notebook. It listed the first-place contestants for the various categories—fastest human-animal team, pet most resembling its owner, most unusual species, and so on.

"How many participated?"

"Dogs or people? Mutt Walk or Frisbee Contest?" he asked. "The entry forms are still in the van. But, man, that's *sooo* not the issue."

"It's not?"

"*Nyet*. It's Penelope. She's upset again."

"So what else is new?"

"Worse this time. I'm telling you, she's having a melt-down." Darrell took Carly's elbow and propelled her toward her office. Her sneakers made skid noises as he pushed her across the eggshell tile floor.

Penny was gazing out the window, her back toward the door. Her cargo pants were about to fall off her hipbones. Half her hair was in a ponytail atop her head, secured by something that resembled a twist-tie for a plastic bag. The other half hung limp down the nape of her neck.

"Hi, Penny!" Carly made her voice upbeat. "How's it going today in the shelter? Is the Expo increasing adoptions?"

Penny turned around. Her normal peaches-and-cream complexion was blotchy. Her eyes were dark and aggrieved. She had the slatternly appearance of someone who hung out in the bathrooms of rest stops and bus stations.

"Penelope, sit down." Darrell moved the two orange chairs side-by-side until they were touching. He walked over to the window, took Penny's hand, and led her like a stray puppy to one of the chairs. Never releasing her hand or her eyes, he lowered himself onto the other chair. "Tell Carly what you saw."

Penny dropped her head to hide behind scraggly wisps of hair. She muttered something.

"Say again?" Darrell stroked the back of her porcelain hand.

Penny gave a barely perceptible shake of her head as she backhanded a strand of hair. Her nails were chewed to the quick.

"Come on, Penelope. This is bothering you. You should tell Carly."

Her response was muffled but comprehendible. "She can't do anything."

Already feeling ineffectual as she stood like a wooden Indian beside her desk, Carly felt even more incompetent after Penny's cutting remark. She wheeled her chair around the desk to place her knees inches from Penny's.

"Penny, what is it?" Getting no response, Carly continued, "Tell me what's bothering you. I'll do what I can to help." She waited for a reply that didn't come.

"Do you want me to tell her?" Darrell asked Penny.

Penny gave a strangled sob as she nodded.

Half way through the story, Penny lifted her head and filled in the details with a choked voice and gesticulating hands. Penny and her neighbor, a spry eighty-year-old named Mrs. Bethke, often chatted on Mrs. Bethke's backyard glider. Mrs. Bethke's dog, Percy, was always at their feet. Mrs. Bethke gave Penny tomatoes and okra from her garden each summer. Penny also received a tin of cookies each Christmas along with a card signed, "Nola Bethke and Persimmon."

Although Penny was occasionally in Mrs. Bethke's house, those occasions abruptly ended when Mrs. Bethke fell last winter and broke her hip. When her divorced son Roger brought her home in a wheelchair from the hospital, Penny took them a casserole. Roger greeted her at the door, took the casserole, and explained that he would be staying with his mother during her recuperation. She asked Roger to convey her best wishes to his mother for a speedy recovery.

Penny rarely saw Roger outdoors, but when she did, he returned her greeting with a condensed wave. No ramp was put over the front or rear steps for Mrs. Bethke's wheelchair. The house took on an abandoned look. The window shades were drawn, the drapes remained closed. During the evening, the only light visible was the blue glow of the television that filtered through the small octagonal window in the front door. Once spring arrived, waist-high Johnson grass and sunflowers overtook Mrs. Bethke's garden. The yard was mowed at irregular intervals, the blade not bothering with the grass under the glider.

To Penny's knowledge, Mrs. Bethke no longer saw the light of day. Percy, meanwhile, was chained to the oak tree on what was once lush grass but was now a circle of barren dirt and feces. The chain link fence did nothing to block his piteous whines from reaching Penny. His coat was missing ragged patches of hair, exposing hide that was scratched bloody in his warfare against fleas.

Penny crumpled into croaky sobs. "Something's wrong over there! Mrs. Bethke, she's so sweet, and I think Roger is doing things to her!"

"What sort of things?" Carly asked.

"I don't know! Being mean to her! And poor Percy!" Her fidgeting hands dropped onto her lap as if her arms were no longer strong enough to support them. Even in her lap, her hands continued to flutter.

"Have you told Juan Pablo about this?" After receiving a shake of Penny's head, Carly dialed Juan Pablo's cell phone. Following a brief conversation, she told Penny that he would be right in from the Expo.

"They're both so helpless. So alone," Penny gulped. "I need to do something, but I don't know what."

While they waited for Juan Pablo, Carly studied Penny. Something was missing, something besides clean hair and rosy cheeks. It dawned on Carly. This was the first time she'd seen Penny without dangly earrings.

Darrell's hand made circles of comfort on Penny's back. The only noise was Mary Louise pecking at his mirror and the faint din of the Pet Expo. Carly searched for the right words to console Penny. The best she came up with was, "Juan Pablo will help us handle this."

"Don't you get tired of this? Just sick-and-tired fed up?" Penny's fists pounded her wafer-thin thighs. "Remember that dog Juan Pablo brought in with both its eyes poked out? And that kitten with the cigarette burns? And the firecracker dog?"

Carly and Darrell vividly remembered these animals. Especially the firecracker dog. It was brought in by Animal Services last July 5th, its rear end nothing but shreds of charred flesh from a firecracker some pervert shoved up its anus.

"You're right, Penny, these are horribly sad things," Carly counseled. "But all of us need to remember the animals we've helped."

Penny's grief was too fierce to be diverted. "What about the ones that we don't help because we never know about them? Dogs on four-foot chains that never get anything more than a bowl of dry dog food. Never a pat on the head. Never a kind word. Or the homeless mama cat having her kittens in the drainage culvert on the coldest day in February, then trying to nurse them when she's half-starved herself. Cats having their tails tied to a rope and then tossed over a branch. Cock fights. Pit bull fights." Her hands flew up beside her head and arched like cat claws. "Why do so many animals have to come here? Aren't there any decent people left?" She circled her arms across her waist and buckled forward. Sobs racked her body.

Carly exchanged a worried glance with Darrell. His hand traveled up and down Penny's spine. "Come on, sweetheart, sit up. Come on, sit up and look at me." Penny allowed him to gently raise her shoulders. He leaned closer to her until their noses were almost touching. He regained possession of her hand. "Look at me, Penelope. That's a girl. Now put your mind to rest. We can solve problems one at a time. And we'll start with Mrs. Bethke and Percy."

Juan Pablo barged into the office. He was as close to being in a huff as Carly had ever seen him. "I swear by the *Virgen de Guadalupe*! Can you believe I just issued a warning for leaving a dog closed up in a hot car?"

Carly cringed. This was exactly what unstrung Penny didn't need to hear right now.

Penny snorted. "Of course I can believe it. People are assholes. Let's euthanize people instead of animals."

"The car was in *our* parking lot. The moron was *here*, at the Expo."

Carly tugged at the neck of her shirt while simultaneously giving Juan Pablo a clandestine finger-across-the-throat can-your-chatter gesture.

Juan Pablo sat on a corner of the desk. The toe of one boot rested on the floor while the other foot hung suspended in midair. He folded his hands atop his massive thigh. "So what's up? Things look a little gloomy in here."

The story was reiterated, and he asked additional questions of Penny. "Does Percy have shelter?" She confirmed he did. "Water?" Yes. "Food?"

"Yes, but not enough. He's down to skin and bones."

Juan Pablo's gaze slipped down to Penny's own skeletal neck and arms. "What about Mrs. Bethke? Have you seen her? Can you find an excuse to get into the house to see the conditions there?"

"Some of her mail was delivered to my place. When I took it next door, I asked Roger if I could come in and say hi to his mother. He said she was sleeping. He took the mail from me and closed the door in my face." Penny's tongue reached out and hooked a strand of her hair. She brought it to her mouth and began chewing on it.

"Cruelty to animals is defined by law as not giving enough food, water, or shelter or abandoning, seriously overworking, or torturing them. Do any of those fit Percy?"

A heartbreaking blanket of hopelessness fell on Penny's face. "The poor old dog is being neglected. He's spent his whole life loved by his owner, and now this. Why do we have to wait for a tragedy to happen?"

"Because the law is very specific and is designed so that when cruelty cases are taken to court, there's enough evidence to convict the suckers."

"Then the law's fucked up! Tell me, Juan Pablo, tell me—isn't there any kindness in the world anymore?"

The room was hushed as her question hung in the air. Even Mary Louise stopped tapping his mirror.

Juan Pablo's folded hands remained reassuringly motionless. "Tell you what I'll do. I'll swing by there this afternoon and talk to Roger. I'll tell him we received an anonymous complaint pertaining to Percy. Then I'll go over proper pet care with him. Could be he's just an ignorant prick and not a true asshole prick."

"And you'll let me know what he says?" Penny asked.

"Of course. And I'll talk to Adult Protective Services and see what they can do for Mrs. Bethke."

"Penny, it's obvious you need a break from this place," Carly said. "You seem so...so...fragile lately. If I send you home for the rest of the day, is there someone you can visit? Or someone that could stay with you?"

Penny's head hung low as her scrawny neck stretched out like a goose poised for the ax. "Maybe."

"What about a little vacation? Doesn't your mother live in California? And your sister?"

The lifeless shoulders shrugged.

Darrell clinched Penny's hand and stood. "Come on, sweetheart. I'll walk you to your car. I have some things I need to finish up here, and then I'll come by your place later. Okay?"

Carly looked at Darrell with astonished admiration. She had never seen this side of the heavy lidded, scruffy bearded, time-warped flower child. Had never suspected it existed. Who'd have thought that someone who spent much of his life swimming outside the mainstream would have the finesse to express so much compassion?

Like a dutiful child, Penny allowed Darrell to lead her across the room. Carly breathed a sigh of relief. That situation was under control for the time being. Now she needed to go outside and make sure the Expo was going smoothly. Plus introduce herself to the Advocates.

She started to rise from her chair but halted in mid-action as Penny and Darrell collided with Sophia Zhirnov and Bullwinkle breezing through the office door. Carly sank back onto the seat. She embedded her incisors into her knuckle to keep her hand from flying up to shield her eyes. Sophia's Capri pants effervesced tequila sunrise orange. A matching bandana circled Bullwinkle's powerful neck.

"Funnel cakes anyone, before I take them to the break room?" Sophia's saffron talons pried open a white pastry box. "I bought them from that cute little *señorita* out in the parking lot."

As she waved the box about, Chanel No. 5 wafted from her wrist. Every time Carly smelled Sophia's perfume, she thought of her mother. When Carly was a little girl, Marge Shannon reserved the fragrance for special events, like New Year's Eve parties and high school reunions. For occasions of lesser importance, she scaled down to Jean Naté.

Carly wheeled her chair back to its rightful position behind her desk. She scribbled a note to herself, underlining the words three times.

**Make flight reservations for Iowa!**

Darrell wiped his palm on the Zhirnov Springs Humane Society logo of his tie-dyed T-shirt. "Why, thanks, Mrs. Z." His eyes rolled gratefully toward heaven as he sunk his teeth into the deep fried pastry.

"Oh, Mr. Darnell! You did a fantastic job on the Mutt Strut! Bullzy and I had a howling good time! And the way you dealt with that bimbo that brought the female dog in heat!"

"Dog in heat?" Carly said to Darrell. "I thought everything went fine."

"Oh, it did go fine! Believe you me! Mr. Darnell handled the situation beautifully when the boy dog chased the girl dog right into the spring."

If it hadn't been for Sophia, the town's namesake would be a thing of the past. The spring had never been large, nothing more than a small gurgle of water originating from a fissure in the bone-colored limestone and forming a puddle the size of a child's wading pool. However, the spring dried up a couple of years ago when Megalopolis's population surge overtaxed the aquifer's capacity to recharge. Zhirnov Springs's grande dame dipped into her own checking account and connected a water line from the spring to the City's Public Utilities. In no time, newly laid pipes belched forth filtered, chlorinated, state-inspected water. Like a primordial artesian outpouring, water gushed from deep between the rocks at a rate never before witnessed.

Sophia turned accusing eyes to Carly. "By the way, why didn't you tell me Mr. Darnell was the resourceful genius behind that larval lamp?"

*Resourceful genius*? Just let it slide, Carly told herself. Just let it slide.

"Bye, Darrell. And thanks." Carly verbally pushed him out the door.

"No prob, man." Powdered sugar clung to his upper lip as he escorted Penny into the hallway.

"So you finished the entire 6K?" Carly asked as Sophia took one of the recently vacated orange chairs.

"Oh, yes!" She turned her attention to the borzoi, stroking his deep chest with the toe of her dandelion yellow tennis shoe. "We didn't finish first, but we did finish, didn't we? We had a grand time until you were a bad boy and went after the cute little bunny that girl was pulling in the wagon! Oh, my stars! I thought you were going to tear that cage right apart." She stopped talking to the dog and addressed the two humans in the room. "Never shows a spit's worth of aggression to anyone or anything except lagomorphs. You know, the breed was developed in Russia to hunt wolves, but they were also used to chase foxes and rabbits."

Juan Pablo slid off the desk and offered Bullwinkle an obligatory goodbye pat on his long, narrow head. "Bullzy can't help but show off his ancestry, can you fella?"

"Carly, I stopped by your office for some advice on the menu for the gala." Sophia  puckered her carnation pink lips. "Harmonious colors on the plates will be critical if we're to expect good bids for A.A.'s artwork."

"She's donating a painting of what?" Carly asked.

"Why, I can't let the cat out of the bag this early in the game, my dear. It would quell the excitement."

Juan Pablo stopped petting Bullwinkle and gave his full attention to Sophia. "You're right. If you're going to get good action on the bidding, the room's energy has to be able to flow freely and not be obstructed by a disharmonious environment."

Sophia lowered her turquoise glasses and studied the cruelty investigator with newfound interest. "I couldn't agree more, Mr. Pablo."

Carly didn't have the heart to tell her Juan Pablo's surname was Ramos.

"Purple would be a good center to build around since it connotes wealth and royalty," Juan Pablo said.

Sophia beamed at Mr. Pablo. He was a man after her ruby red heart. "Precisely. After all, it is the extreme value of red's energy and power. The trouble is that purple foods are so few and far between."

"Well, let's see, there's plums, eggplant, purple onions, grapes," Juan Pablo said.

"Does wine count?" Carly chimed in and was ignored.

Sophia continued with, "Currents, blueberries, blackberries."

"Grape Tootsie Pops, Kool-Aid, jellybeans," Carly persisted merrily since she was being disregarded anyway. She wished they'd quit their yapping so Sophia would take the tempting pastry box of lard to the break room.

Another face appeared in her doorway. "Can I join the party?" Alan Drake asked.

Carly's forehead scrunched up. This office was like Grand Central Station, considering she wasn't even supposed to here.

"Of course. Come in! Mr. Pablo and I were just planning the purple menu for the gala. Care for a funnel cake?" Sophia proffered the white box with its expanding circles of grease.

"Thanks, but no. I just stopped by to talk to Carly for a minute."

Bullwinkle padded over to Alan and looked up at him with soft, intelligent eyes. Alan gave the aristocratic animal an obligatory pat on the head before easing into an orange chair.

"We'll get out of your hair. Say tootaloo to everyone, Bullzy." Sophia waved her sapphired fingers. Juan Pablo trailed them out the door.

Carly was always glad to see Alan. Over the past four months, she had developed both a professional respect and a personal liking for the man. He promptly answered her e-mails and returned her phone calls. His advice was prudent and grounded in reality, and he was solicitous of the fact that Carly was a novice at her job.

"Since you're here, I have some questions I want to ask you," Carly said. "But you go first."

"You're being sued."

"What!" After she regained some of her composure, she said, "One of the things I've learned to appreciate about you is your tendency to skip the chitchat and get right down to business. But couldn't you have been a little more delicate in your approach this time?"

"Apparently you fired an employee named Scotty Janacek?"

"Sure did."

"Dottie Newman's nephew."

"You're kidding." Carly hoped Dottie had risen above the personal affront she felt over Carly's suggestion to transfer *Paw Prints* to a professional publisher. But Dottie had simply hunkered down while she waited for an opportunity to ambush the interim Executive Director.

"Wish I was. The bad news is she's footing the bill for Janacek to sue you, the organization, and the Board for discrimination. She's doing it out of pure cussedness. The good news is I told her that her involvement with this lawsuit was a conflict of interest since, as a Board member, she'd be suing herself. She agreed to voluntarily resign. Which is no loss. We need some new blood on the Board."

"You said, 'Discrimination'?"

"Americans with Disabilities Act."

"The only thing disabled about Scotty Janacek is his brain."

"Precisely. Scotty is, shall we say, a little slow."

"As in moron."

"As in low IQ. As in he claims he wasn't given adequate training to compensate for his being a tad mentally challenged."

"Mentally challenged? That's a bunch of cock and bull! First, he was too lazy to clean the hair out of the drains, and we had to pay $200 for Royal Flush Plumbing to roter-rooter out the drain lines. But I let that incident pass with just a written reprimand. Then he was caught red-handed with three of the shelter's Doberman puppies at his house."

"Without permission to take them home to foster care?"

"Foster care? He put a For Sale ad in the newspaper classifieds. He was cashing in on the purebreds."

"A Doberman heist, eh?"

"Ruby and I fired him together. He got real nasty and called us every name in the book. Mary Louise didn't help matters when he had grand illusions of being Leslie Gore and began singing 'Sunshine, Lollipops, and Rainbows.'"

Alan let out a whoop and a breath mint flew from his mouth. "What a bird! At least there's something funny in all of this. Anyway, don't lose any sleep. It's a frivolous lawsuit and, if it goes to court, the judge will probably throw it out. In the meantime, let me look over your personnel manual to make sure we have all our bases covered."

"Which reminds me of one of my questions for you. Everyone who works in this shelter interacts with the public at some time or other. Would it be unlawful to require that employees have hair the natural color of the human race? And for females to wear a bra?"

"You're treading on thin ice, my dear." He bent over to pick up the wayward mint.

"I figured as much. Next topic. I've been advised by a City Councilman that the Humane Society should give the City Council a short talk about the good works we do—including how much those good works cost—prior to the Council adopting next year's budget. Since Hugh won't be able to do it, I defer to you."

Alan lowered his chin and looked at her from under dropped eyebrows. "You *defer* to me?"

"Okay. Okay. I'm begging you to do it."

He gave her a generous, confidence-boosting smile. "Carly, I know you can handle it. But I'll do it if you want me to."

She gave him the date, and he pulled out his PDA. "Sorry, I'll be somewhere between Cozumel and Belize City, a tropical drink in my hand with 'nothing but blue skies do I see.'" He spun around and pointed a warning finger at Mary Louise. "That wasn't an invitation for you to start crooning."

"So you're going on a cruise and I'm going to a City Council meeting. You're answering all my questions the way I expected. Final question. I know the Humane Society is responsible for its employees' physical safety. But what about their mental and emotional safety?"

"You've lost me."

She explained how Penny's roller coaster mood swings had gravitated to rage and hopelessness. "I think, for her own good, she should find a job somewhere else. Should I make her leave? Or at least require her to get counseling?"

"We can't require her to get counseling, but we certainly should offer it to her as a first step. Do you know any counselors or therapists?"

She shook her head.

"Me neither. But let me work on it." He rose to leave. "Be sure to document this behavior in her personnel record, including the fact that we're pursuing counseling for her."

At last everyone was out of her office. But she didn't go outside to the Expo. Instead, she closed the door and dialed Eddie's home number.

Damn. An answering machine.

"Hi. It's Carly. Just wanted to let you know that I plan to paint the porch tomorrow, Sunday, in case you were serious about replacing those boards. And you're welcome to hunt around for your coin collection."

There. Short and sweet.

Someone knocked on her door. Ruby stuck her head in. "You'd better come to the cat ward. We've got problems."

**13**

S hould anyone ask, she'd tell them that she overestimated how long it would take to stop by the dry cleaners and the ATM. That's why she was accidentally-on-purpose sitting in her car in front of City Hall fifteen minutes before it opened Monday morning. It had nothing to do with Eddie's law office being a half-block away and this vantage point offering an excellent view of his renovated building. Not that she was particularly curious, but as long as she was here, she might as well take a gander.

She swiveled to the right, hiked up her skirt so she could prop her knee on the center console, and pivoted her neck toward the 1890's limestone storefront.

She wondered what he paid for that building. And what it cost to renovate it. Knowing Eddie, he probably got one heck of a bargain on the building or the remodeling or both. Was that a historic plaque beside the front door?

Suddenly from behind her. *Tap, tap.*

The back of Carly's head smacked the driver's side window. Her face whipped in the direction of the noise. Her hand, as it flew from her lap to the radiating pain in the back of her skull, clobbered the rear mirror, sending it akilter.

Charlie VanCleave's nose was inches from the glass. He waved his fingers at her.

As decorously as possible, she lowered her knee, placed it under the steering wheel, and tugged at her hemline. She rolled down the window. "Hi, there!"

"Good morning."

"I, uh, I'm just waiting for City Hall to open. To get on the agenda for the next Council meeting. Taking your advice." She wondered if she'd ever outgrow sounding like a blathering idiot.

"Glad to hear it. You're a bit early, though." He glanced at his watch.

"Oh, well, the early bird and all that." She gave a casual toss of her hand. "You're out and about rather early yourself."

"I'm headed for Amaya's." His head nodded toward the restaurant a few doors down the street, the opposite direction from Eddie's office.

"Oh." To keep from rubbing the painful knot on the back of her head, her fingertip traced the undulating handgrips of the steering wheel. "So. Did lemonade sales hit an all-time high yesterday?"

"I wouldn't sign the contract to build that addition to the shelter just yet, but the lemonade stand reaped a tidy profit. How did your porch painting go?"

"Not very well. I spent all day on my hands and knees scraping. I never even got to the painting part. Which, to be honest, I don't want to start until I get two rotten boards replaced." Eddie hadn't returned her call.

"Are you handy with a hammer and saw?" Charlie asked.

"Are you kidding? But I have a friend who will help me." The sentence reeked of "boyfriend." Oh well, she was content to let Charlie VanCleave draw his own conclusions. "While I was scraping, I thought about what I should say to the City Council. The presentation should be how long?"

"Not long. The Council has a lot to cover at each meeting, and the Mayor likes to keep things moving along. Plus you'll want to leave time for questions."

"Questions?" Panic rose in her voice.

"Tell you what. You've got a few minutes before the City Secretary gets here. Why not join me for breakfast? I'll give you some pointers."

Carly debated the wisdom of sharing a meal with this man with the gray cashmere eyes and day-brightening smile. Dallying around with a married man was like to participating in a jalapeno pepper-eating contest. Once the excitement wore off, there was always a price to pay. But there'd be no dalliance, flirtation, or risqué innuendos at this morning's breakfast. Just friendly conversation between two business associates. She'd make certain of that.

As they walked to Amaya's, Carly shot a glance over her shoulder at Eddie's office. Wouldn't that be a piece of superb timing—for him to happen to see her with an attractive man. But no one was in the vicinity of the stone building.

Amaya's was a bare-bones mom-&-pop restaurant that served Tex-Mex breakfast and lunch. The little storefront drew a diverse crowd that wore everything from wing tips to flip-flops to cowboy boots. Every time the door opened, passersby were snared by the smell of coffee, sausage grease, and fried potatoes-and-onions. Low-fat, low-carb, and low-cal weren't part of Amaya's vocabulary. At peak times, the bruised and battered wooden tables were in such high demand that strangers were glad to sit together, if it meant getting a seat.

Carly hoped that wouldn't be the case this morning. Although she'd barely acknowledge it to herself, she wanted a private thirty minutes with Charlie VanCleave. Not that she'd ever act on her attraction to the City Councilman. Years ago, she marked all married men as off-limits. Ever since the beginning of the end of her wedded life. Yes, she blamed Eddie for the dissolution of their marriage by blatantly violating their sacred vows. But it was her exploits that started the downhill slide.

Four years ago, she flew home to Dora for her cousin's wedding. Eddie was on the fast track at Pocahontas and declined the invitation in favor of a six-day workweek. Beer flowed at the wedding reception, and Carly sallied around the dance floor with a variety of men but principally with her high school sweetheart, the unmarried Junior Swenson. The beer, the music, and the old flame made them as spunky as schnauzers. Tongues wagged, but Carly and Junior didn't care. Hey, if they were up to monkey business, would they do it in full sight of half the county?

The brewing trouble came to a head the evening before her flight back to Texas. Junior asked her to meet him for dinner at an upscale hotel in Des Moines. Over a leaded crystal candleholder and two bottles of wine, they reminisced, forehead to forehead. The candlelight melted away the years, and time's winged chariot did some serious backtracking. But despite the flood of nostalgia, the ambling trip down memory lane was innocent enough. Well, maybe those parting embraces weren't entirely innocent.

But the event wouldn't have altered either of their lives if one of Carly's cousins—who was also visiting Iowa for the wedding—hadn't been staying at the same hotel. As luck would have it, this particular cousin happened to have worked with Eddie when he was employed at Agri-Cuts. Because Pocahontas supplied Agri-Cuts with turkeys, the two men still had professional dealings with one another. Via this circuitous route, the rumor reached Eddie 800 miles away that Carly and Junior had rekindled their former good times.

After a week of door slamming and—in Carly's estimation—childish melodramatization, Eddie eventually believed her when she insisted nothing except dinner transpired between her and Junior. However, Eddie claimed she was amiss in going to an expensive, candlelit, out-of-town restaurant for a two-and-a-half-hour clandestine dinner with a former boyfriend. He asserted it was a sneaky, scheming, underhanded thing to do, and it undermined the foundation of trust upon which their marriage was supposedly built.

"Trust is the easiest thing in the world to lose, and the hardest thing in the world to get back," Eddie quoted, although he couldn't remember who the sage was.

Life never quite returned to status quo as a subtle reservedness lingered between them. Unable to shake the final twinge of unwarranted guilt, Carly committed a second reprehensible act. She breached their long-standing agreement to forego birthday presents for each other in favor of socking away money to build their new home. She chanced upon a grossly underpriced weight bench in a pawnshop, just like the one Eddie coveted. Overanxious to return to her husband's good graces, she plunked down the money and wedged the weight bench into her Mazda.

Eddie threw a vindictive fit that was infinitely beyond the severity of her wrongdoing. He again spouted off his breach-of-trust quote. Eight times. The weight bench was returned to the pawnshop, and Eddie upped the amount of time he spent at work and at the health club. Four months later, Jocelyn parked herself under the mistletoe.

Carly liked to believe herself to be the tragic heroine. After all, her transgression wasn't of the grievous type. In the hierarchy of sin, it was only a venial offense. However, Carly kept bumping into the same questions. Would the marriage have spiraled into distrust and betrayal if she hadn't indulged in wistful musings and embraces with an old boyfriend? Or was the incident merely the straw that broke the camel's back for a marriage that was already showing signs of wear and tear?

The bottom line was that Carly learned her lesson. Violate the sanctity of marriage and eventually you'll suffer the consequences. But breakfast with Charlie VanCleave was different. This was strictly a business meeting. Nothing more. The man just happened to be very easy on the eyes.

They slid into the only available table-for-two, the seats still warm from their previous occupants. A perky waitress was immediately by their side, her order pad poised for action. Carly drooled while she scanned the dog-eared paper menu. She let Charlie order first while she reached under the table to grab the thigh that spread across the seat of her chair. She speculated that was how shrink-wrapped Crisco felt.

"Separate checks, please. I'll have a breakfast taco. Egg and bean. And a cup of tea." She didn't try for chamomile. She'd be lucky if Amaya's had regular tea.

Charlie's eyebrows rose. "Hot tea?"

"Yes. Don't forget, I'm a Yankee."

"That explains a lot of things." Even behind his glasses, his charcoal eyes had the ability to disarm.

"Oh? What's that supposed to mean?"

"Just teasing, Ms. Shannon."

"Tell me what to expect from the City Council." Best just to get to the *raison d'être* of this early morning business meeting.

Carly flinched as a lightening bolt flashed off a silver belt buckle the size of a turkey platter. She looked up and saw the walrus moustache of Sonny Parmer from the Board of Directors. The techno-cowboy held his sweat-stained Resistol cowboy hat against his chest like he was saying the Pledge of Allegiance.

"Mornin'. Gonna be hotter than blue blazes today, ain't it?" He mopped his neck with a rumpled red kerchief.

Her internal voice screamed, No! Go away! while she introduced Sonny and Charlie.

"How's the Web site coming along?" Sonny asked.

"The folks at CyberLinks said it will be ready for us to look at next week. Perhaps you and a few other Board members would beta test it?"

Sonny placed his hat brim-up on the table and leaned an extended arm on the back of her chair. He was settled in for a long chat. "Some of those dern Board members are straight out of the Stone Age. They wouldn't know a pixel if one bit 'em in the ass."

Sonny began to babble about intricacies of Web site design. But "babble" wasn't an accurate term. More precisely, he moseyed, delivering one drawled-out syllable at a time, stretching each vowel like strands of black, gooey tar as he considered the wisdom of using dynamic HTML. JavaScript. Cascading Style Sheets. And there wasn't no two ways about it—gotta have an interactive map.

Doesn't he have some hay to bale or cattle to feed or fence to fix or *something*, Carly wondered as she tried to gracefully interrupt him.

But Sonny plowed right along. "We'll be pissing in the wind if all those animal pictures make the pages too large. They'll load slower than molasses in January, and people will go elsewhere—you know how impatient city folks are."

Despite her rural upbringing, Carly had no choice but to believe that she must be city folk. She was so brittle with impatience, she was ready to pour her hot tea over his dillydallying, lollygagging head.

When his lull between words stretched into a hiatus between sentences, she seized the opportunity. "So I can count on your help next week?"

"Darlin', you can bet your bottom dollar on that."

"Great! I'll let you know when it's ready. Good seeing you, Sonny."

Sonny must have pieced together the meaning of her social cue because he replaced his hat and tipped the brim in a so-long gesture.

She turned her attention to Charlie. "Where were we?"

Charlie grinned. "City Council meeting."

"Ah, yes. You were giving me pointers."

"The main thing to remember is this: you'll be competing for a piece of the money pie with the police department, the street department, the park department, and so on." His eyes roved over the assortment of breakfasting construction workers, secretaries, teachers, small business owners, and other citizenry of Zhirnov Springs. "Most people think the City is just stingy with its bottomless pot of tax dollars. The truth is the City has to budget its money just like the rest of us."

"It certainly feels like we pay more than our fair share of taxes. Seems like there ought to be more money available."

"Seems like it, doesn't it? One of the problems is that you live in a bedroom community." He smiled at her wrinkled forehead. "Zhirnov Springs's population has tripled in the past ten years. It's *population*. Not its businesses or its industry. That translates into a low tax base."

"I have to admit—politics is a black hole for me."

"Think of it this way. If you're painting your porch, I take it you own your own house. And you probably feel you pay a fortune in taxes for the right to own that house?"

She was so disoriented by the twinkling of his eyes, she was slow to register that he expected an answer. She nodded.

"But the taxes businesses pay—including the sales tax they collect—dwarfs the amount you and I contribute to the city's coffers. And how much industry does Zhirnov Springs have? A smidgen more than *nada*. That's one of the challenges facing the Council and the City Manager. How to lure more companies into our community."

"But that's why I moved here. I like small towns."

Charlie leaned back so the waitress could set down his plate of huevos rancheros. "I hate to have to tell you this, but if you want to live in a small town, you'll have to move a lot further from Megalopolis. There's already a developer who wants to build a mall in Zhirnov Springs. And we've been wooing a big name maker of semiconductors, plus some other light industry."

"All of this sounds good for the City but not for the citizens." She drizzled salsa over the steamy contents of her tortilla.

"Depends on how you look at it. While most people want Zhirnov Springs to remain a small town, they also want more services. Better schools. More books in the library. Another soccer field." He pointed the tines of his fork at her. "Better animal control. So your challenge is to convince the City Council that, even if the City pays the Humane Society more money, your non-profit group is providing a tremendous service at a fraction of the cost of a government-administered program."

"By tremendous service, you mean like how we kill three out of every four animals that enter our facility?"

He gave a soft whistle. "Three-fourths? How does that compare with other animal shelters?"

"We're just," she raised and lowered her shoulders, "average. Do you know what the number one killer of dogs and cats is?"

"I'm guessing, based on this conversation, it's euthanasia."

"That's right. Not heartworms. Not cancer. Not old age." She pointed to her breastbone and continued in a voice strangled with resentment. "The number one killer is people like me. And that doesn't even include the strays that starve to death or puppies and kittens that are drowned at birth, etc."

"So the key is to prevent the puppies and kittens from being born."

"That's certainly a primary factor. You see, every litter hurts. Every single litter. Most people just can't seem to grasp population dynamics. They think it's okay for *their* dog or *their* cat to have a litter. They can probably find homes. Or they can take them to an animal shelter, and *surely* it will find homes for them."

She shook her shoulders as if loosening an unwanted burden. "Sorry. I shouldn't be so sarcastic. As you heard from my conversation with Sonny—or rather Sonny's conversation with me—our Web site will be on-line soon. I've included an animated version of what I teach school kids. One dog turns into five. Then each of those five has five puppies. Next, those twenty-five puppies give birth. So now there's 125. Then 625. Meanwhile, there's fifteen people who want a new dog." She was being gabby, even preachy, but she didn't care. He was such a good listener.

"I gather the Humane Society is more than just a job to you."

"Yes, it is." She rubbed her forehead. "But I guess I'm losing faith."

"In?"

"In my ability to make a difference. In anybody's ability to make a difference. Serving as Executive Director has given me a bird's-eye view of how insidious and complex the problem of pet overpopulation is. The throw-away mentality is so deeply ingrained in our culture, most people are more reluctant to toss away out-of-style shoes than they are to getting rid of a pet that's no longer convenient. How do you change the ethos of an entire society?"

"For an Iowa farm girl, I'd say you have a pretty long row to hoe."

"I mean, look at the anti-smoking and anti-litter campaigns. How many decades have they been around? And how much money—both public and private—has been thrown at those problems? And still people smoke like chimneys while they toss fast food wrappers out their car window."

"*Buenos días.*"

Carly's head swung around. How the heck had 200-plus pounds of Latin lover snuck up beside her unnoticed? "Good morning. Surprised to see you here."

"Surprised to see *you* here," he countered. He extended his hand. "Juan Pablo Ramos."

"Charlie VanCleave." The two men shook.

"Juan Pablo is our cruelty investigator," Carly explained. She watched in stunned disbelief as he grabbed an empty chair from the next table. He didn't intend to join them, did he? No! No! No!

Juan Pablo put the chair backwards at the table and straddled the seat, resting his arms on top of the ladderback. "I'm just waiting for my to-go order of breakfast tacos."

Carly nodded her general agreement with his short-term plan. "Were you able to talk to Mrs. Bethke's son on Saturday?"

"No. No one answered the door. There was no car in the driveway. That's the first place I'm headed when I leave here."

"Have you been to the shelter this morning?"

"Yeah. When I left, Penny was cleaning the kennel and mopping her eyes at the same time."

"I was afraid of that." She turned to Charlie. "Saturday, after the fun-filled Pet Expo, we had the pleasure of euthanizing every single cat in the cat ward."

"What?"

"Every single one. Cats are very susceptible to a condition known as upper respiratory infection. It's kinda like a bad kitty cold. All it takes is one sneezing cat with a virulent strain of the germ and pretty soon every cat in the room is sick. Since there's no effective antibiotic or cheap and easy treatment, the only way to break the cycle is to put down every cat that might be carrying the bug and then disinfect the whole ward. Do you know what killing every single cat does to employee morale?"

"And the decision is yours to make—to put down all those cats?"

"Fun job, huh?"

"Isn't there some way to prevent the disease?"

"Yeah. Sure," Juan Pablo said. "Bulldoze that worn-out facility and replace it with a new one."

She explained, "To control disease and smell, we need air exchange systems that completely change the air twelve to fifteen times an hour."

"You're telling me animal shelters should remove all the heated or air conditioned air and replace it with more heated or cooled air every five minutes? My God, what that must cost in the summer and in the winter!"

"No kidding. Tell Allison to keep selling that lemonade." She cocked her head in thought. "Think I should ask the City Council for a new HVAC system and money to pay for the utility bills?" She turned to Juan Pablo and explained that she would be addressing the City Council and Charlie was coaching her.

Juan Pablo grinned sardonically. "You know what I think you should do? Let the City Council see for themselves what it's like to work under lousy conditions. Or rather, smell for themselves. At that meeting, pass around a box of newspaper soaked in tomcat urine."

Charlie reared back and bayed like a coonhound. "I can picture it now. 'Yes, Mr. Mayor, that's your picture on the front page at the ribbon cutting for the semiconductor facility. The yellow stain? Oh, it's nothing. Just part of the job.'" He brought his clenched fist to his lips to stifle the laughs. "I suspect there might be better ways to get your message across. My father used to tell us kids that complaining does about as much good as the barking of a far away dog. A very apropos analogy in this case, don't you think?"

Juan Pablo's receipt number was called from the counter. "I'll fill you in later on what I find at Mrs. Bethke's," he told Carly as he replaced the chair at its rightful table.

After the waitress removed their plates, Carly leaned forward, forearms on the edge of the table. "Here's the deal. If we don't get an increase in our contract with Zhirnov Springs, we can no longer shelter animals for the City. We cannot, simply *can not*, continue to foot the taxpayers' bill."

"I'm already convinced. It's the rest of the Council you need to work on." Charlie gave her some tips for her presentation, then said, "Above all, be sure to include slides of animals. You're the only agency in town that's able to incorporate big brown eyes in its appeal. That gives you an edge. And include kids in those animal pictures. Kids and animals—an unbeatable combination."

"You know, that's so basic, and I would have never thought of it."

"Keep it simple. You'd be surprised how uninformed some of the Council Members are. If you want to practice on an audience, I'd be happy to accommodate."

Suddenly the joy left the conversation. His proposition sounded too much like a come-on. Carly's hackles intuitively rose. Certainly he didn't make that offer to every group that wanted to tap into the City's bank account. Where was Mrs. VanCleave while her hubby was breakfasting with his constituents?

"Thanks for the offer. I'll give you a call if I need any pointers." With both hands, she smoothed nonexistent wrinkles from the red-checkered vinyl tablecloth. "Guess I'd better head over to the City Secretary's office."

**14**

As if her boatload of anxiety over tonight's Council presentation wasn't bad enough, she spent the day on an emotional roller coaster, starting with her voicemail.

"Hi. It's Mom. Thought I might catch you before you settled in for your day. Just wanted to let you know that Dad's cataract surgery went just fine. He's already in the recovery room."

Carly chastised herself for forgetting to send him a get-well card. How could she be so callous toward her own parents?

The next voice was Eddie's.

"Hey. It's me. Want to go out for dinner? And afterwards, I'd like to look for those coins. Remember how we used to blow our entire 'eat-out' budget every Wednesday? Mickey D's, Wendy's, Taco Bell, Kentucky Fried. We hit them all, didn't we? Tomorrow's Wednesday. But no fast food. How about Romano's? I'll be hard to get hold of so just e-mail me."

She replayed the message, listening not so much to the words as to the timbre of his voice. If Amaya's aromas could morph into sound, the result would be Eddie's voice—comfy, familiar, and laden with delicious but deadly goodies.

She turned to her computer. Her thumbs drummed the keyboard frame as her sense of caution came to blows with her desire to see Eddie. She typed a draft response. She sipped her tea. She edited the draft. She called her mom, who held the cell phone next to the ear of her recumbent husband. In a groggy voice, he told Carly that nowadays cataract surgery was as easy as falling off a log, leaving her less vexed at her greeting card oversight.

Ruby poked her head in the door. "I've got a guy on the phone who says six cows are starving on his neighbor's place. Any suggestions?"

Ruby's predicament was that Juan Pablo was recuperating at home with sutures and a bruised rib. He had been attacked—not by an animal but by its owner. While he was investigating a report of a man beating his dogs, the man turned his baseball bat on the cruelty investigator. Juan Pablo was the only person at the Zhirnov Springs Humane Society with enough savvy about the legal intricacies of cruelty investigation to respond to a complaint.

"First ask him if they're Longhorns. If they are, tell him Longhorns are supposed to look like a rack of bones," Carly said. "If they're not Long-horns, give him the phone number for Megalopolis Animal Control. Bob Hicks told me he'd do what he could whenever we needed help."

Her e-mail response impatiently hummed to be sent. She tortured a paperclip while she studied the ten-point Arial letters.

> Dinner Wednesday sounds good. Afterward we can scav-enge through the entire house if you want. You're right, those coins have to be there. Just let me know what time to meet you at Romano's.
>
> By the way, I got the porch scraped but not painted. If you happen to get an urge to tackle those boards sometime....

After deleting the second paragraph, she poised the mouse arrow over the Send button. Eyes closed, she clicked like she was testing whether an electric wire was hot. She wanted to slam her head against the monitor. She was too old to be doing things as stupid as going out with her ex-husband.

All day she was dogged by thoughts about dinner with Eddie and pointless speculations of if-he-said-this-then-she'd-say-that. Just as she left the shelter for the City Council meeting, the low clouds let loose a steamy drizzle.

Once inside City Hall, she made a beeline to the restroom. The heel of her hand hammered the button on the blow dryer. She turned the jet of hot air toward the rain droplets clinging to her mascara and blush. Then she focused the blast on her blouse. IShe asked the reflection in the mirror why she hadn't thought to wear a raincoat. Because she never had time to watch the weather. Because she was always at work.

While Carly removed her smudged mascara, a woman glided into the restroom. She was the polar opposite of Carly—a complexion that looked dewdrop radiant even under the unforgiving fluorescent lights, lipstick held in place with lipliner, a voile dress—dry, no less—that curved around her breasts and hugged a waist no bigger around than a Q-Tip. She was the epitome of a woman ease with herself and her surroundings, a virtual Vanna White who effortlessly spun City Hall's letters.

Carly slouched into one of the stalls and sat down. She bent forward, jammed her elbows into her knees, and tunneled her fingers into her hair. Her thoughts were self-flagellating. She was running with the big dogs now. Way out of her league. What right did she have to tell the City Council how to spend their multi-million dollar budget when she was so dumb as to accept a date with her lying, cheating former husband?

Okay, okay. She reminded herself that Eddie wasn't the issue at the moment. Right now, all she had to do was deliver a simple three-minute presentation. Which she had practiced ad nauseam. In front of a mirror.

But what if the Councilmen—er, Council Members—had questions? She could have asked Charlie to role-play potential questions, but his offer to preview her presentation flashed with red neon lights. He had everything going for him—personality, intelligence, magnetism, good looks. And he was probably just as deceitful a husband as the one she was going out with tomorrow night.

A *pphssh pphssh* outside the stall was followed by a whiff of hairspray. Vanna White's heels clicked out of the lavatory.

Carly looked at her watch. It was time to pry herself from the little girls' room. She stared at the stainless steel latch on the stall's door as if an automatic timer would flip it open. It sat cold and immobile. Maybe it was telling her to stay locked in her sanctuary?

She chose a seat toward the back of the Council Chamber. A couple of Council Members were on the dais but not Charlie. The City Secretary bustled about the room as if she were on several simultaneous missions critical to world peace. Carly remembered the morning she signed up to be on the agenda and told the Secretary she'd be using slides. Initially stunned to speechlessness, the woman eventually stammered, "Slides? Don't you have PowerPoint?"

Charlie came through the door behind the dais and took his seat. He was wearing a navy blue sport coat. Looking good, as usual.

She glanced around the room, her eyes catching on a camera that was too large to be a camcorder. A TV camera? She wasn't expecting that.

Between the attendees and the dais loomed the menacing podium. What if she tripped on her way there? She perused the gangplank aisle for cords, purses, snags in the carpet, anything that might confirm she was a klutz. She telescoped her neck into the aisle and surveyed the daunting array of buttons and switches on the podium. She couldn't get a good view. She extended her head further, like a stork looking for a place to drop a baby.

Her bizarre pose captured Charlie's attention. He smiled and gave her a thumbs-up. She smiled back and reeled in her neck so it sat over her shoulders. She retrieved her notes from her briefcase and pretended to study them. She knew them by heart. Even though speakers were allowed five minutes, Charlie advised to keep her talk to three minutes and allow two minutes for questions.

The mayor called the meeting to order, and a quorum was declared. Everyone rose for the Pledge of Allegiance. The minutes from the previous meeting were approved. Wilhelm Vorwerk was appointed to the Planning and Zoning Commission. A property tax abatement was requested by Baxter Electric. The Council considered terminating the contract with Yamamoto Cleaning Services for park restroom maintenance.

Carly crossed one leg over the other. This was downright boring. And the plastic chairs were as uncomfortable as the orange ones in her office.

"Item eight," the mayor said. "Presentation regarding the Zhirnov Springs Humane Society."

Carly rose and walked down the aisle. Getting from Terminal B to Terminal E at the DFW airport was shorter and less daunting.

Someone dimmed the lights. Oh, no! She couldn't see her notes! Out of nowhere, the City Secretary appeared at her side and flipped on the reading lamp. A long tapered fingernail pointed to two buttons. "Forward. Backward."

Carly poked the forward button. Her tongue was as thick as molasses when the first slide—the familiar Humane Society logo—miraculously appeared on the screen.

For 180 seconds she skimmed through the mission of the Zhirnov Springs Humane Society, its administrative organization, its limited sources of revenue, the number of animals it handled, and the services it performed. "In closing, I'd like to thank the City Council Members for this opportunity to address them. And I'd especially like to thank those of you who participated in our recent Pet Expo. I'd be happy to answer any questions."

When the lights came back on, a Councilman said, "I have a question. By the way, Charlie, I'm glad that was you and not me in that dunking booth. Some of those balls looked like they were aimed at your head." The polite laughter that rippled through the room loosened Carly's tense muscles. "First I'd like to tell you, Ms...." he glanced down at his papers, "Shannon, how much I personally appreciate the fine work you people do. It's a hard, thankless job." Carly unwound further. "Now, if you could tell me, why doesn't your organization hire more minorities?"

*Why doesn't your organization hire more minorities?* What kind of question was that? Her mind whirled like a pinwheel as it tried out various responses. "Am I assuming correctly you're referring to racial diversity? Our staff of twelve includes one black and two Hispanics. Our cruelty investigator is Hispanic. You might have read about him in the paper last week. He was assaulted by an angry dog owner. He's on medical leave, and therefore, we are temporarily unable to respond to complaints about alleged cruelty." She mentally stuck a sock in her mouth. Stop babbling. Stick to the point. "The Zhirnov Springs Humane Society is an Equal Opportunity Employer, as long as the employee treats animals with compassion and does the job that's expected of him or her."

The Mayor acknowledged another Council Member. It was Vanna White from the restroom. "I've been listening to spay/neuter orations for twenty years. If we still have too many animals, obviously spay/neuter isn't doing any good."

"Oh, but it is! It alone can't solve the problem, but it helps. Tremendously. Why, without it...." Carly struggled to unjumble her sentences. "Animals multiply exponentially. One female cat and her offspring can result in four-hundred-and-twenty *thousand* offspring in seven years. Spaying and castrating pets *does* make a difference. It's very hard to see what's not here, what was never manifested."

Charlie raised a half-opened hand to head level.

The Mayor nodded. "Go ahead, Councilman VanCleave."

Charlie intertwined his fingers on the countertop in front of him as he leaned into his microphone. "I tried to find your Web site and couldn't. Don't you have one?"

The corners of her mouth curved up at the freebie question. He was a nice man, even if he was a probable two-timer. "Actually, that's one of our current projects. It should be up and running later this week. It will contain pictures of all the animals that were picked up as strays as well as the animals that are available for adoption."

"Good work." Charlie nodded and leaned against the tall back of his chair.

"Any further questions?" The Mayor looked at his fellow Council Members on his left and then on his right. "If not, I have one. I understand your organization is requesting a substantial increase in next year's contract. How do you justify your request?"

It was a tough question but one she anticipated. "All the residents of Zhirnov Springs have felt the town's growing pains. The funds the Humane Society receives from the City haven't kept pace with the demands placed on the organization, both in terms of the volume of animals we handle and in the diversity of services the citizens expect from us."

Her tone, at first empathetic, became clipped and blunt. "Our Board of Directors has determined that the organization cannot remain solvent if it continues to provide services to the City at the current reimbursement. If the Humane Society is to survive, either we will have to receive additional revenue or we will have to discontinue housing animals picked up by the City. If the second option occurs, the City would not only have to provide sheltering 24/7, it would also lose the services of our cruelty investigator, whom I mentioned earlier. The citizens expect cruelty laws to be enforced."

She counted to three before continuing, just as she had rehearsed. Her voice slowed and became like the top of a billiard table—velvety on the surface, solid underneath. "Animal shelters are a drain on taxpayers brought about by society's misplaced values. At the Zhirnov Springs Humane Society, we are working toward a community that doesn't need an animal shelter. We are a non-profit humane society trying to create," she paused again and enunciated each word with quiet gravity, "a truly humane society."

During the ensuing silence, she forced herself to look each Council Member in the eye. But the silence continued inordinately long. She feared that perhaps they had they taken a personal affront to her "misplaced values" statement. But it wasn't an insulted silence. It was more like the hush of a crowd that had expected a nuts-and-bolts rebuttal but, instead, are confronted by the emotional truth.

Finally the Mayor said, "Thank you for the informative presentation, Ms. Shannon, and for sharing your organization's worthy goals with us."

"Thank you. And I'd like to invite each of you to our upcoming gala and art auction, An Evening in St. Petersburg."

With a heady, drunken sensation, she sashayed back to her seat.

She pinched herself. She did it! And she did it reasonably well. That minority question threw her a little off base, but she handled it okay.

She was as giddy as a kitten with its first snort of catnip.

**15**

The morning after the meeting, Carly honed in on two of her twenty-seven e-mails.

> You could have heard a pin drop when you delivered the line about a truly humane society. A real show stopper! You deserve an Academy Award except I know you weren't acting.
>
> Charlie

There was no mention of get-togethers for further strategy sessions. Good. Maybe Mr. Niceguy has moved on to easier pickin's.

The second e-mail was from the director of Zhirnov Springs Animal Services, a man named Fernando Cisneros. During the time that Carly served as interim director, Fernando went from being a Hi-How-You-Doing acquaintance to being a true ally.

> Carly,
>
> The Animal Advocates of Central Texas happened to see the City Council meeting on cable TV last night. They're not happy that the Humane Society can't respond to complaints of animal cruelty. Also they heard (I don't know how) about all the cats being euthanized a couple of weeks ago. They're mad as hornets. They've already gotten hold of the mayor and the city manager. There's a meeting set up with them for 4:30 this afternoon at City Hall. It will take at least an hour, maybe two. You and I are expected to be there. Have a nice day (Ha!)
>
> Fernando

She e-mailed Charlie to thank him for his help, replied to Fernando that she'd see him at the meeting, and finished off the rest of her e-mails.

Mary Louise supplied background music. ♫ *It's gonna be a bright, bright sunshiny day.* ♫

Flush with last evening's success, Carly rolled up her sleeves and dove whole hog into something she had put off far too long—reviewing the Humane Society's past financial statements. Thirty minutes later, she whistled the equivalent of *holy mackerel!* No wonder the treasurer was afraid of spending money. According to the monthly balance sheets, the organization teetered on insolvency.

Carly turned to the old bank statements, hoping they'd chronicle the cash flow saga. She leafed through the pages of the previous year. Then back another year. A third. The pattern didn't vary. The treasurer paid the bills the moment the account balance was sufficient. Sometimes sooner—scattered here and there were bank charges for overdrafts.

It was only by the grace of sheer luck that the twice-monthly payroll was met. She thought about the paychecks. What if they bounced, her own included? What if the Humane Society fell into arrears and had to shut down? The City would have no option except to assume responsibility for sheltering the animals. Would government employees have the same compassion and commitment as the Humane Society employees and volunteers? And would the City conduct cruelty investigations? Or would it simply let the reports go unanswered like it had in the past?

Eyes burning from the parade of endless numbers, Carly hid behind the coolness of closed eyelids. She wished she could still her frenzied mind. Financial ignorance had definitely been bliss.

Carly revisited the discussion at the last Board of Directors meeting when the topic of money was once again brought up. Ideas for fundraisers had come fast and furious.

Cute doggie containers at convenience stores & veterinary offices to collect people's unwanted change.

Alan pointed out that the money would get stolen unless someone regularly picked it up. "And the staff doesn't have time to make the rounds," thank goodness he was quick to add.

"Couldn't we find volunteers?" Lady Stetson asked.

Carly thought of Joe Becker and the freezer.

A softball tournament, someone else suggested.

Who among us knows anything about softball?

A photo op with Santa Claws. Howliday Photos of your pet.

How about Puppy Love Photos for Valentines Day?

Let's get the kids involved with a car wash.

A silent auction.

A golf tournament.

A charity motorcycle rally, like they do in California. Hogs for Dogs.

Antagonism roiled along the table as each board member expounded the merits of his suggestions and condemned the half-baked ideas of his colleagues. In the end, nothing was settled, which, Carly had come to realize, was status quo.

She turned her untrained eye back to the sea of numbers that covered her desk. Those fund-raisers were like spitting in the ocean compared to the Humane Society's needs. What was clearly required, besides more income, was a large nest egg—say the size an ostrich would lay—that would supply a steady source of investment income. Inside Carly's head, a light bulb came on—the mega-watt mercury vapor kind. She suddenly saw what Sophia meant at that first Board meeting when she talked about wills and bequeaths.

Carly tapped her pencil against the center of her chin. The financial key to wellbeing for charitable organizations lay in planned giving. But how do you go about that?

Juan Pablo stuck his head in Carly's door shortly before 3:00. "Guess what little honey-bunch I found hitchhiking." He winked at her.

"Juan Pablo! What are you doing here? You're supposed to be home nursing your ribs."

His shoulders came within centimeters of brushing both sides of the doorway. "Just stopped by to pick up my paycheck."

Visions of a rubber paycheck bounced across Carly's mind. "Come over here and let me see those stitches."

As he moved from the doorway, someone else took his place. Carly arched her neck to look around the mass of muscle. With the scowling expression of a screech owl, Ruby propped her thick slab of a torso against the door jamb.

"Is that the honey-bunch you picked up?" Carly asked.

"A cheerful ray of sunshine, isn't she?" Juan Pablo strolled over to Mary Louise and opened the cage door. "Come to Daddy."

Mary Louise gave a flirtatious come-hither tilt to his head.

"You think you're as pretty as a peacock, don't you?"

The parrot stepped onto the stout stogie of a finger. Juan Pablo moved the bird to his shoulder and braced his rib cage while he eased into an orange chair. Mary Louise rubbed his yellow forehead along the stubble of Juan Pablo's beard. After the two boys cooed at each other, the dark tip of the bird's beak probed Juan Pablo's hair as if searching for nits.

"Why were you hitchhiking?" Carly asked Ruby.

"I wasn't hitchhiking. The van died at Twelfth and Pecan Street."

The van died. Crap. Carly put her elbow on the desk and dropped her forehead to her fingertips. What were they going to do without a van? The van hauled animals somewhere everyday, such as to the veterinarian for neutering or to the mall for mobile adoption days.

Ruby continued to hold up the doorframe. "I had the clunker towed to Walt's." Walt, of Walt's Service and Repair, was kind enough to charge the Humane Society for parts-only when he worked on their van.

"Why are you standing in the doorway?" Carly asked. "Come on in."

"She's sulking. She's jealous because they interviewed me in the newspaper. Did you read it?" Juan Pablo's onyx eyes were as round and bright as a Dandie Dinmont terrier's.

Carly, an avid avoider of newsprint, knew about the article because someone tacked the clipping on the corkboard in the break room. "Of course I read it. I even told the City Council about your escapades."

Ruby defended herself as she tore away from the doorframe. "I'm not sulking. Why would I be jealous of someone who was in the newspaper only because he got beat up?" Ruby plopped down on the second orange chair.

"I'm just kidding you, angel puss." His huge paw patted her knee. "Teasing you tickles me like a peacock feather skimming along my—"

Ruby jerked her leg away. "I don't want to hear it. Understand?"

"Wanna see my bruise?" He started to lift his shirt.

Ruby turned her head in revulsion. "Spare us."

"See, dumplin'. I told you, deep down inside, you don't like men."

"You want some stitches on the other side of your face to match the ones you already have?" For all her scowls and growls and threats, Ruby seemed in good humor. In fact, her smiles had outnumbered her glares for several weeks.

"Hey, dude, glad you're back!" Darrell loped into the office. He had a new look. The entire back of his head was shaved, leaving only a crimson rooster comb on top. His T-shirt proclaimed

Your animal shelter
Where the most eligible singles hang out
Adopt a friend for life

Juan Pablo's mitt swallowed up Darrell's extended hand. "I'm not really back, man. Just came by to pick up my paycheck and any hitchhikers I came across." His finger jabbed Ruby's fleshy upper arm.

Ruby curled her stubby fingers into a fist and pounded it into the palm of her other hand. "You're cruisin' for a bruisin'."

"Have you tasted what's in the break room?" Darrell asked. "Mrs. Z and that Russian wolfhound of hers brought in a humdinger of an American flag."

Three pairs of ears waited for him to go on.

"Care to explain?" Ruby finally asked.

"A real doozie of a cake! Up here in the corner," Darrell turned his back to the group and raised his left hand as if he were writing on a blackboard, "it has fifty little blueberries." His fingers flickered like little stars. "And all across here," the distended fingers of his right hand swept out in three horizontal waves, "are strawberries lined up stem-to-stern. For Memorial Day. It's the cat's meow."

"But Memorial Day is still two weeks away," Ruby said.

Juan Pablo smirked at her. "So don't eat any, lamb-cakes."

Darrell did an about-face toward the group. "You guys need to get some before it's gone. You know the expression—he who hesitates misses the boat."

A hush fell as everyone pondered Darrell's turn of the phrase.

Seemingly out of desperation to break the protracted silence rather than a desire to correct Darrell, Juan Pablo said, "By the way, you mean 'borzoi,' not 'Russian wolfhound.'"

Darrell looked flummoxed but stood his ground. "No. I mean Russian wolfhound."

"The breed used to be called Russian wolfhound. Now the proper term is borzoi," Juan Pablo said.

Darrell gave the matter thoughtful consideration. "No. Mrs. Z is Russian. And her dog is Russian."

"It's a borzoi," Juan Pablo said as Mrs. Z's twitter filtered in from the hallway.

Darrell stood his ground. "*Nyet.*"

"*Sí.*" Juan Pablo said.

"*Nyet.*"

"*Sí.*"

"*Nyet.*"

"Greetings everyone!" Sophia blew a kiss in the direction of Juan Pablo, but the aerial smooch was probably targeted at the bird on his shoulder. Bullwinkle's feathered tail gave each person a cursory salutation as he made the rounds for his obligatory pets.

Carly sighed. So much for getting any more work done. She had hoped to review last year's Annual Summary and the current budget numbers before the meeting with the Advocates. Plus she wanted to rehearse tomorrow morning's presentation for the Sunrise Lions Club.

"Mr. Pablo, my poor boy, let me take a look at those stitches." Sophia perched her chained reading glasses on the tip of her nose and examined the sutures. She gasped. "Why, they're black." Sophia stepped back and dropped her glasses onto her chest.

"Yes, ma'am, they are."

Her mouth moved as it searched for sound. "Didn't the doctor have any other colors?"

"I don't know. I didn't ask."

Sophia came to her senses. "Of course you didn't. You were injured at the time. Probably dazed. What color are your bruises?"

"How are the gala plans coming along, Sophia?" Carly intervened on Juan Pablo's behalf.

"That's exactly what I wanted to talk to you about. I'm so glad we chose a Russian theme for the gala. Slavic food is so colorful. I'm thinking red and black caviar for color balance." She looked at Juan Pablo for his concurrence. "And beets and red cabbage for the purple focal point of the main course."

"Perfect choice." Juan Pablo's thumb and forefinger circled in an a-okay.

"And carry the purple through dessert with blueberry cheesecake."

"Wish I could afford to go. I like purple food." Darrell swung his arms in front of his hips. "Gotta get back to work. *Dasvidanya*, Mrs. Z, and thanks for the cake. It's the bees' knees!"

"I thought it was the cat's meow," Ruby wisecracked, setting Darrell momentarily adrift.

"*Dasvidanya!*" Sophia waved to Darrell and turned to Carly. "Guess what? A.A. has agreed to have a book signing at the gala. Oh, I declare! The excitement of it all! Her first book! If we advertise the book signing on our Web site along with some pictures of her paintings, I know we'll bring in the artsy crowd from Megalopolis. I told Reinhardt we priced the tickets too cheap. Carly! You must sit at my table. I won't take no for an answer. Don't worry about a ticket. It's my treat. And bring a date."

Sophia's face, which was flushed pink with pride, abruptly switched to doleful hangdog. "I've run into a snag. The band backed out. They were going to concentrate on Tchaikovsky with some traditional Russian folk music thrown in. Maybe a little *trepak*." Sophia folded her arms across her chest and kicked a leg forward in a micro-burst of the famous

Russian folk dance. "But the group has split up. Something about hanky-panky between the cellist's wife and the violinist. Anyway, they've left me up the creek without a paddle."

"Your paddle just left the room," Ruby said.

"Pardon me?"

"Darrell."

Sophia flexed one brow. "Mr. Darnell?"

"Right."

"Ruby, Sophia has a serious problem," Carly interjected. "Stop horsing around."

"She's not joking," Juan Pablo said. "Darrell's a genius on the guitar."

"'Genius' is a bit of an exaggeration," Ruby countered.

"Why must you always be a sourpuss?" Juan Pablo said. "It's not an exaggeration."

"It is."

"Is not."

"Is too."

"*Nyet,*" Ruby mimicked Darrell.

"*Sí,*" Juan Pablo followed suit.

"*Nyet.*"

While the two mortal enemies battled it out, Sophia looked to Carly for confirmation of Darrell's talent. Carly could only shrug her ignorance.

Sophia broke into the squabble. "Are you absolutely positively certain he can play classical music?"

"As certain as sunrise," Juan Pablo replied.

"Then I must talk to him." Sophia motioned for Bullwinkle to heel, and they went in search of a guitarist.

"Speaking of the gala," Ruby rose and walked over to the bookshelves to retrieve the digital camera, "A.A. phoned to ask for some pictures of the neighborhood before she designs the mural."

"I thought A.A. took pictures when she was here," Carly said.

"She did, but only of the wall. She needs pictures of the surrounding area because she wants the mural to be an extension of its community."

"An extension of its community?"

"Right." Ruby plopped back down on the chair and stretched her stumpy legs on top the metal desk. "A.A. feels it's essential that the mural integrate a visual-spatial relationship with the adjoining planes to allow its message to transcend the boundaries of species segregation. How else can it be part of its collective culture?"

Eyes curved into half-moons, Carly gaped at the Operations Manager.

She regained her mental footing in time to respond to the ringing phone. Walt had bad news. The problem was the timing belt. "When the timing belt goes, it can damage the valves."

"Damage the valves?"

"Yeah. The pistons can smash into the valves if the cam stops turning. Kaput. You could end up with bent or broken valves or a shattered piston."

"Walt, can't you please speak English and tell me what it's going to take to fix the van's innards?"

"You're looking at either spending some big bucks or carting the old van to the salvage yard. I'll call you with an estimate in the morning after I get a chance to look at it further."

She hung up the phone and gave the sigh of the weary. It was asking too much of her brain to leap from visual-spatial integration to smashed valves and kaput cams.

"What are we going to do?" she asked Ruby and Juan Pablo after explaining the situation. "We can't afford a new van. I'm not even sure we can afford to fix this one."

"Just wait and see what Walt says," Juan Pablo advised. "You might be making a mountain out of a molehill."

Carly heard his words but was too tied up with worry to heed their message. She rubbed her forehead. Money could be taken from the gala's proceeds—nothing like counting your chickens before they're hatched— but that money was needed to build up the reserves in the checking account. One of the main reasons she agreed to take this job was to help animals. Which she didn't have time to do because she was too busy worrying about money. And without money, she couldn't help the animals.

"What else can go wrong?" Carly's question was rhetorical. "Is Penny back from vacation? Has anyone talked to her?"

"Haven't talked to her. She's due back tomorrow," Ruby said.

"Does she seem relatively stable?" Carly asked.

"I said, I haven't talked to her."

"Keep an eye on her, will you?"

"Of course."

Carly glanced at her watch.

"Going somewhere?" Juan Pablo asked.

"I have a meeting in forty minutes with the Animal Advocates group." She wondered if they'd take the hint that she had things to do, i.e., it was time for the two of them to leave.

When Ruby and Juan Pablo remained firmly soldered to their seats, she continued. "The Advocates have complained to the Mayor about the shelter." She picked up a pencil and tapped her nervous energy onto the top of the desk. "Geez, what do they expect from us? Our budget is half what we need." She winged the pencil. It skidded across her desk and tumbled to the floor.

Juan Pablo told Ruby to pick it up.

Ruby's head drew back in disbelief. "Pick it up yourself!"

He stroked his bruised ribs. "I can't bend over. Plus Mary Louise is on my shoulder."

"If you're on sick leave, shouldn't you be at home? As in, *adiós muchacho.*" Ruby pulled her feet off the desk and retrieved the pencil. Her finger flicked it across the faux-walnut laminate to Carly.

Carly intercepted the pencil and flicked it back. Their bickering was getting on what was left of her nerves. When were they going to leave? Didn't Ruby have work to do? And for someone who "just stopped by," Juan Pablo seemed to have as much motivation to move on as a turtle sunning itself on a rock.

Ruby and Juan Pablo watched the pencil roll off the desk and onto the floor.

"Carly, I'll be straight with you," Juan Pablo said. "You need to chill or you'll end up as unraveled as Penny."

"What do you mean?"

"I mean this." He raised his voice two octaves. "'Ruby, Sophia has a serious problem. Stop horsing around.'" His voice resumed its normal pitch, a cross between the muted throatiness of Marlon Brando's Godfather and an eighteen-wheeler's air brakes. "Stop being so serious, would you? If we stop joking in this place, we'll all be in trouble."

"I take my job seriously," she defended her actions.

"That doesn't mean you can't have a good time. A seriously good time." He grinned at his joke, but she didn't. "If you're going to be serious, so am I. You're a whirlwind of motion every second you're in the shelter. This is the first time in months I've seen you sit at your desk and not try to do three things at once. And you actually laughed a few times. I'm serious when I tell you, your life will not bear fruit until you learn the art of lying fallow."

"For once, I have to agree with him," Ruby said.

Carly tried to lighten the mood. "You're ganging up on me."

"Damn right." Ruby crossed a foot over her knee and grabbed her ankle. "So who you taking to the gala?"

Carly gave a lip fart. "Can you believe Sophia?"

"Sure can," Juan Pablo said. "Who's your date?"

"Like I have time to date." Her leg bounced under the desk.

"Ah-ha! You've just confirmed my point!" Juan Pablo said.

"I don't know anyone I can ask to go with me to an art auction." As Carly said these words, she thought about Eddie. Maybe?

"What about Charlie VanCleave?" Juan Pablo asked.

Carly stiffened. "Charlie VanCleave?"

"Yeah, Charlie VanCleave," Ruby said. "He's hot."

Carly rolled her eyes. "He's not hot. He's a Brownie leader."

"What would you know about hot men?" Juan Pablo asked Ruby.

Ruby raised a warning finger. "Don't start on me."

But Juan Pablo forged ahead. "Just ask yourself this, dollface. 'What are the true consequences of this choice that I am making?'"

"I'm warning you. If you don't button your mouth, you'll be on medical leave the rest of your life."

Like flies around a cow, Juan Pablo wouldn't let up. "Better to let it out and bear the shame than hold it in and bear the pain."

"Back off. Or you'll find out just how many different colors of suture material the doctor has."

"Acceptance of yourself is the key."

"I oughta knock the snot right out of you."

"Acknowledge your true essence, then give someone else access to that essence."

"Don't you ever shut your mouth?"

"Turn on the faucet and let your genuine self come out."

Ruby exploded like a Roman candle. "Give me time, would you!"

Juan Pablo's mouth snapped shut like an alligator's. Carly's leg stopped bouncing. Was Ruby actually peeking out of the closet?

Ruby shifted in her chair and returned to the original topic. "I'm telling you, Carly—Charlie VanCleave is hot."

"He's not hot. But he *is* married."

Both Ruby and Juan Pablo squinted at her.

"Since when?" Juan Pablo asked.

"Why are you asking 'since when'?" Ruby asked. "Are you interested in Charlie VanCleave for yourself?"

Juan Pablo ignored his tormentor. "I don't think he's married, Carly."

"He's married. He has a daughter and a wedding ring."

"He's a widow," Juan Pablo said.

Ruby gave a sigh of exasperation. "He's not a widow. Only women can be widows. He's a widower."

"He's a widower?" Carly asked.

"Don't you ever read the newspaper?" Juan Pablo asked.

"No."

"Don't you ever listen to the news?"

"No."

"Don't you pay attention to what's going on in your town?"

"*Nyet!*" Carly said. "*Nyet! Nyet! Nyet!*"

"Geez Louise. Yell at me, why don't ya?" Juan Pablo sighed in exasperation. "Anyway, his wife was killed two or three years ago in a plane crash. Remember that little commuter that went down somewhere in Arkansas?"

"*Nyet*," Carly said flatly.

"It was probably two years ago," Ruby said.

"More like three years," Juan Pablo said.

Carly was tempted to ask for an expansion of the slender account of the crash, but that would merely incite Ruby and Juan Pablo to contradict each other's versions. "Are you sure he's not married?" She looked from one to the other.

"I assume he hasn't remarried." Ruby shrugged. "Not that I keep up with the social lives of our elected officials."

"Such a horrible thing!" Carly said.

"Not so horrible for you if you'd get off your fanny and put a move on the Councilman." Ruby rose from her chair.

"I assure you, I'm not interested in Charlie VanCleave." Carly felt her mouth twist into a pucker. She had so little practice lying, she wasn't sure how to do it. "And I can't believe I'm actually seeing you, Ruby, help Juan Pablo to his feet. Have you two kissed and made up and I missed it or what?"

After Juan Pablo returned Mary Louise to his cage, he turned and pointed a finger at Carly. "Ask him to the gala." He hoisted his hand in the air and waved. "*Hasta la vista.*"

Carly grabbed the budget folders, the Annual Summary, and her notes for the Lions Club presentation and tossed them into her briefcase. Then she headed to the front office and rifled through the file of adoption forms.

VanCleave
Employer: Prime Realty
Number of adults in household: 1
Number of children: 1
Pets: 1 gerbil

On the way back to her desk, she retrieved the fallen pencil. It was an absentminded reflex; her thoughts were preempted with far more critical matters. Charlie was a widower. Maybe he wasn't a wife-cheater. Maybe he was just as nice a guy as he appeared to be.

A widower.

Widowers were supposed to be septuagenarians. How horrible to lose your wife at that young an age! The grief he and Allison must have gone through. And might still be going through.

If she thought it was such a terrible misfortune, then why did she feel riotously happy?

She needed to figure out the significance of this latest information. But not now. Now she needed to head to City Hall to meet with people who thought she was Beelzebub himself. She opened her big mouth at the Council meeting about being unable to respond to cruelty complaints and look what happened. She got flipped out of the frying pan and into the fire.

Carly gave herself a once-over in the mirror on the back of her door. She craned her neck forward to study the four or five silvery hairs that shouted their presence at her crown. The early crow's feet reminded her of the facial masque that was still sequestered in her bathroom cabinet. Her pale lips needed a touch of lipstick.

She straightened but continued to stare at her reflection. Her lips needed more than lipstick. Her lips needed kissing. Her skin needed touching. Her—

Enough! She flipped off the light switch and went to her car. Any and all delectably wicked musings evaporated in the smoldering afternoon heat.

**16**

Representing the establishment were Carly, Fernando, and the City Manager, Jesús Villanueva. On behalf of the Advocates were two women and a man. The corner of Villanueva's mouth twitched when the man introduced himself as the Advocates's legal counsel. Carly figured Villanueva was kicking himself for not having the City Attorney at the meeting. Just like she wished the Humane Society's legal counsel was sitting at the table rather than on a deck chair sipping a fruity Caribbean drink.

Villanueva's offer of coffee was politely and unanimously declined.

The older of the two women—the steno pad scribbler at the Pet Expo—handed Carly a yellow legal pad and pen. "We'd appreciate your name, title, phone number, and e-mail address."

"Thank you for meeting with us on such short notice," said Patsy McNeal, a woman Carly judged to be around forty and smelled of money despite her casual Dockers, pullover shirt, and sandals. She had the silky, wheaten trusses of an Afghan, rendering Carly instantly green with envy.

Villanueva smiled. "Short-notice is usually a good thing. Fewer people can work the meeting into their schedules, meaning we're not impeded by an army of bureaucrats."

The Advocates's chuckle was courteous and brief.

Carly felt some of the tension leave her back. These people didn't seem too awful. And after all, the Humane Society and Advocates wanted the same thing–what was best for the animals. How much hostility could there be?

"The Mayor said he would be late. Shall we get started without him?" Villanueva took on the role of leader.

Patsy McNeal didn't allow him to hold that position for long. "Yes, let's." Flinging her wrist, she slid each person a single piece of paper. "These are our concerns."

1. Excessive euthanasia
2. Failure to sterilize all adopted animals
3. Lack of Advisory Committee
4. Failure to vaccinate all incoming animals
5. Failure to scan all strays for microchips
6. Failure to make use of available resources (i.e., Internet)
7. Failure to provide 24/7 response to suspected animal cruelty
8. Failure to prosecute to the maximum allowed by law.
9. Failure to have a disaster response plan
10. Failure to provide humane education to school children

The sinking feeling in Carly's stomach reached down to her toes. She'd never make it to Romano's by 7:00.

"Excuse me." After Patsy's authoritative voice, Carly hated the timidity of her own. "I'd like to suggest that we discuss item #1 last. The other items should move along more quickly. I don't know. It just works better for me to get some of the small things off my plate so I can concentrate on the bigger issues."

The lawyer shrugged. "Fine with me." Everyone else followed suit.

The scribe scribbled on her steno pad with such a fury, Carly's hand cramped just watching her.

Patsy snapped the list in front of her and held it at arm's length. "Item #2. Failure to sterilize all adopted animals."

"We already do that."

Patsy swirled her chair toward Carly. "No, I don't believe you do."

Carly felt the wind knocked out of her, both by the woman's tone and her eyes. She had the green, far-seeing eyes of a cat. Eyes that could be as enticing as emeralds or as caustic as bile. Eyes that could castrate a man with a single sidelong glance. Right now, those eyes were carving Carly up into bite-sized pieces.

"Yes, we do." She felt like she was one step away from a *Sí, Nyet* debate with Patsy.

"All the animals you adopt?"

"All the dogs and cats we adopt. Occasionally we have some livestock or birds pass through the shelter. We don't spay or castrate them."

"What about puppies and kittens?"

"Yes, as long as they're over two months of age."

"So you're telling me you don't adopt out anything under two months of age?" Patsy had the tenacity of a bulldog.

"Rarely."

Patsy's eyebrows arched.

"I mean, sometimes we have some seven- or eight-week old puppies or kittens that we place up for adoption. We send them home with a voucher so the new owner can get it done later by their vet."

"And do you follow up to make sure those surgeries are actually performed?"

"Yes. Most of the time." Carly hated how mousy she sounded.

"*Most* of the time?"

"We have limited staff and limited time—"

Patsy jumped on her like a duck on a June bug. "But you have the time to take in and care for the future off-spring of these animals that you adopt out unsterilized? Ever hear of the 'revolving door syndrome'?"

"We do the best we can." Carly had always taken pride in the Humane Society's progressive policy of adopting out only spayed or castrated animals, or at least *mostly* animals that were spayed or castrated. Her blood began to boil. She shouldn't have to defend the Humane Society's policies to this do-gooder who sat at home writing lists of shortcomings instead of getting out in the real world and working to make it a better place.

Patsy threw Carly's own words at her. "Every litter hurts."

Carly swallowed her pride. "Yes, it does."

"What about rabbits? Do you sterilize them?"

"Rabbits? Why, no."

"Do you euthanize rabbits?"

"Yes."

"Do you take more rabbits into the shelter than you can adopt out?"

"Y-y-yes."

Patsy's eyelashes fluttered. "Do you see my point?"

At a loss for words, Carly raised her hands in helplessness.

"Any further discussion on item #2?" Patsy effectively dismissed Carly by addressing the group as a whole.

From the opposite end of the table, Carly heard the angry sound of knuckles being cracked. She looked at Fernando. His mouth was a grim, straight line. Although Fernando was a city employee, he was as loyal as a brood hen to the partnership between animal control and the Humane Society. As such, he was intolerant of criticism of either.

Patsy moved right along. "Item #3. Lack of Advisory Committee."

"State requirement. Chapter 823 of the Health and Safety Code." The lawyer intoned the memorized mandate. "The governing body of a county or municipality in which an animal shelter is located shall appoint an advisory committee. The advisory committee must be composed of at least one licensed veterinarian, one county or municipal official, one person whose duties include the daily operation of an animal shelter, and one representative from an animal welfare organization. The committee shall meet at least three times a year."

Villanueva gave a tight smile. "State requirement. Then by all means we need to comply. Fernando, would you and Carly take the lead on this? Let me know by the end of the month how you'd like to proceed."

"Item #4. Failure to vaccinate all incoming animals." Patsy's eyelashes fluttered again, this time with the intensity of a hummingbird's wings. "Obviously this refers solely to dogs and cats. Not livestock or rabbits."

Carly responded with, "We vaccinate all the dogs and cats that are placed up for adoption against all the common infectious diseases that can be acquired in a shelter setting."

"We want *all* the animals vaccinated. It would cut down on disease." The hard line of Patsy's mouth made it clear that her convictions offered no leeway.

"Many of the strays are euthanized as soon as the legally required three-day holding period is over. It would be a waste of time and money to vaccinate them."

"And meanwhile the ones that you *do* place up for adoption break out with the diseases they're harboring."

Villanueva cleared his throat. "Once a veterinarian is appointed to the Advisory Committee, perhaps we could seek his input? Shall we table further discussion on item #4 until then?"

"Item #5. Failure to scan all strays for microchips."

"Microchips?" Villanueva asked.

Carly was fed up with trying to communicate with Patsy McNeal. She looked to Fernando to answer the question.

With steam about to rise from under his collar, Fernando explained that many owners have microchips inserted under the animal's skin. Once the pet was registered with the microchip company, a hand-held scanner passed over the body of a stray animal allowed the owner to be located.

"And we don't scan all the strays?" Villanueva asked.

Carly said, "Some animals, particularly the feral cats, are just too fractious to handle."

"Then how do you euthanize them, if they 'are just too fractious to handle'?" Patsy's sarcasm dripped.

"We sedate them first by simply…" What was the phrase Carly wanted to use? Jabbing them with a syringe as best they could while the animal tried to claw out the technician's eyes? "by simply injecting the sedative as humanely as we can."

"After they're sedated, could you scan them?" Villanueva stood his pen on one end, then flipped it to stand on its other end. The pen remained at attention, poised for an answer.

"Yes, I suppose so. But there's really no need. These are essentially wild animals. No one owns them." Carly could tell by the look on Villanueva's face that she was making no headway whatsoever with him. He wanted to concede this one to the Advocates. "Yes, I suppose we could." She tried to rein in her hostility by staring at the dusty fake ficus in the corner of the room.

"Item #6. Failure to make use of the Internet."

"I thought you saw Carly's presentation to the Council last evening," Villanueva delivered a glancing blow to Patsy. "The Humane Society plans to have its Web site up within a week. Guess you missed that part."

Patsy, bristling at the not-so-subtle swipe, proceeded with the righteous indignation of a Persian. "Item #7. Failure to provide 24/7 response to suspected animal cruelty."

"There *are* laws against cruelty, you know," the lawyer said.

"We have only one cruelty investigator," Carly said. "Although he is on-call, obviously he can't be available 365 days a year."

The scribe finally spoke up. "Could you cross-train another employee?"

"No." Carly's voice was unyielding. "We're short-staffed as it is. I defer this question to Mr. Villanueva. Perhaps the City would like to take over cruelty investigation."

The City Manager's eyes shifted to Fernando, who looked like a train was bearing down on him at full speed. Villanueva used the handiest escape route. "The City is in the process of reviewing its contract with the Humane Society. That issue will be addressed."

"Item #8. Failure to prosecute to the maximum allowed by law."

"That's out of our hands," Fernando said.

"Pardon me?" Patsy asked.

"I said, that's out of our hands." Fernando had the body language of a snake ready to strike.

"I believe what Fernando is saying," Villanueva explained, "is that the Municipal Judge is the one who determines the fine."

"We understand that. But what good are laws if the judge merely slaps the offender's wrist?" the lawyer asked.

Fernando addressed Villanueva, turning his back on Patsy and the lawyer. "I've talked to Judge Shipley. I've tried to explain the public health importance of leash laws and rabies vaccinations. But he treats noncompliance like it's a joke compared to other, what he calls 'serious crimes' that pass through his court."

"Let me work on that from my end," Villanueva said.

Fernando shifted his eyes but not his body toward Patsy and the lawyer. "You know, you're not the only ones who would like to see those laws enforced." Rather than use a tone of like-minded solidarity, he spewed the words like he was name-calling on a playground.

"Item #9. Failure to have a disaster response plan." Patsy rested her folded hands in her lap, the very essence of patience as she waited for the excuses.

Carly didn't know how to respond. It wasn't an issue she was familiar with. Or had even considered. She glanced at Fernando, who looked like a crowbar would be required to pry his lips apart.

Villanueva spoke. "That's an oversight on my part. Animal Control should be part of the City's disaster plan."

Carly still was unclear about the topic. "You mean, if there's a tornado or something?"

"Any type of disaster," the lawyer said. "A train wreck involving a hazardous gas, a bioterrorism incident—"

Fernando's sardonic laughter interrupted the lawyer. "Bioterrorism in Zhirnov Springs?"

"Megalopolis. Houston. Dallas. Wherever. An airplane disseminating bubonic plague organisms will send people running for their lives. Some of the people who are incubating plague will wind up here. And it's my understanding plague is readily transmitted between humans and animals, both pets and wildlife."

"Fernando, Carly, the City's Disaster Coordinating Council meets here the second Wednesday of every month at 9:30. You'd better bone up on terrorism as it relates to animals." Villanueva gave a throaty chortle at his pun. "Bone-up. Get it?"

"Item #10. Failure to provide humane education to schoolchildren."

"It's a budget issue," Carly said lamely.

"It's a budget issue that will have to be resolved. Item #1. Excessive euthanasia." Flames burned inside Patsy's green eyes.

Carly had reached the point of belligerence. "Euthanizing even one healthy, well-adjusted animal is excessive."

"Agreed. So what do you plan to do about it?"

"We try as hard as we can to find good owners for the animals under our care."

"Such as?"

"Such as we work with the *Courier* for a Pet-of-the-Week picture."

"Have you asked the *Courier* to run free found ads, so when a person finds an animal, maybe he'd keep it a few days and place an ad rather than taking it to the shelter?" Patsy rattled off the names of several Texas newspapers that provided the service free of charge.

Carly unclenched her teeth. "No, but that's a good idea." She fumed that the home team the only one making concessions. Why was this meeting so lopsided?

"Megalopolis plans to hire an animal behaviorist." Patsy threw the words out like a challenge.

"I'm aware of that," Carly spat back, wanting desperately to knock the bitch off her high horse.

Patsy's eyes burned holes into Carly. "And there are plenty of other things you could do."

"I'm open for suggestions."

Patsy had a ton of suggestions, all of which involved additional money and staff time. Expanded hours. Increased use of foster homes. Discounts for seniors. Patsy's passionate naiveté struck a chord with Carly. It wasn't that many months ago she sat in Hugh's office, buoyant with confidence that she could make a difference. But reality was doing a dynamite job of wiping out her quixotic ambitions.

"It's late," Villanueva said. "I guess the Mayor isn't going to make it. Why don't we plan on meeting again after some of these ideas have been implemented. The Disaster Response Plan. The Advisory Committee. By then we'll have a better idea of how next year's budget looks."

Patsy didn't respond to the City Manager's suggestion. Instead, she played her trump card. "We have a permit to hold a demonstration rally front of City Hall three weeks from Friday. However, we'd prefer to hold it in the grassy area at the Humane Society."

Indignation coursed through Carly. "That's private property. I have no intention of allowing you to stage a—"

"I'm certain the reporters will find it interesting that you denied our request. That should be *real good* for your public relations."

Villanueva looked like he wanted nothing more than to go home and pop a top on a cold beer. "Look, Carly, a demonstration is a demonstration. As long as it's peaceful," he shot a warning look at the lawyer, "what's the difference where it is. Let them have it at the pound."

The scribe looked up from her steno pad long enough to shoot him a withering look. "The animal shelter."

Villanueva accepted the reprimand graciously. "My error. The animal shelter."

The lawyer pointed out a technicality. "The Humane Society, because it has a contract with the City, is in essence an extension of the City, that is to say, public property. So there's really nothing to prevent us from holding the rally there."

"I'd have to get our City Attorney's opinion on that," Villanueva said.

Patsy wasn't interested in waiting for a lawyer's opinion. Her tigress eyes narrowed as she went down a more direct path. "Here's the deal, Ms. Shannon. If you oppose our rally at the shelter, word will reach every reporter in the area that you recently issued a death sentence for a whole roomful of cats. An entire roomful. Reporters, by their nature, are curious people. They'll want to know what else is going on at the so-called Humane Society."

# 17

Carly headed straight from the conference room to the restroom. She splashed cold water on her face, but a mere smattering of water wasn't sufficient. She doused her face with handfuls of water, then scoured it with a brown paper towel. But what she really wanted was to claw her cheeks with her fingernails and leave long angry streaks.

Instead, she yanked a nylon makeup bag from her purse. With enraged strokes, she applied layer after layer of color, stopping just shy of becoming a Fabergé egg.

She snatched the scarf from around her neck and stuffed it in her briefcase. After pouring over her limited wardrobe for an excessive amount of time this morning, she selected a scarlet blouse that exposed too much cleavage for businesswear. However, like the extra glaze of makeup, it was just right for the kind of business that transpired in a dim Italian restaurant.

Scarlet. She figured she couldn't have chosen a more appropriate color, considering she felt like she'd been ripped to bloody shreds. Her fist whacked the tile countertop. She shouldn't have even been at that bloodbath. Hugh should have been there. Or Alan. Or somebody. Why was she being blamed for problems she inherited?

She stuck out her tongue at the mirror. Her hair had sprung loose from this morning's twist and now looked like it belonged to an Old English sheepdog in need of a good brushing. She ripped the bristles through the tangles, digging them into her scalp like she was raking them across Dragon Lady McNeal's face. She pitched the brush into the porcelain sink where it circled a few times before settling above the drain. The roots of her hair screamed as she spiraled her hair onto the back of her head.

Purse slung over her shoulder, she grabbed her briefcase and turned for one last look in the mirror. Her face was still blotchy with anger, which made her angrier. How dare that bitch ruin her evening!

During the drive to the restaurant, she fumed about the Advocates's condemnation of the Humane Society, *her* Humane Society. Certainly she could understand why they'd be unhappy with Megalopolis Animal Control. The department lay at the rock bottom of a sluggish bureaucracy. As a result, Megalopolis Animal Control was crippled with red tape. Changing a basic procedure required an act of God and several months of paperwork. On the other hand, the Zhirnov Springs Humane Society lacked the dead weight of a vertical hierarchy, granting the organization the flexibility to respond quickly. So why were the Advocates slamming the Zhirnov Springs Humane Society?

Carly raged to herself how stupid it would be to allow a sanctimonious do-gooder to spoil her evening. She punched in a smooth jazz station on the radio and took a gulp of bottled water to cleanse the bitter taste from her mouth. Without stopping, she chugalugged the whole bottle.

She thought about Villanueva. Beneath his conciliatory jargon, his reaction was one of tolerant annoyance. Carly hadn't detected any anger. She decided she'd adopt the same attitude. Those pushy fanatics weren't worth the wear and tear on her nerves. And they sure weren't worth a wrecked evening.

To get to Romano's, she had to drive past Amaya's. Everything in the little diner had been shut down since 2:00 that afternoon except the back-lit sign over the counter—Sussex Creamery Premium Ice Cream. But Carly could smell the spicy grease, hear the clink of dishes, feel the sear of hot sauce. She could see the checkered curtains that framed Charlie VanCleave's easy smile and dusky eyes. She could hear her curt response to his well-meaning offer. *I'll give you a call if I need any pointers.* Carly felt chagrined. She was as big a bitch as Patsy McNeal! And furthermore, she asked herself, why was she thinking about Charlie VanCleave while she was on her way to a dinner date with Eddie?

A dinner date with her ex-husband. She shouldn't be having a date with her ex-husband. She should be buying his favorite coffee at the Sup-R-Val-U. She should be watching their son climb on his back for a horsie ride. She should be pressing Eddie to get out of bed in the morning while the curves of her body tempted him to stay. She should be doing all the comfortable, commonplace things that make up the lives of happily married people.

The last thing she should be doing is dating. Dating had been so easy as a teenager and so miserable in her thirties. Annalisa occasionally invited her over for dinner at the same time she conveniently invited some eligible man. None of them interested Carly, and for the most part, the reverse was also true. Only one man actually asked for a date. She told him she was already seeing someone. Of course, she didn't elaborate that he had yellow eyes and his name was Yuri Andreyevich Zhivago.

When she worked at the veterinary clinic, she accepted a date with a particularly appealing client. But he turned out to be so burdened with kids and hang-ups about his ex-wife that Carly quickly pulled the plug. And since the first day she stepped through the door at the Humane Society—zilch. Unless your imagination was broad enough to regard an offer to patronize a lemonade stand the equivalent of being asked for a date.

She wasn't made for casual dating. And she wasn't interested in mediocre dating. She could do a fine job of being mediocre on her own.

She arrived at Romano's on the strike of seven and sank onto the bench by the hostess station. What was the first thing she should say to him? What should they talk about? Old times or new times? Say, remember the time when...? So, what's new in your life? Where's Jocelyn nowadays, if you don't mind my asking.

Five minutes after seven. Ten minutes after. Carly got tired of imaginary conversations with a man she barely knew anymore, a man whose tardiness was rekindling the smoldering rage detonated by Patsy McNeal. As the minutes ticked away, Carly wondered if she had the right night, the right time, the right restaurant. Her stomach contracted into a hard knot.

He blew through the door. As soon as he saw her, a smile lit up his face. "Forgive me?" In a fanfare welcome, he extended both arms toward her. She had forgotten how Eddie filled any room the moment he entered. She had also forgotten how full he was of vim, vigor, and himself.

Were the open arms a signal he expected a hug? She grasped each of his hands with hers, maintaining a safe two-arm distance from him.

Once seated at the table, Eddie said he tried to call her at work to let her know he'd be a little late, but she had already left the office. "They refused to give me your cell phone number, but they said they'd try to reach you. You've trained them well."

*Trained them well?* She found the remark to be incredibly condescending and placed the staff at the same level as a well-behaved pet.

"Got off early today, did you?" he asked, shaking out his napkin.

"No, I was at a meeting. At City Hall." She couldn't resist adding the last phrase, even if it was somewhat snobby. "I switched my phone off—courteous person that I am." At the same time she was winking that her words were tongue-in-cheek, she was kicking herself for forgetting to turn her phone back on after the meeting.

"How about if I order some wine?" he asked.

"I'd love some." The words came out rushed and breathy like she needed some booze before she crawled out of her skin. Maybe she did.

While he skimmed the wine list, she scanned his face. His cheeks and the tip of his nose had a sun-kissed look, but the lines radiating from the corners of his eyes stood out from his tanned skin like crackles in porcelain. His hair was thinner on top, no longer affording him the luxury of letting it fall over the early traces of horizontal etchings on his forehead. Eddie was aging. What a strange thought. She remembered his father as a hodge-podge of wrinkles and crevices. In Mr. Chevalier, had she caught a glimpse of what Eddie would look like in his later years? She wrinkled her brow as she tried to capture the images. Eddie driving a golf cart rather than a ski boat. Eddie swinging a five iron in lieu of a tennis racket.

"Any preferences?" he asked.

"Huh?"

"On the wine?"

"No. You choose." And make it snappy.

She opened the menu's padded, simulated leather cover. Her stomach rebelled against the heavy pasta dishes. Despite being empty, her belly felt like a boulder was wedged in it. She had no more room inside her than a goose's stomach that had been brutally over-distended to satisfy people's penchant for foie gras. The only thing she craved was the anesthesia offered by wine.

While her thumb rubbed the brass corner of her menu, her eyes wandered down the right hand column. The prices were ridiculous. She had planned on Dutch treat, but yikes! She'd been living off her previous salary while stashing away her temporary raise for a new roof. A fresh surge of indignation cascaded over her. How do restaurants have the nerve to charge that much for pasta and tomato paste! She'd far rather have a new roof than an overpriced meal.

She had the sudden urge to be at Amaya's, where you could stuff your stomach to bulging on just a few dollars. And you didn't have to worry about spilling anything because the tablecloth was vinyl and the old-timey dispenser contained an endless supply of the thin-ply napkins. And one fork, one spoon, and one knife per person eliminated the guesswork.

Carly ordered eggplant Parmesan for no better reason than Sophia would have been proud of her purple choice. Eddie ordered veal braciola.

Veal!?!? Her lip curled. Didn't he realize where veal came from? Maybe he didn't know the cruelty that lay behind the pale piece of meat.

Maybe she could find a tactful way to explain the short, miserable life that calf led in a crate so small, it couldn't even turn around. Maybe she was as sanctimonious as Goody Two Shoes McNeal. Maybe she ought to just keep her mouth shut.

"I think I'll run to the ladies' room while we're waiting for the wine."

Luckily, the restroom was empty. She leaned against the faux patina wall, breathing in the rose petal air. The obstinate knot in her stomach refused to untangle.

The amount of time she was spending in restrooms lately was a little worrisome. She tried to figure out what was going on. Was she in over her head at work? Was serving as the interim Executive Director of a tiny nonprofit agency more than she could handle? Why were things bothering her so much? Why did she wake up at night worried that the Humane Society didn't have enough money to pay its bills? That Penny was becoming so emotionally incapacitated she'd have to be dismissed. That the City would decide to not renew its contract. That the van was fit only for the junkyard. That Dottie Newman's nephew would be successful in his lawsuit. That the Advocates would tarnish the Humane Society's good name and donations would shrivel up. Worst of all, she wasn't accomplishing diddly-squat for the animals. Top all that off with the need to visit her family in Iowa, keep in better touch with Annalisa, and get more exercise.

Patsy McNeal had browbeaten her so badly, not only was she not enjoying this evening with Eddie but was irritated with him. If she didn't lower her off-the-chart anxiety, she'd blurt out something rude to Eddie, and that would be the last she'd see of him. She wished she could splash cold water on her face again, but she refused to apply her makeup three times in one day. Carly continued to take in long, calming lungfuls of air. It will all work out; it will all work out, she repeated like a mantra.

As she tossed back her head with conviction, she caught sight of the glittering specks on her earlobes. Would Eddie recognize the diamond studs he gave her on their first anniversary?

As she approached the table, Eddie's eyes roved south of her earrings to explore her scarlet blouse and form-fitting skirt. In the old days, she liked to flaunt her body in front of Eddie. He had been such an appreciative observer. But these weren't the old days, and she wished her meager cleavage was still modestly concealed beneath a scarf. He continued to reconnoiter as she slid into her seat. She smoothed her napkin over her lap, toying with the idea of throwing decorum to the wind and tucking the napkin into the plunging neckline.

She guzzled her glass of wine like it was a mug of beer. She set down the half-empty glass and smiled at Eddie.

"I *was* going to propose a toast." He swirled his wine.

"Oh, sorry. Guess I was thirsty." To prove her point, she took a sip of water.

"You've kept yourself in pretty good shape."

His smile showed the entire breadth of his straight, white teeth, made straight—Carly knew—from braces when he was thirteen and made white from periodic bleaching.

She took another robust slug of wine and thought about his comment. What was this cock-and-bull about *pretty* good shape? She lost a full ten pounds in anticipation of this evening. Why couldn't he have said "good shape" or even "great shape"? She tipped her glass until the last drop of the Zinfandel slid down her throat.

"So, you're in charge of the pound while the head honcho is away?"

"As I mentioned before, it's an animal shelter. Referring to it as a pound is like calling this place a pizza parlor." She immediately wanted to take back the words. Lighten up, Carly-girl. Lighten up or he'll go running off into the night. "I'm sorry. I didn't mean to sound so nitpicky. I'm a little overly sensitive because of that meeting at City Hall."

"What happened?" he asked while he refilled her glass.

"There's this group of extremists known as the Animal Advocates. Have you heard of them? No? You will if you watch the news. They're going to stage a protest at the Humane Society. They think they know everything about how to run a good animal program. They mean well, but they're malicious and idealistic. They think if we did our jobs properly, there wouldn't be a pet overpopulation problem and everything would be right with the world."

"When's your boss coming back?"

"I don't know. Poor guy. His wife had a stroke. His grandson has leukemia."

"Geez. Rotten luck. What if he doesn't come back? Would you want the job permanently?"

The wine and Eddie's interest in her career were mellowing her. "You know, I'm really not sure. There are moments when I'm scared to death. Like last night. I had to make a presentation to the City Council."

"And that scared you to death?" He phrased the question as if she might also have a phobia about spiders.

"Not exactly to death. But really, really nervous. And I have some personnel issues that could blow up. I'm getting sued for one thing."

"In that case, I know a good lawyer." He gave his famous toothy grin.

She paused, waiting for him to ask about the lawsuit. But he didn't. He just went full throttle with his grin—dimples, crinkled eyes, deep-throated chortle. He was cute when he did that. The problem was, he knew it.

She drained her glass again. The heat from the wine unwound the coiled tension in her throat. Then it began to work its magic on her chest. She needed to slow down. Alcohol on an empty stomach was a recipe for disaster. She was probably the only person in the shelter who hadn't pigged-out on the star-spangled cake.

"Shall we finish off that bottle?" He poured the last of the wine. "Believe me, I sympathize with you about personnel issues. At my office, I'm already on my third secretary. Had to give the first two the boot."

As the waiter brought their salads and Eddie requested another bottle of wine, it dawned on her that he was turning this conversation about her into one about himself. She wasn't going to let him get away with that.

"To answer your question, I'm not sure if I'd want the job or not. There are times when everything falls into place, and I feel real good about what I do. About what the organization does. For instance, there was this real sweet dog that we named Hailey because she was found as a stray during a horrendous hailstorm." She could tell by the flatness behind Eddie's eyes that he wasn't connecting with the story. "Really big hail, like golf balls. Anyway, nobody wanted to adopt her, and just as we were on the brink of euthanizing her, someone gave her a super home."

His eyes narrowed in thought.

"What is it?" she asked.

"I'm confused. What's the big deal about one dog? Even if it was a nice dog. I mean, you euthanize dogs all the time. What's one more?"

Carly counted to three before answering. Otherwise, she would have knocked those straight, white teeth right out of his picture-perfect smile. For anyone to consider docile, affectionate Hailey as just one more dog was insufferable.

"The employees, and that includes me, work there because we like animals. Yes, we have to harden ourselves so that we can do the job society requires us to do, as despicable as that job is. But deep down, we're all soft-hearted."

"So what are you going to do about those humane-iacs?"

"Humane-iacs?"

"Those Advocate people."

"We'll concede on some of the things that they want and tell them 'tough cookies' on the things we simply can't do. For instance, I need to talk with the editor of the newspaper and see if they'll run free Found ads for people who find animals. It's on my to-do list for next week."

His fork poised in mid-air. "You know something? Now that we've had time apart, you know what I've figured out about you?"

"What?"

"Everything's on your to-do list."

"What?"

"It's like you want to do all these good and wonderful things, but you just never get around to most of them."

"Pardon me?"

"You just can't seem to prioritize. To set goals."

Under the table, she tightened her fist until her fingernails dug into the flesh of her palm. With her other hand, she speared a cherry tomato.

"I'm not sure I follow you." *You miserable prick.*

"For instance, you're so busy writing your to-do list, you don't know what you intend to do when your boss returns. Or if he doesn't return. A decision like that is a big-ticket item. Do you want to continue at the Humane Society? Or use this experience as a catalyst to a decent paying job?"

His implication was clear—her paychecks had always been sub-decent. She bit her tongue, dying to ask just exactly why she wasn't marketable for better paying jobs. Because she curtailed her education for an asshole like him.

Her emotions must have been transparent because he reached out and traced the back of her hand with his finger. "I didn't mean to upset you."

She toyed with the idea of ramming the tines of her fork through his hand. Fortunately, or perhaps unfortunately, he withdrew his hand before her impulse became a reality. Elbows spread-eagle, he rested his forearms on the table. He bent over his laced fingers. "You're such a capable woman. I never understood why you lacked confidence in yourself."

This twist in the conversation left her bewildered and even angrier than she had been. "So far you've told me I can't prioritize, I run around like a Pocahontas turkey with my head chopped off, and I have a pathetic self-image. Anything else?"

"No, no! You took what I'm saying all wrong."

Carly replayed his words. *You took what I'm saying all wrong.* Interesting choice of words as opposed to, *I didn't make myself clear.* Had he always been that way? The fault inevitably lay with the other person? What about those two secretaries who *got the boot.* Were they really so bad they needed to be fired? Or did the blame—the lack of proper training or maybe failure to check their references—really belong to Eddie Chevalier?

She stared at the entree the waiter brought. The eggplant Parmesan looked as appetizing as this conversation. She motioned for the waiter to take away her half-finished salad. She returned her gaze to Eddie, her eyes skirting the young calf that lay on his plate.

"What I meant was that you are an intelligent, attractive, principled, hardworking woman. You can do anything and be anything you want."

"I never had your self-conviction. Or your self-motivation."

"And truthfully, I never promoted that conviction in you. We were both so busy launching my career that yours got buried in the bottom drawer. You were always there to help me, Carly. I appreciate that now, even if I didn't at the time."

At least she heard one good thing from him. Somewhere over the years he learned to acknowledge her contribution to his chosen vocation and resultant financial achievements.

"You're right. I don't have a lot of self-confidence. Dealing with city managers and mayors and newspaper editors isn't the sort of thing I'm used to doing. But I am getting better."

"I'm glad to hear that."

"The next thing is this big gala fund-raiser that the Humane Society is having at the Country Club. It's called An Evening in St. Petersburg. Sophia Zhirnov is on our Board of Directors."

"Oh," he said, as if the name Zhirnov explained the Russian theme.

"Tickets are $150. And there'll be an art auction."

Eddie stopped chewing. "A hundred-and-fifty bucks a ticket?"

"Yeah. Even though I've been given tickets for myself and a friend, I still have to buy a dress. Not to mention getting my hair done, maybe my nails. All of which makes the cost of a ticket look cheap."

"I guess there'll be a lot of big shot, rich people there?"

"I guess. Poor people like me don't usually patronize art auctions."

"So who are you going to take?"

"Pardon?"

"Didn't you say you're expected to take someone with you?"

She cleared a frog from her throat. "I haven't figured that out yet."

"Too many to choose from?"

"Hardly." She let her sarcasm imply the opposite.

"Let me know if you get desperate."

"You'd go with me?"

"Now why did you say it like that? There you go again with that low self-image. Of course I'd go with you. As I told you, Carly, despite every-thing, I'd like to think we could be friends."

"You'd have to wear a tux."

"No problem. I have one."

"You own one?"

"I decided to buy one rather than to keep renting. Jocelyn's family was involved in all that social stuff."

She poked at her eggplant while she summoned her courage. "I take it Jocelyn's out of the picture."

His eyes grew hooded. "We split almost a year ago. It just wasn't working out. She changed."

"You mean you grew apart?"

"She got to where she was working six days a week. And she spent the rest of her time taking care of her grandparents after they got sick. She wouldn't go water-skiing any more."

"I'm sorry to hear that things didn't work out. No, I really am!" she said in response to his look of skepticism. "It hurts when a relationship breaks up. Deeply hurts. No one knows that better than a jilted spouse."

Something she said must have struck a chord with Eddie. His voice grew low. "Did you know it was your face I fell for, Carly? From the first time I saw you. I'd never before and I've never since seen a face as honest as yours. And right now, that face is screaming how much I hurt you. The truth is, I never deserved someone as kind as you."

Whoa! Time to slow down. Those words felt too good. The thing about Eddie was that she could never fully trust him. He'd always been able to charm her with his words, his nuances, his smile. She wasn't about to let him wrap her around his little finger again.

"Without question that's undoubtedly true! You never deserved me!" She laughed. "And you thought I had self-esteem problems!"

He laughed along with her. "Hey! Guess where I'm headed in July."

"Where?"

"Guess."

"I have no idea. Why don't you just tell me."

"The Hawkeye State."

"You're going home?"

He nodded. "Spend some time with my parents at their lake house." His eyes focused in the distance, back in time. "Remember when we used to go fishing? Lazy afternoons on the dock? Or tooling around in that little johnboat of theirs, looking for good fishing holes? Those were some of the best times, weren't they?"

"Yes, they were." She took a sip of wine. Eddie's face, the busboy filling her water glass, the couple at the next table, the evening as a whole—everything looked slightly hazy, like those glamour photos that blurred out the rough edges. Life in its entirety was looking rosy, and she was feeling back on top of things. But she'd been around this block enough times to know where these feelings were coming from. It was called exhilaration-in-a-bottle, and she needed to stop drinking before she got snockered to the gills and couldn't drive home.

"You know what!" Eddie's eyes lit up like a young boy who had just hit his first homerun. "Let's go fishing! You and me. You'd love the coast. Have you ever fished for snapper? I have a buddy whose brother runs fishing charters. Thirty-two-foot boat. You and I could go out for a day."

"You and I? Fishing?"

"Sure! It will be like old times!"

Carly wrinkled her forehead. Like old times? Old times involved a Zebco rod-and-reel and a carton of night crawlers. That was a far cry from a thousand-dollar jaunt into the Gulf of Mexico.

He flipped open his cell phone "Let's see. This weekend is out. Next weekend is the ski tournament." He kept stabbing the keypad. "The following weekend, oh yeah, there's that." Whatever *that* was didn't hold much excitement for him. "How about the weekend after that?"

"I've lost track. Which weekend is that?"

When he told her the date, she shook her head. It was the weekend of the gala.

"The gala?"

Had he already forgotten their conversation of five minutes ago? "Evening in St. Petersburg? Remember?"

"Oh, yeah, with the rich artsy people." He put away his electronic toy. Apparently planning more than a couple of weeks ahead was more than he or his Random Access Memory could manage.

She asked the waiter for a doggie bag. Half her meal sat untouched on her plate. Tomorrow's lunch.

The discussion about fishing started a cascade of tender reflections. While she sipped chamomile tea and he had a cup of mocha java, they followed trail after trail of memories of their life in Iowa. Her family. His family. Their mutual friends. Necking in the car at red lights. Their claustrophobic apartment in Iowa City. Their celebration following Eddie's job offer from Agri-Cuts. Today's world ebbed away as the recollections came gushing back—good ones and bad ones, mainly good ones. Her old clunker car. His old clunker motorcycle. Snowball fights. Real fights. The orphaned squirrel they raised in their bathtub. Sunday morning hang-overs. All the delicious, nostalgic things that youth is composed of.

Eddie paid the bill, insisting it was his treat. The meal plus tip topped a hundred dollars. Penny's words echoed through Carly's mind. *Owners won't spend the money to have their pets fixed but they'll drop a hundred bucks at a restaurant.*

It was almost 10:00 when they reached her house. She motioned for him to follow her to a corner of the porch where she tapped a wine-numbed toe.

"Boards need replacing."

"Aw, not tonight, honey," he joked.

The hinges on the front door squeaked like a rusty coffin. Funny she hadn't noticed that before. As she turned on a lamp, she sniffed the air. She had always liked the smell of old houses, an indeterminate mixture of wool carpet, thirsty wood, fireplace smoke, and Pine-Sol. But tonight, the house she and Eddie had shared didn't seem the least bit quaint. It just seemed like an old, tired house.

"Got plenty of time on your hands, do you?"

She turned from putting the doggie bag in the refrigerator to see Eddie grinning over the partially completed jigsaw puzzle. She started to explain that it had been there, more or less in the same unfinished state, since Christmas. Instead she merely laughed. "Life in the fast lane."

She excused herself and rummaged through her medicine cabinet for some aspirin. On the way home, the oncoming headlights had bored into her head. Alone in the car, she thought about Penny and what shape she might be in when she returned from vacation tomorrow. Dwelling on Penny started a torrent of worries about work. She came up with several things to add to her to-do list. As she fumbled around in her purse for a pen, Eddie's cutting remark came to her. *Everything's on your to-do list. It's like you want to do all these good and wonderful things, but you just never get around to most of them.* By the time she pulled in the driveway, her head was throbbing.

When she returned to the living room, Eddie was sitting on the sofa with Yuri in his lap, stroking the length of the cat's back. The yellow eyes were closed in utter bliss. The only movement in the bundle of fur was the contented twitch of his tail. Carly silently called the cat a spineless traitor.

Eddie patted the cushion next to him. "Care to join us boys?"

Carly eyed the cushion. Sitting next to Eddie looked so treacherous. But so tempting. "Would you like something to drink? I don't have any mocha java, but I have regular coffee." She scrunched her eyes closed as she tried to remember whether the statement was true. "Maybe I have coffee." The darkness felt cool and inviting. She reluctantly lifted her heavy lids. "If I do, it's left over from you."

Eddie screwed his face into a thousand furrows. "Three-year old coffee? I think it's outlived its usefulness."

The bird popped out of its clock. Each of its cuckoos was like a jack-hammer to Carly's head.

"I hate to be rude but can we look for those coins another time. I'm really bushed, and I have to give a presentation in the morning to the Sunise Lions Club."

"Oh, sure. I know you've had a rough day." He moved Yuri off his lap. "A cool morning would be a better time to be in the attic anyway."

They stood awkwardly by the door. Or at least Carly felt awkward. Eddie looked as unfettered as an Irish Setter.

"I meant what I said. If you want me to go to that gala with you, all you have to do is call."

"Thanks. I appreciate the offer."

He ran his tongue along his lower lip, leaving a moist sheen behind. "I really did enjoy tonight, reminiscing about the good old days."

Her voice was a hoarse murmur. "Everything about the old days seems good, doesn't it, even though we know how far from the truth that is."

He took hold of both of her shoulders. "I want to thank you for all those good years. I am what I am today because of you." He grinned. "You can take the credit or you can take the blame!"

Her tongue was tied in a knot that wouldn't unravel. She felt over-whelmed by the lure of his touch and his persona.

He put his hand on the side of her face. His thumb stroked her cheek. He lowered his thick eyelashes and tilted her chin up.

Her heart pounded like a stampede of cattle, drowning out the soft voice that cautioned, Back away, Carly-girl. Back away now!

The familiar softness of his lips brushed against hers.

He slid his arms around her. His mouth covered hers.

She felt blasted with longing. It had been an eternity since her body pressed against another person. She had forgotten the sensation of being folded in a man's arms.

She wrapped her arms around his neck. His mouth grew hungry and hers responded. She longed to tell him with her eager lips that things could be better between them.

His hand caressed the length of her back. Heat started in her chest and radiated outward. His taste, his smell, his reassuring touch. They were all so familiar.

So were her feelings. They were the twin of her emotions the first few times he took her in his arms—the evocative sensation of subjugating her desires to a creature far more beautiful and more compelling than she could ever hope to be. Her knees went weak, just as they had back then.

Or was it that *she* was weak? And always had been? Even as her lips were responding to his, the nagging qualm tugged at her, refusing to be pushed aside.

She lowered her head so her brow pressed against his chest. "I can't do this."

He was quiet for a moment before putting his mouth next to her ear. "But it feels right, doesn't it?"

Her throat constricted into a tight half-hitch. The words wouldn't come.

He returned his hands to her shoulders and held her away from him. Those blue eyes. That fabulous face. His infectious joie de vivre. How she'd love to believe in a fairy-tale world where she could crawl into those comforting arms and never leave.

His eyes searched hers. "You can't do this tonight? Or you can't do this ever?"

"I don't know," she whispered.

Over the past few months, she rounded an invisible corner of her life. She wasn't at all certain Eddie belonged anywhere on her to-do list.

18

She'd simply have to stand her ground with Sophia and tell her that yes, she would be attending the gala, but no, she wouldn't be bringing a date. It's not like a person couldn't exist without being part of a couple. "One" was a real number, as real as "two." "Single" was a fine word. As was "alone." Certainly the dictionary defined neither word as "half a duo."

Something about inviting Eddie to the gala just didn't set right. Too many emotions tumbled around in the hopper last evening for her to make sense of them. She had prepared herself to be swept off her feet, ever wary of a probable crash landing. Instead, she felt impatience and resentment. And yes, some tenderness and lust. Certainly it would be easy to blame her peevishness on the residual effects of Patsy McNeal. And an evening with the man who had been her true love would fill any woman with angst. The tenderness had a direct tie-in with the memories they shared. And the lust, well, no explanation needed. Until she sorted out her genuine, authentic, bottom-line feelings, she wasn't about to ask anything of Eddie Chevalier.

And she just didn't have the nerve to invite Charlie. Oh, sure, lots of women asked men on dates, but not this woman. If any asking were to be done, Charlie would have to initiate it. It's not like he's bashful, she told herself. He's a politician, for Pete's sake. With the exasperating stubbornness of a Pekingese, politicians dug in their heels until they got what they wanted. Charlie VanCleave clearly wasn't scratching at the door, begging to be let into her life.

These thoughts rumbled around while she drove away from the Sunrise Lions Club meeting. Her talk had gone well. Particularly after the four aspirins kicked in and an equal number of glasses of water rehydrated her wine-dry mouth.

Eddie's voice began ricocheting in her head. *It's like you want to do all these good and wonderful things, but you just never get around to most of them.*

Not this time, buddy, she snickered. There's at least one thing I'll scratch off my to-do list *today*. She switched direction and headed to the Zhirnov Springs Courier to talk to the editor about free Found ads.

To her surprise, the editor was one of the Lions. He complimented the Humane Society on its contribution to the community. "My reporters will just have to give you folks a little more coverage."

"I hope it will be *good* coverage." Carly laughed like she was an old hand at public relations. She explained that the newspaper would soon be contacted by a group known as the Animal Advocates of Central Texas. "They're intent on the Humane Society getting more than its fair share of bad press."

The editor thanked her for the heads-up. She discussed the need for free Found ads. She could see the wheels in his head spin for all of two seconds before he said he saw no reason why the paper couldn't perform that service for the community.

"I'll talk to Charlotte in Classifieds. Unless she has a problem with it, you can expect to see it start up next week."

He walked her to the front office. "Let us know if there's anything else we can do for you. Help yourself to a copy of today's paper."

Back in the car, she tossed the newspaper and her purse onto the passenger seat and gave a saucy lift of her shoulder. "Tada!" she crowed aloud. Not only had she achieved her objective of free Found ads, but she also primed the pump to thwart the Advocates when they began their full assault on the Humane Society. She beat Patsy McNeal at her own game! And as for Eddie Chevalier and his crass statement about how she never gets around to all those good and wonderful things, well, he could just eat his words.

She hated to admit it, but the idea about free Found ads was probably a good one. The animals would benefit, which was the point, wasn't it? Maybe she was on a roll now. Maybe she was on track to accomplishing all sorts of good things. Heck, maybe someday the Zhirnov Springs Humane Society could afford to have an animal behaviorist on staff, just like Megalopolis. Hey, the sky's the limit!

As she rooted in her purse for her sunglasses, her eyes skimmed across the *Courier*'s headline. Her mouth went dry.

### Elderly Woman Victim of Abuse

Without touching the paper, Carly raced through the first three paragraphs. Her mind registered key words like "Nola Bethke," "hospitalized," "emaciated," "spent her days on a portable toilet in her living room," "son under arrest," and "neighbors alerted by stench of a dead dog in the back yard."

She dug her cell phone from her purse and hit speed dial for Ruby's pager. When asked to leave a message, she punched 911 followed by her own cell phone number. Within thirty seconds, Ruby returned the call.

"Is Penny there? No? Is Juan Pablo there? Give me both their home phone numbers."

Ruby wanted an explanation, but Carly said she didn't have time and she'd call her back if there were trouble.

When she didn't receive an answer at Penny's, she dialed Juan Pablo. She got his answering machine.

"Juan Pablo! It's Carly. If you're there, answer the phone! It's an emergency! Juan Pablo, can you hear me! Answer the phone!" The machine beeped that she was out of time. She redialed. This time he answered with a voice dull with sleep.

"Juan Pablo. Wake up and listen to me. Did the police call you last evening about a dead dog?"

"Say again?"

"The police were investigating a dead dog and found Mrs. Bethke. She's hospitalized. Elder abuse."

"Holy shit."

"Penny's not at work. I can't reach her at home."

"Holy shit."

"I'm on my way to her place right now. I know you're on medical leave, but you have to meet me there."

She prayed with a fervency she hadn't felt since she begged God to stop the divorce proceedings. Her prayer this time was a simple one—that she was overreacting. But something deep in her gut told her she wasn't. Penny, who was on the verge of an emotional meltdown when she left on vacation, was due back at the shelter this morning. She was never late for work.

Penny lived not far from Carly in the original section of town built before subdivisions ate up the surrounding farmland. As Carly waited for Juan Pablo in front of Penny's, she longed to close her eyes, put her forehead on the steering wheel, and blot out her fears. Instead, her gaze settled on the clapboard house to the left of Penny's. That must be Mrs. Bethke's—a one-story bungalow with old-fashioned gingerbread on the wraparound porch. The house with the pulled window shades and the bedraggled flowerbed.

Carly propped her elbow on the armrest. Her fingertips pushed around the slick perspiration on her forehead. Self-contempt revived her headache. If anything had happened to Penny, the blame rested with her. Her thoughts had been so immersed with Eddie Chevalier and her ego had been so tied up with concerns about her job performance, that she ignored the needs of a fellow human being. She should have insisted Penny obtain counseling and said to hell with the legal ramifications. Her fist pummeled the dashboard. You stupid, self-centered bitch!

Finally—Juan Pablo! She was reassured to see that the off-duty cruelty investigator was in uniform. Although he wasn't a peace officer, it gave him the appearance of one.

Even before he clicked his remote to lock the pickup's doors, she thrust the newspaper under his nose. Her shoulders sagged with relief as he skimmed the article. He was trained to handle these situations. He'd know what to do. He was always calm and in control. His bulk, his massive hands, his bull-like shoulders, they all radiated invincibility. He was a buttress against anything and everything.

His head motioned for her to follow him to a flight of wooden stairs that led to a second story landing. He pointed toward a compact car on the gravel driveway beside a decaying garage that was missing half its roof. It was Penny's car.

While she climbed the stairs, Carly looked down into Mrs. Bethke's backyard. The chain-link fence hadn't seen a WeedEater since last fall. The glider looked like an abandoned orphan as seed heads poked through the seat's slats. Carly gripped the handrail as she caught sight of a circular grassless area under a pecan tree. One end of a rusty chain was fastened around the tree; the other end lay empty.

With knuckles like a heavyweight boxer, Juan Pablo rapped the wood frame of the screen door. When he didn't get an answer, he opened the screen and knocked on the inner door. He rapped harder. He tried the doorknob. It turned. Her heart quickened as he opened the door a crack.

"Penny?" his baritone voice called.

He pushed the door open further.

"Penny? Are you home? It's Juan Pablo."

He turned to Carly. "Do you want to go with me? Or wait here?"

The uplift of her chin indicated she'd go with him.

The shade was drawn over the single window in the kitchen. Carly pushed her sunglasses to the top of her head. The floorboards under the linoleum protested each step as they crossed the room. The sink was clean of dishes. A half-empty bag of microwave popcorn sat on the counter, its top neatly secured with a chip clip. The cats' food and water bowls were full.

Carly sniffed the air. It struck her as an overly dramatic thing to do, as if she were a cow entering the slaughterhouse, picking up the scent of blood from its own kind.

Juan Pablo poked his head into the living room. "Penny?"

The living room was as tidy and dim as the kitchen. An air conditioner hummed in the side window. The drapes were open just wide enough for a tabby to sit on the sill that overlooked the street. He glared at the intruders. A small calico was curled on top of a carpeted kitty playscape. Carly thought Penny had three cats. The third was nowhere to be seen.

A door slammed in the downstairs apartment. Carly almost jumped out of her skin. The cats and Juan Pablo were unruffled.

Her eyes caught sight of a smashed pot in a corner of the floor. The glossy leaves of a philodendron lay atop a heap of black dirt and crumbs of white perlite. The plant had met its demise very recently.

Juan Pablo walked into the short hallway. Carly turned him into a bulwark as she crouched inches behind him, her legs wobbly. She glanced in the tiny bathroom, its blinds closed to the sunlight. The room looked like it belonged in a different apartment. Clothes were heaped on the floor and over the shower curtain rod. The toilet bowl was a grimy khaki. The sink and the back of the toilet were littered with pill vials, toothpaste, a comb, a pink disposable razor, deodorant, makeup, and dangly earrings. Long tangles of brown hair lined the grime-caked sink. The light in the overhead fixture outlined the desiccated corpses of bugs.

Carly wiped her clammy palms on her skirt and walked past open shelves in the hallway that housed books, knickknacks, and framed photos. The litter box was tucked under the bottom shelf. She bent to examine it. Buried in the litter were one moist spot and one turd. Considering this was a multiple cat household, the box had been cleaned recently.

There was only one room left in the apartment. Visceral fear clutched at her as she followed Juan Pablo toward the door. Would they find an empty bedroom with floral wallpaper and an eyelet bedspread? Or Penny with her wrists slit? Carly kept telling herself the bedroom would be empty. The bedroom would be empty. The bedroom would be empty.

Each beat of her heart throbbed up her neck and into her head. She peered on tiptoe over Juan Pablo's shoulder into the dimly lit room.

Two rail-thin, blue jeaned legs lay splayed on the bed.

Gasping for breath, Carly fell back against the hallway wall.

She heard Juan Pablo shout Penny's name and slap her face. The bedsprings creaked as he shook the body, followed by more orders for her to wake up.

Then there was silence. Carly knew what he was doing. They had both killed enough animals to know how to verify death. She could picture him tapping her motionless corneas, feeling for a pulse in her neck, placing an ear on her chest in search of a heartbeat.

The click of a cell phone clip being ripped from a belt cracked like thunder.

"Rosa, this is Juan Pablo Ramos. You'd better dispatch EMS and a police unit to 916 Voelter Avenue. I came here to check on a coworker of mine and found her dead."

Light-headed, Carly pulled herself away from the wall. She inched her way toward the bedroom. She couldn't go farther than the doorway. She stared at the body of Penelope Downing, centered on top of the ivory coverlet, her head on the pillow. Beside her lay a syringe.

Carly's legs would no longer support her. Her back slid down the doorframe until she was on her haunches. She dropped her face first into her hands and then onto her knees. Penny's instrument-of-choice was Blue Juice.

C arly got through the next few days by tending to the affairs of a life suddenly ended. She ordered flowers, which she paid for out of her own pocket even though the card said the arrangement was from the Humane Society. She asked Ruby to revise the work schedule to put a skeleton crew on duty the morning of the funeral so that most of the staff could attend the service. She called an impromptu meeting of the employees to discuss collecting a memorial donation among themselves. They decided the contribution should be split—half to Penny's wildlife rescue group and the other half to ElderAngels, a nonprofit organization that assisted victims of abuse.

After obtaining a search and seizure warrant for Penny's apartment, Juan Pablo and Carly picked up the three cats, their food bowls, and their kitty playscape, all of which took up residence in her office until homes could be found. She also retrieved the philodendron from Penny's living room and hung it in the shelter's reception area.

Darrell passed word of Penny's death to the Legacy Care Center where Penny took shelter animals for visits. He suggested the nursing home acquire a resident cat to provide emotional therapy for the socially isolated residents. With great peace of mind, he reported to Carly that the Care Center would give one of Penny's cats a try if it was healthy, docile, and declawed. Fortunately, the little calico fit the bill.

From the Internet, Carly printed a recipe for homemade dog biscuits, which she thumbtacked on the bulletin board in the staff break room. The next day, it was gone. She smiled, knowing the hardtack would show up in the kennel next Christmas.

Also from the Internet, she downloaded information about the link between animal cruelty and elder abuse. She learned that during the insular years of old age, seniors often depended on pets for intangible comfort—stress relief, humor, protection, a sense of purpose, and links to the past. The elderly person's psychological dependence on the animal made the pet an easy target for anyone looking to exert power and control. Through abuse or threats of abuse to an elderly relative's pet, a family member could seek retaliation, exact financial assets, or vent frustration over their caretaking responsibilities.

Juan Pablo found out from the police investigation that Roger, who was currently incarcerated and undergoing psychiatric evaluation, had been seeking retribution from his mother for the wrongdoings that she— in his mind, anyway—had supposedly committed when he was a child. Juan Pablo's police contacts also told him that Mrs. Bethke was expected to leave the hospital before long to move to the assisted living section of the Legacy Care Center.

Tormented by both the obligation and the need to visit Mrs. Bethke, Carly forced herself to the hospital. Nola Bethke was as sweet as Penny had described her. Tears streamed down the creases of her face and onto her washed-out hospital gown when Carly told her about Penny's death. It was Carly's turn to wipe her own eyes as she told Mrs. Bethke how sorry she was to hear about Percy.

Carly learned that Mrs. Bethke had only a nephew in Louisiana to help her tidy up the loose ends of moving from her home of forty-five years to an assisted living apartment. Carly reached for Mrs. Bethke's hand. It was so soft, it felt like powder. Carly promised to visit often and help in any way she could. All Mrs. Bethke had to do was say the word and Carly would deal with the realtor, have a garage sale, transfer the utilities, fill out change of address forms, amend insurance policies, whatever. As soon as Carly got home, she phoned Mrs. Bethke's nephew and made him the same offer.

Carly let Ruby handle the police investigation but hovered in the background in case she was needed. Because euthanasia solution was a controlled drug, the law required it be kept inside a locked safe, which was in turn kept inside a locked room. The Drug Enforcement Administration demanded that meticulous records document each time the drug was used. But so what? It was easy to write "8 ml" when dog received only six. Over a few months, those couple of milliliters accrued to an amount sufficient to meet Penny's needs.

Carly secured counseling for the staff and required their attendance at two group sessions, one that discussed how to cope with suicide and one on how to mitigate the stress associated with killing animals for a living. The psychologist seemed well versed about suicide but lacked advice about euthanasia. He mainly listened to the employee's stories, validated their feelings, and gave some general guidance on the importance of a proper lifestyle, including a social support system, spiritual grounding, and adequate playtime.

She sent an e-mail to Bob Hicks suggesting the shelters in the metroplex area co-sponsor a half-day workshop for their employees. The topics would be how to cope both with the day-in, day-out trauma of euthanasia as well as with the cruelty mankind inflicts upon the animals it domesticated. Not only was he enthused about the idea, but he gave her the name of a person with a national animal welfare organization who would be a good facilitator for the workshop. Then his e-mail took on an unexpected tone.

> The public has no idea what it's like for people who work day in and day out in animal control—the intensity of the helplessness and hopelessness. It's no wonder we have such a high turnover rate among our personnel.
>
> At sometime in our careers, each of us suffers compassion fatigue. Some people crash and burn like Penny. Others develop a tough coping mechanism—thick calluses to protect the sensitive area underneath—and end up devoid of feelings. Only a fortunate few eventually obtain the sense of balance and peace that is essential if we are to stay our course.
>
> My deepest hope is that you'll be among the healthy survivors.

Although Bob's note had been sent with the best of intentions, it slashed her heart. An experienced manager like Bob would have recognized Penny's symptoms and obtained the needed help. That's what tore through Carly's insides—the remorse that she should have done more.

During the moments her time and mind were engaged with busy-work, she was able to ignore her own role in Penny's death. Taking care of the final details of Penny's life made Carly feel noble. As did helping the staff deal with both the suicide and the incessant depression of their own jobs.

But nonstop activity was nothing more than her own coping mechanism, a way to hide the hideous truth with honorable intentions. And the hideous truth was that guilt tore at her. For the rest of her life, she'd be plagued by the gnawing remorse that she had been negligent in preventing Penny's death. She had been so self-absorbed with her own state of affairs that she had ignored Penny's eleventh-hour cries for help. It had been the equivalent of Penny tumbling into an abyss and just as she was about to hit rock bottom, Carly, with her typical lack of assertiveness, called, "What can I do to help you?" Like the continuing story of her life, she had hung back and been the observer rather than participant, this time with fatal consequences.

On the Monday after the funeral, she received a phone call from Penny's father. He called her every name in the dictionary of swearwords. Carly kept her composure and repeatedly expressed her condolences but refused to place any of the blame for Penny's death on the Humane Society. She did this on Alan's advice. Just as Alan predicted, Mr. Downing's final words were that he had an appointment with a lawyer as soon as he got back to Dallas. The Humane Society, the Board of Directors, and Carly would all be hit with a lawsuit.

The personnel file contained documentation that she and Alan had actively pursued counseling for Penny, which somewhat calmed Carly's anxiety. Plus her years at Doc Griffin's veterinary clinic taught her that anger was one of the five stages of bereavement. Inconsolable rage could be directed at anyone—the doctor, the hospital, God, the dead person, the grieving person himself, the drunk driver, the National Rifle Association, or, as in this case, the employer. Nevertheless, the encounter with Penny's father left her shaking. She was still trembling when a woman stormed unannounced into her office and slammed the door.

Carly recognized Penny's mother from the memorial service. She lived in California and had the bronze, leathery skin to prove it. She splayed her fingertips at the edge of Carly's desk and bent halfway across the top. The stale smell of cigarettes explained her gravelly voice.

"Before I get on that plane to go home, I wanted to take a good, long look at the individual who is personally responsible for my daughter's death."

"Mrs. Downing, please allow me to express—"

The woman exploded. "I can assure you, I haven't been Mrs. Downing for years!"

Mary Louise's wings fluttered.

"Excuse me for a second, please." Carly rose and slid the blanket over the bird's cage.

As she turned back toward her desk, Penny's mother collapsed into an orange chair. She reached into her purse. Carly hoped it was for a handkerchief and not a gun. She debated whether to sit in the second orange chair so she might better express her sympathy or if she was safer behind her desk in case the woman turned violent. She chose the desk.

"My name is Carly Shannon. And your name is?"

"I know perfectly well what your name is!"

Carly kept her silence until the woman answered her question.

"My name is irrelevant to this issue. The point is that my daughter is dead because she worked in this slaughterhouse hellhole!"

"No words can describe how sorry—"

"How can you be so insensitive toward your employees as to expect them to kill animals every day? That's what pushed Penny over the edge! That's mismanagement if ever I saw it, and you can be sure I'll find a way to get you terminated!"

"Everyone at the Humane Society feels Penny's death very deeply. If there is anything we can do—"

"Anything you can do? Anything you can do? It's a little late for that, isn't it?" Tears were audible beneath the cigarette chafe in her throat.

"Please believe me when I say you have my sincerest condolences as well as those of the rest of the staff."

The woman sat stone still except for the contortions of her mouth as she struggled to keep her sorrow at bay.

"When will you be returning to California? Would you like some help cleaning out Penny's apartment?"

"I'm sure I can manage my daughter's things just fine."

"As far as her cats go—"

"Cats?"

My God, thought Carly. The woman hasn't given a thought to the fact that Penny had living creatures that depended on her.

Carly nodded toward the playscape where two wide-eyed cats blinked at the screaming woman. "If you'd care to leave the cats here, I assure you I'll find homes for them. Otherwise, you're certainly free to take them with you."

"What the hell would I do with two cats?" Her voice returned to its initial gruff rasp.

"Actually, there's three." Carly didn't mention that the Legacy Care Center had already taken the calico. But it didn't matter. This woman didn't care how many pets her daughter had.

"You might as well find homes for them."

Carly nodded. Apparently leaving the cats at a slaughterhouse hellhole was preferable to hauling them back to California.

Despite the mistreatment she was suffering at the woman's hands, Carly felt infinite sympathy for the mother in the rigid orange chair. Her swollen eyes were ringed with red. Her hand shook as she dabbed her dripping nose. The death of a child had to be one of the most painful, if not *the* most painful, of life's traumas. And to have the death occur by the child's own hand had to cause unfathomable agony.

Penny's mother sniffled and stuffed her monogrammed handkerchief back in her purse. She grabbed hold of the edge of the desk with to help her rise. Once standing, she continued to grasp the edge while she swayed like the purposeless, bare mast of a sailboat. Finally she spun about on her heel and walked to the door, holding her head held high and vigilantly placing one foot in front of the other.

When Carly realized the woman intended to leave without saying another word, she called out, "Is there anything I can do to help you?"

The woman swung the door open and with her hand still on the knob, turned in slow motion toward Carly. "Resign." She slammed the door behind her.

Following her divorce, Carly sobbed until no tears were left. During the intervening years, sad movies, heartrending events, and small fits of melancholia caused a few tears to escape down her cheeks, but she hadn't had a full-fledged, gut-aching, hiccup-inducing crying jag in over two years.

She slid to the floor, put her head on the frayed cushion of her chair, and made up for lost time with soaking tears of blame and failure and remorse.

**20**

On the Friday afternoon three weeks after Penny's funeral, a caravan of Advocates's cars pulled into the parking lot at 4:30 even though the demonstration wasn't scheduled to start for another hour. Carly peeked through the miniblinds as Advocates swarmed like bees on the grassy area in front of the shelter. They hauled small white crosses and sledgehammers from a pickup.

She planted her fists on her hips. "Would you look at this!" she told Mary Louise. "They're punching holes in the lawn!"

Carly retrieved the bird from his cage and placed him on her shoulder. Mary Louise curled his head down and around to get a good look between the slats. Together they watched as the Advocates stuck the crosses in the ground in orderly rows. The Advocates had an easy job of it. The soil was soft to the point of being sodden. Over the past week, it rained more days than not. Carly had crossed her fingers in hopes that the protest rally would get rained out, but no such luck. A white sun was boring through the clouds.

"Hello, Sunshine!" Mary Louise hollered to someone entering the room behind them.

Alan stepped next to Carly. His first and middle finger, still the color of pumpernickel from his Caribbean vacation, parted two of the blinds' slats. "At least they didn't stage a candlelight vigil."

Juan Pablo sidled to Carly's other side and likewise squinted through the cranny. "Heaven help them if they trample Sophia's flowers."

Carly and Alan's strategy was to keep the number of shelter representatives at three to avoid the appearance of defensiveness. Plus the fewer people speaking with the press, the less chance that misinformation would be given out. They handpicked Juan Pablo because not only was he the cruelty investigator—which made for good press—but he could stare down just about anyone.

Carly's eyes roved over the gathering crowd, instinctively looking for an attractive man with grey eyes. Fernando from Animal Services had told her that Charlie was the sacrificial lamb for Zhirnov Springs's elected officials. There he was—smiling and pumping the hand of one of the Advocates. Always the politician.

At 5:15, vans from two television stations pulled in the driveway followed by Fernando in an Animal Services truck and the City Manager in his personal car.

"Well, fellas, time to face the music," Carly told Alan and Juan Pablo as she put Mary Louise in his cage.

As they were leaving the office, her phone rang. She signaled for the men to go ahead.

"It's Bob Hicks," said the harried voice at the other end of the line. "Have you been watching the news?"

The news? Were the Advocates already on TV? "No. Why?"

"That hurricane has made a surprise turn to the north. It's gaining strength, and the entire coast from Galveston to Matagorda Bay is being evacuated. How many can you take?"

"How many of what can I take?"

"Dogs. Cats." Bob's speech was short and clipped.

She pulled her mind off the impending rally and tried to process Bob's words. The first hurricane of the season had been predicted to make landfall in the cattle-populated curve of south Texas. But it changed course and was now expected to slam into glass skyscrapers, residential subdivisions, fishing ports, and tourist mecas. And animal shelters.

"Carly? You there?"

"I guess...I guess we can take a few."

"Good. I'll call Michael from Bay Pointe on his mobile and let him know. He's already on the road—about an hour from here. I'll tell him to take his animals straight to your place."

An hour? "But Bob, the Advocates are here!"

He snickered. "Isn't that how it always goes? When shit happens, you can pretty well figure you'll get covered head-to-toe."

Apparently she wasn't going to get any sympathy from him.

"I understand the Bay Area SPCA recently seized a bunch of horses in a cruelty case. Can you take some of those?"

"I guess so."

"How about dolphins?"

"Dolphins?"

"Just joking. The Aquarium and the Zoo have had their emergency plan in place for years."

"How many animals can we expect here?" she asked.

"I'll call Michael and get back with you."

But I'll be outside with the Advocates! But she didn't say that. Instead, she gave him her cell phone number.

She stared out the window at the thigh-high forest of crosses. Why did everything always have to happen at once? What should she do? Her first obligation was to be outside with Patsy and her disciples. The Bay Pointe situation needed to be turned over to the Operations Manager. She phoned Ruby, who had the day off, and explained the situation.

"I can keep the horses at my place," Ruby said. "How many dogs and cats are we getting?"

"Bob's supposed to get back with me on that. I don't think there will be very many. Bay Pointe is pretty small."

"I'll be there in twenty minutes."

Carly exhaled relief. Ruby might be hot tempered and pigheaded, but she could handle the unexpected.

Carly stepped outside and into a sauna. Little pockets of steam rose from the waterlogged ground. She just finished briefing Juan Pablo and Alan on the hurricane when Patsy McNeal stepped onto a homemade black platform not much bigger than a covered kitty litter box. Her Advocate T-shirt was tucked into a calf-length gauzy skirt. A glorious cascade of curls tumbled over her shoulders.

The fifty or so people gathered around Patsy. Approximately two-thirds of them wore Advocate T-shirts. The rest were police, reporters, or representatives of the City or the Humane Society. An Advocate handed out red folders to each member of the press. Media kits, Carly assumed.

The dead air was oppressive. Carly looked at the trees. Not a leaf moved. Merely the calm before the storm, she thought as Patsy tapped the microphone to make sure it was working.

Patsy's malevolent cat-eyes performed a 180-degree sweep. "Ladies and gentlemen, we have come together this afternoon because we are the voice of the voiceless. Our animals are begging us to stop the slaughter!"

The Advocates applauded.

"Each of these crosses behind me represents 100 animals that were killed at this facility last year. That's 9,000 lives that were needlessly taken. I'd like to ask that we observe a moment of silence out of respect for the millions of animals whose last breath was drawn in an animal shelter anywhere in this nation." Patsy bowed her head. Her audience followed suit.

When her head bobbed back up, fire bolts shot from her luminous, hypnotic eyes. "Why does this slaughter happen? Why does our society condone it? Condone it? No! Our society requires it!" She pounded her palm with her fist. "Enough is enough! There are ways to prevent future massacres. Here's a prime example of what's not working." Patsy's arm swooped toward the building. "That door was locked at 5:00. Five o'clock! What time do their customers get off work? People who want to reclaim lost pets? People who want to adopt animals? Yet they close their doors to those very people at five p.m. on the button. Un-be-leev-a-bul."

Five o'clock! Carly began to broil from the inside outward. What about Monday through Thursday when we're open until 6:00? And Saturday 10:00 until 4:00! And Sunday afternoons!

"Let me give you another example of what's not working. This organization," Patsy's arm made another theatrical sweep toward the building, "takes in animals not just from within the City but also from the County. Do you realize the County doesn't pay a thin dime to shelter its animals? Do you realize once you step outside the city limits, animal control ceases to exist? This county is no longer just cedar trees and goat-roping ranchers. It's modern suburbia. I want to know—why isn't the County footing its own bill?"

Patsy waited for the smattering of applause before continuing. "A shelter doesn't have to be an Auschwitz for animals. It can be a sanctuary where the tenets of responsible pet ownership are promoted. Those basic tenets are—"

Her index finger stood like a proud phallus.

"Sterilization."

A second finger joined the first.

"Education."

A third finger went up.

"Legislation."

She gestured toward a picket sign with those very words. While the two cameramen pivoted to get footage of the sign, Patsy fell silent and scrutinized the faces in the crowd. Her calculating, merciless eyes skimmed over Carly with complete disregard. As far as Patsy was concerned, the interim Director was persona non grata.

When the cameras returned to Patsy, she went after the shelter, the City, and the County like a terrier after rats. Carly noticed that Patsy referred to "them" as if the three entities were all one-and-the-same, like one big, conniving Mafia family.

For the next five minutes, her accusations shot out like enemy gunfire. Weak, ineffective laws. Police and judges who refused to enforce the existing laws. Animals leaving the shelter unsterilized. No humane education outreach to schoolchildren. Uncontrolled disease in the kennels. Failure to solicit citizen input through an advisory committee.

Carly's phone rang. She stepped away from the crowd to talk to Bob. One vanload of animals was headed to Zhirnov Springs. Plus six horses.

Ruby arrived as Carly was confirming the arrangements with Bob. After updating the Operations Manager, Carly turned her attention back to the Advocates just in time to catch an entertaining bit of Patsy's finger-pointing.

"Our City and County Fathers must accept responsibility for the problems faced by the human and animal residents of this town and this county." Her voice dropped to a stage whisper. "Did you realize that one of Zhirnov Springs's City Council Members breeds cats?" She went after the offender with both barrels. "Kittens are being brought to this facility in laundry baskets to be killed, and one of our City Fathers (or should I say City Mothers) is setting the audacious example of breeding cats! Un-be-leev-a-bul!"

Patsy concluded with an offer for the Advocates to work with the City, the County, and the Humane Society to rectify the problems. As she shook her fist above her head, her closing words were "Sterilization! Education! Legislation!"

She still had one foot on the speaker's platform when Alan leapt onto it. Patsy's head swung to gape him as she stumbled off the wooden box.

"I'm Alan Drake, Chairman of the Board of Directors of the Zhirnov Springs Humane Society. I have a couple of announcements. First, it's extraordinarily hot this afternoon. There are ice chests full of soft drinks for all of you. Over there to assist you is Mr. Juan Pablo Ramos, the Humane Society's cruelty investigator. Mr. Ramos, if you'd wave so people know who you are. He can also answer any questions about our," Alan slowly enunciated the next two words, "cruelty mitigation program."

Carly's eyes shot open. Cruelty mitigation program? Leave it to an attorney to come up with a fancy term like that.

Alan continued. "Second, I'd like to point out Ms. Carly Shannon, the Humane Society's Executive Director. She'll be happy to give a tour of the shelter to anyone who wants one. Third, the animal shelters along the Gulf Coast are evacuating in response to the hurricane. The Zhirnov Springs Humane Society is opening its doors to offer refuge. We need to give the arriving vehicles access to the building, so if I could ask the owners of those cars parked near the kennel to please move your vehicles. Thank you."

Carly tried to suppress her grin but couldn't. *Opening its doors to offer refuge*. Oh, Patsy, there's no way you're going to come out on top this afternoon. Not when the Humane Society is ready, willing, and able to offer assistance and compassion to those in a crisis situation. And the media is here to record it.

Carly's shelter tour had the two TV reporters with their cameramen, a man from a talk radio show, a reporter from both the *Courier* and the Megalopolis newspaper, and the scribe from the Advocates, who abandoned her steno pad in favor of a camcorder. Also present was Charlie VanCleave. Where reporters go, so go politicians.

Carly's voice and spine were rigid as the cameras focused on her while she lead them through the shelter and answered their inquiries. No puddles of cleaning water had been left on the floor for someone to slip on, right? And all the poop was scooped up? And all the animals were properly playing their parts, looking happy and healthy while at the same time staring with infinitely sad eyes from behind bars?

Anxiety gripped Carly's throat when the *Courier* reporter asked her what Patsy McNeal meant by "uncontrolled disease in the kennels."

"The animals come from a variety of diverse backgrounds. Some of them are harboring diseases but don't show any signs of illness, like just before you get that scratchy throat that tells you a cold is on the way. And just like a cold, the disease can spread to others despite rigorous sanitation."

Charlie jumped in. "Is this building adequately designed to prevent the spread of disease?"

"There are definitely changes we would like to make, such as adding a new air exchange system that would remove the germy air and replace it with fresh, clean air." She gave the reporters a maudlin smile. "Items that cost tens of thousands of dollars will have to remain on our Wish List for the time being."

When they stepped back outside, a breeze was plastering Patsy's skirt against her legs. Carly looked up at the gathering thunderheads. Just what the saturated ground needed—more rain. It wasn't unusual for hurricanes pounding the Texas coast to spin off thunderstorms, even tornados, as far inland as the central part of the state.

The van from Bay Pointe arrived. Behind it was a pickup pulling a horse trailer. The media clustered around as the driver, Ruby, Juan Pablo, and Fernando unloaded animals. Carly stopped dead in her tracks. There had to be at least three dozen pet carriers. And not nearly that many empty cages inside the shelter.

The man from the talk radio station snapped closed his cell phone and announced to his fellow newsmen, "If any of you are tornado chasers, there's one plowing into Prairieland right now, moving this direction."

**21**

P rairieland?" questioned Michael, the driver from Bay Pointe. "We've got a van full of animals headed that way!" He whipped the cell phone off his belt. While he punched in numbers, he asked Ruby, "Can he bring his load here?"

Ruby paused for the briefest of seconds. "Of course." She turned to Carly, her bugged eyes exclaiming, Holy cow! Where are we going to put another load of animals?

The first angry pellets of rain hit Carly's face.

"Ruby," Carly said, "take the horses to your place. We'll finish up here."

"But that leaves just you and Juan Pablo."

"We'll handle it. Now go on. Get those horses to safety." Who was speaking, Carly wondered. Certainly that voice of confidence and authority didn't belong to her.

Ruby verbally beat herself up. "I had no idea they'd bring so many animals. I should've called in more staff to help."

"Don't worry about it. Now get going."

Despite her strong words, Carly's stomach sunk as she viewed the mayhem around her. The invigorating breeze had turned into a gale. Trees were bent over at their waists, their leaves cutting loose from the branches. Most of the Advocates scattered like a covey of quail. A few diehards scrambled to rescue the ninety white icons of slaughter, which were tilted like Iowa corn after a hailstorm. Alan and Charlie hauled the ice chests into the building. Fernando, Juan Pablo, and Michael, the van driver, transferred animal carriers into the building.

The clouds dumped their load. Carly grabbed the handle of a cat carrier with each hand and raced inside. The men had simply placed the carriers on the first available floor space inside the door. Carly peeked in the carriers' little holes. Some of the crates contained multiple animals— two cats, a litter of puppies. Carly shuttered. Oh, God, please get me through this evening. Then she scowled as the realization struck her—Patsy McNeal was right. The shelter needed a disaster plan.

The racket from the animals and the storm was twisting her mind all helter-skelter. She closed her eyes, shut down her ears, and tried to calm her overwrought mind.

First of all, breathe.

Second. Gather all available flashlights from within the shelter as well as from car glove compartments. She found six.

Third. Turn on Darrell's boombox. The advice she received from the radio was for everyone in the station's listening area to take cover, which meant she couldn't call in additional staff. Using her thumb, she ticked off her helpers—Juan Pablo, Alan, Fernando. That's all she had to work with?

Fourth. Figure out where to stash six- to eight-dozen additional animals, almost as many as the Humane Society typically housed. The problem was, she spent her days in her office and Juan Pablo was usually in the field. No one present tonight was familiar with the current occupants—which one was a fear biter, a bitch in heat, a tom cat itching to pick a fight.

Fifth. Review the shelter animals' records to identify which ones were docile enough to be safely caged together. She'd assign that task to someone. Alan.

And while he reviewed the records, he could also ascertain which strays had been in the shelter longer than seventy-two hours and one minute. Those could be euthanized immediately. She exhaled long and hard. God, this was a miserable job. Who in their right mind would choose this line of work?

Where was she? Sixth. Euthanize. Who would hold the animals for her? Fernando.

As she replaced her sandals with black rubber boots, someone walked up behind her. "What can I do to help?" It was Charlie, drenched to the bone.

"Um, I don't know yet. For the time being, bring in the rest of the animals. Then I'll have something else lined up for you." She flashed him a hurried but grateful smile.

She continued piecing together her action plan. While Alan reviewed the records, Charlie and Juan Pablo could use their male screws-and-bolts intellect to put together the collapsible cages and puppy pens that the shelter used on mobile adoption days.

After the men combined the Humane Society's more tractable animals so there were two or three per cage, the emptied cages could be cleaned and disinfected for the Bay Pointe animals. She'd have to show the men how to use the disinfectants, how to squeegee the runs, where to find food, how to fill in the basics on the animals' records.

Once the vans were unloaded, the two drivers couldn't be dissuaded from trying to get back to Bay Pointe to their families. Carly gave them some colas from the ice chest and the bag of Cheetos that had been in her office, unopened, since who could remember when.

At that moment, the electricity went out and flashlights clicked on.

Like miners in the bowels of the earth, Carly and the four men followed the beams of their flashlights. Thunder cracked and rain pelted the metal roof. Some of dogs howled with fear. Others chewed and clawed the chainlink in their desperate efforts to escape the threatening noise. Carly and her team had to scream in order to be heard.

Never had so much been accomplished in so little time at the Zhirnov Springs Humane Society. And no one was bitten, although a cantankerous gray cat gave Alan some souvenir claw marks down the length of his forearm. Within two hours, every animal was bedded down and the boombox's batteries were dead.

Winded, Carly, Alan, Fernando, Juan Pablo, and Charlie stood in the kennel and, under the dim light of the flashlights, looked at each other. Without saying a word, she motioned the men to the employee break room. At the table, Charlie took the seat next to hers. His thigh was a full hand's length from hers, but she swore she could feel its radiating heat.

Charlie telephoned Allison to make sure she was okay. Alan and Fernando also checked in with their families. Carly wondered who would care that she would be late getting home. She supposed she could call Yuri and Camey, but probably neither would bother to answer the phone. She glanced over at the other person who had no one waiting at home. The Latino hunk was emptying ice chests by distributing the soft drinks around the table and transferring the leftovers to the refrigerator.

Alan popped a Wint-O-Green Life Saver in his mouth and offered the roll to the others. They devoured the mints like hungry wolves. Alan plunked two more rolls on the table. In no time, the small, unventilated room was saturated with the aroma of a peppermint factory.

"So this is what you folks in the business refer to as 'raining cats and dogs'?" Charlie asked.

Carly grinned, partially at the poor pun but mainly at their accomplishment. She had led the little band of five to victory. What a glorious feeling to be so completely pooped but so totally pumped.

She allowed her gaze to linger an extra moment on the man next to her. He looked nice in a suit and tie, but he looked better with the top two buttons of his rumpled shirt open and his hair tumbling rascally over his brow like a little boy's. Her imagination played with images of what he would look like on a Saturday afternoon in a T-shirt and shorts. Wait a minute, she caught herself. She knew what he looked like in shorts, and it was pretty darn good. So that led to the next question. What did he look like without shorts?

While the unrelenting wind and rain battered the building, the group verbally patted themselves on the back over what they pulled off during the past two hours. The conversation segued into the Advocates's protest demonstration. Although each person had his own perspective, they all agreed on three things. First, the rally seemed like it happened two days ago, not two hours. Second, the hurricane unmistakably showed how off-target the Advocates's allegations of ineptness and lack of compassion were. Third, Patsy pushed it too far when she attacked a City Council-woman for breeding cats.

"I have to ask," Carly said to Charlie. "Which of the two women is it?"

"Want to take a guess?"

"The one that glides around like she's Vanna White?"

Charlie threw his head back and brayed. When he came back upright, his hair fell even more rakishly over his eyebrows. "I've never heard a better description of Loretta!" He grew serious. "If I'm any judge of my fellow City Councilmen...I'm sorry," he deferred to Carly, "Council Members, we should probably thank Patsy McNeal."

"Thank Patsy McNeal?" Fernando spat the words. "That bitch was frothing at the mouth with her lies."

Charlie held up his hands in a bear-with-me gesture. "The Advocates may very well be the catalyst we need to get things rolling."

"Huh?" Juan Pablo asked.

"When people scream, things get fixed. Which means you," he nodded at Fernando, "get what you asked for in your animal control budget. And you," he nodded at Alan, "get an increase in your contract plus some money from the County. These Advocates may be outspoken and con-frontational, but they're not stupid. As far as the fiscal year goes, they timed their little display perfectly."

"Sounds like the tail wagging the dog," Alan said. "But, hey, if it works...."

While the tip of her tongue stabbed the hole of her Life Saver, she watched the silhouette of Charlie's moving lips and how the wan light suggestively deepened his five o'clock shadow. Her skin felt steamy. Was it because of her damp clothes? Or was it due to the room's stuffiness? Or was it the closeness of Charlie VanCleave?

As though he felt her gaze, he turned toward her. The muted blackness of his eyes made her breath catch. They held the promise of something waiting just over the horizon—a full moon, perhaps, or a meteor shower, or Fourth of July fireworks.

As the auspicious eyes searched hers, she grappled for something to say. "We're lucky the flashlight batteries held out this long."

Fernando used his cell phone to call his buddies at the police station. From his end of the conversation, the group learned that the tornado warnings were still in effect. Electrical lines were down everywhere. The streets under all the viaducts were flooded and barricaded.

Fernando leaned back in his chair and stretched his arms back from his shoulders. "I guess I'll go down to the police station. There'll be a shitpotful of calls about loose dogs once this storm plays out. Fences blown down. Scared dogs busting off their chains."

"I'll go with you. Ain't got nothing better to do," Juan Pablo said.

Alan's cell phone rang. "Hi, hon." A frown descended on his face. "Aw, no." The frown deepened. "I'll be right home." He disconnected. "Tree limb blew down. Went right through one of our windows."

Charlie glanced at the fluorescent numerals on his watch. "I'd better be leaving." He twisted toward Carly and put a bent elbow on the back of her plastic chair. "Can you get home all right?"

"No way you're going home in this toad-choker," Juan Pablo said. "You heard Fernando. All the streets under the viaducts are barricaded."

"You live on the east side of the railroad tracks?" Charlie asked.

She nodded. "I'll just wait out the storm here."

"Even after it stops raining, it will take hours for the water to drain away." Juan Pablo rose to retrieve his yellow slicker from coat rack.

"Then I'll just stay here tonight."

"You can't stay here!" four men bellowed.

"I can lay my head on my desk."

"Carly. Carly, honey," Juan Pablo addressed her as he would a baby sister. "You know as well as I do this place comes alive with cockroaches at night." He added for emphasis, "The size of Chihuahuas."

She recoiled, her plan axed.

"In fact, there's one right now." From behind her, Juan Pablo's fingers did an itsy-bitsy-spider crawl on the nape of her neck. A parade of goose pimples followed.

As she flinched, her shoulder brushed Charlie's fingertips dangling from the back of her chair. Her goose bumps doubled.

"You're welcome to wait it out at my house," Charlie said. Her ears pricked up like a Doberman's. "I live less than a mile away."

"Or you can come home with me," Alan volunteered. "You'd have your choice of entertainment—help me nail up the plywood or pick glass out of the carpet."

"Or you can come with us to the police station." Juan Pablo winked.

"Allison and Hailey would love to see you," Charlie said as if that were the pièce de résistance.

She turned full-face toward him. His hand was a mere cat's whisker away from her chin. Even without weighing her other options— Alan's, or maybe Annalisa's—she knew her answer.

Her tongue gave a nervous swipe at her lips. "Well, okay, if you're sure it won't be an inconvenience."

"No inconvenience whatsoever."

She tried to inject a little silliness. "You're really-truly sure?"

His response didn't contain a trace of flippancy. "Really. Truly."

## 22

It was eerie without a single streetlight to light the way. The streets were deserted except for the flashing beacons of patrol cars. Jagged spears of lightening ripped the darkness, outlining the black houses and making the yards glow white with hail. The hail had stopped, but not the rain or the wind. Torrents of water coursed down the slightest incline. Trees cowered in the face of the tempest.

Carly hunched over the steering wheel, straining to see Charlie's tail-lights. The wipers couldn't keep up with the deluge, and it was a 50-50 toss-up whether the condensation or the defroster was winning the battle for the inside of the windshield.

Before they left the Humane Society, Charlie explained that on the days he worked late, Allison went to her friend Claire's house, just a half block from where they lived.

When they arrived at Claire's house, Carly waited at the curb, engine running. A blast of wind rocked the car. She shivered. The rain had slashed through her clothes in the short time it took to lock the shelter's door and waded across the lake in the parking lot. She cranked up the car's heater to full speed.

Hoping to get a good look at Charlie's neighborhood, she wiped a hole in the fog of her side window. The curtain of rain and the inky blackness made it a wasted effort. Not that it mattered. She was familiar with the subdivision. The upper middle-class development contained what realtors described as "the type of home your family deserves."

When Charlie finally emerged from the house, he was leading two girls, not just one. Carly resumed follow-the-leader behind his taillights. He pulled into the garage, and she nosed up the driveway as far as she could and made a dash for cover.

Charlie explained that playing by candlelight was just too cool to have the evening end so early, so the girls begged to have a sleepover at one of their houses. His voice dropped. "Considering the circumstances, I thought it best if they spent the night here."

"What circumstances?"

"I didn't want you to misinterpret my invitation tonight."

She tried to figure out if she was glad or disappointed that Charlie's intentions were honorable. She couldn't come up with an answer.

As Carly followed him inside, she discretely beamed her flashlight around the two-car garage that held his SUV on one side and miscellany on the other. Garden tools. A radial arm saw. Cans of paint. A Barbie helmet hanging from the handlebar of a girl's purple bicycle. Two adult bicycles—a man's and a woman's—suspended upside down from the ceiling.

Hailey was waiting for them in the kitchen. Her front legs pranced up and down like she was stomping grapes. She had turned into a butterball. Carly stooped to pet her.

"Poor girl. Don't they feed you? Ha! We should have named you Pork Belly!" She buried her fingers in the thick fur around the dog's shoulders and shook a roll of fat.

Allison was handed a flashlight and told to put Hailey outside so she could go potty "whether she wants to go out in the rain or not" and then take Claire's backpack upstairs.

Charlie excused himself and disappeared deeper into the house. He returned carrying a small pile of gray clothes. "Here's an old sweatshirt and some sweatpants that have shrunk over the years. They should come fairly close to fitting you."

"I didn't come here to inconvenience you."

"You can't stay in those wet clothes, at least not if you intend to sit on my furniture!" He took her shoulders and spun her around. His hand warmed her lower back as he directed her to a half-bath under the stairs. "I just hope there aren't any holes in embarrassing places. After you've changed, I'll meet you in my study. It's that direction." He pointed to his right and made an outsized gesture of flipping on a light switch. "I'll see what I can do about light."

In the shadows of her flashlight, she slid out of her blouse and slacks. Her bra and panties were damp, so she removed them as well. She folded her underwear safely and securely inside her slacks.

She pulled on the sweat suit. It was definitely a man's. The pants were tight in the hips while the top hung off her shoulders. At least the sweat suit wasn't his dead wife's. Charlie was right—the clothes were old and far from plush.

Carly turned her side to the mirror and pressed the sweatshirt against her ribcage. The material wasn't so thin that her nipples were visible. That was probably a good thing. Maybe.

She found Charlie had indeed turned on a light in the study. The room flickered with the ochre glow of an old oil lamp. She made a small mountain on the ceramic floor of the hallway, first her sandals, followed by her clothes, and finally her purse and flashlight. She gave the pile a nod of her head. Good. Very good. This way, she'd remember to take everything with her.

The study was too dim to make out the details but the desk held the usual—computer, phone, and stacks of papers. She walked over and picked up the phone. No dial tone. The room contained a sofa, recliner, television, stereo system, and bookcase. Various items hung on the wall. She wished the light were a tad brighter so she could see the pictures or diplomas or whatever was in the frames. But then again, she reasoned, the diaphanous light of the oil lamp had its advantages. Not only did it whisk away physical imperfections, it paved the way for romance. If, that is, one were inclined toward romance. Was she? Maybe. Maybe not. Probably. But not definitely.

She walked over to a window that stretched almost from the floor to the ceiling. She pulled aside the drape. The glass was opaque with sheets of water. She let the material fall back into place.

Where to sit? The couch? The flickering sienna light made the sofa look seductively soft, perfect for sinking into an undertow of cushy fantasies and sturdy arms. She told herself that it was too soon for the couch. The chair was safer, at least for the time being.

She slipped into the recliner and settled her head into a hollow in the cushion. She smiled. The divot must have been made by Charlie's head resting here for hours—a TV-watching head, a dozing head, a reflective head. She kneaded her shoulders into the pliant cushion.

Arms and legs suddenly flew across the room. Allison hurdled herself into a cartwheel then thrust her arms heavenward into a victory V. Not to be outdone, Claire threw her legs in the air in a toe-touch that almost achieved its objective. She then dropped to the floor in a somersault.

"It looks like you're both going to be cheerleaders," Carly said.

Allison raised her clenched fist across her chest, then brought it up beside her head before shooting her arm straight into the air. "Hey! Hey! What do you say! We'll go all the way!"

"Were you a cheerleader?" Claire asked.

"No. I never could do a toe touch like you can."

"Neither of us can stand on our hands yet, but we're learning," Claire said.

"Stand on our hands?" Allison snorted like a piglet. "We can't even stand on our heads."

"I can help you," Carly said. "That's one thing I did learn how to do."

The girls took turns balancing upside down while Carly offered stabilization and reassurance. It was some time before she noticed a pair of socks in the doorway. Her eyes wandered up to black sweat pants and finally onto a sweatshirt the color of oatmeal. Charlie was leaning against the doorframe, arms and feet crossed, watching the action.

"Can you take a break from practice to let your dog in?" he asked Allison. "Towel her off and leave her in the garage until she's dry."

While the girls pirouetted from the room, Charlie moved toward the couch. Carly was hit with a bout of cold feet. She dove for the recliner, avoiding the perils and possibilities of the couch.

"It's nice to see a parent make the child assume responsibility for the pet," she said.

The leather cushion gave a muffled creak as he settled onto the sofa. "She's a pretty responsible kid for an eight-year-old. She wasn't always like that, but we've had to make some changes."

Carly wondered if the "changes" referenced their lives after his wife died. It was a door-opener to a topic that, if this relationship were to go any further, would have to be discussed sooner or later. She took a chance.

"I was terribly sorry to hear about your wife. I just recently learned about your loss." She lifted her shoulders like she was born an idiot and managed with very little trouble to stay that way. "I guess I'm a little behind on things."

"Thank you for mentioning it. I find the subject difficult to work into a conversation." He paused for a crescendo of thunder. "And you have my condolences on the Humane Society's recent loss. Having a coworker commit suicide has to be hard on the staff."

"Very."

"And hard on you."

"She had some emotional problems, but I never dreamed...." Suddenly she saw a clear picture of Penny in repose on her ivory coverlet, a spray of freckles across her pale checks. The familiar tingle of ripening tears assaulted Carly's nose. She swallowed hard and tried to speak, but her voice jammed up. "I'm sorry." She cleared her throat. "I don't know why I'm getting worked up now. I thought I was all cried out."

"Don't apologize. Whatever you do, don't apologize. Alicia's death taught me many things, one of which is I learned how to cry. Big boys don't cry, you know." He gave a wry grin. "But this boy learned real fast the value of tears. The necessity of tears."

She was reprieved from responding by the sound of footsteps on the kitchen tile. She raised a finger to her lips and crept to her stack of clothes for her flashlight. She held the light under the tip of her chin. The beam skimmed upward across her face as the girls rounded the corner.

"Ah ha! I've got you now, my pretties," she said in her best Wicked Witch of the West voice.

Both girls screamed.

Charlie busted a gut laughing while the girls hid their embarrassed faces in their hands.

"I'm uglier than warts on a hog. And just as mean!" Carly chortled like an old crone. "Quite a stormy night we're having. The kind of scary night a warty old witch like me likes." Fingers crooked like cat claws, she reached out and tickled Claire's tummy.

Both girls burst into giggles and ran to the safety of the center of the room.

Allison dropped to her knees and put her forehead on the carpet. "Let's practice some more."

Her father said, "Maybe the warty old witch had a long day at work and would like to sit quietly for a while."

Allison, head still catawampus, looked over at Carly in disbelief that anyone would prefer sitting on one's bottom to standing on one's head.

"I'm not that tired," Carly said.

"Here's the deal," Charlie said to the girls. "You have thirty minutes before bedtime. Decide what you want to do. Cheerleading? Barbie dolls? Whatever. But you're going to bed at 9:30."

While they pondered their options, Claire chewed on a strand of hair. Carly was knocked off balance by a swell of visions of Penny during her final few weeks. She averted her gaze until she heard Claire's voice.

"How about cards?"

"Yeah!" Allison seconded. "Okay, Dad?"

"Are you up for a half hour of Crazy Eights?" he asked Carly.

"And Spoons?" Allison asked. "Do you know how to play Spoons?"

At Carly's nod, Charlie told Allison to get the cards while he moved the lamp to the kitchen table.

"Nooo," Allison protested, still upside down. "Let's play on the floor."

Charlie raised his eyebrows at Carly.

"I'm game," she said.

The next half hour was as relaxing as a pot of chamomile tea. The cards gave her something to focus on. There was much teasing and laughter. Claire kept her hair out of her mouth. And Carly loved sitting cross-legged across from Charlie, close enough to be able to look up from her cards and see what was going on behind those glasses, but yet not so close that she could feel, real or imaged, his body heat.

Charlie made them adhere to their 9:30 curfew. After bringing Hailey in from the garage, Allison asked if Carly wanted to see Rocky.

"Rocky?"

"My gerbil. He's in my room."

"Sure."

Allison gave her father a goodnight peck on the cheek. Carly waved her flashlight at him as she and Hailey trailed after the girls. "Be back in a little while."

As the beam shone into the cage, Carly admitted that Rocky was a particularly handsome gerbil. "And you're sure he's a boy?"

Allison nodded. "Want to see?" She started to reach in the cage, but Carly said she needn't bother. She'd take her word for it.

"Did you know that male gerbils are called bucks?" Allison asked.

"No, I didn't. But I do know they like to stay up all night and make a lot of noise in their cage. Doesn't that keep you awake?"

"No, I'm used to it. I've had him since he was a baby. Sonia gave him to me."

"How old is he now?"

"About, like, hummm, a year maybe."

"How long will you two stay up talking?" Carly asked with the hushed voice of confidentiality.

"Not too long."

Claire giggled at her friend's understatement.

"How long will you and Dad stay up talking?" Allison asked.

"Only until the rain stops. Then I'm going home."

"So you won't be here in the morning?"

"Oh, no."

"But you can come back tomorrow afternoon. We're having another lemonade sale."

"Really? For the Humane Society? Your dad didn't tell me that."

A look of consternation settled on Allison's face as she looked at Claire. "I hope he didn't forget to buy the lemonade again."

Hailey jumped on the double bed.

"Does Hailey sleep with you?" Carly asked.

"Sometimes."

"Does she sleep with your dad?"

"No, he doesn't let her sleep in his bed."

Who does he let sleep in his bed? But of course the question remained unasked.

"Good luck with your lemonade sale. The animals need all the help they can get. Goodnight Rocky. Goodnight Hailey. Goodnight Claire. Goodnight Allison."

*Goodnight Rocky. Goodnight Hailey. Goodnight Claire. Goodnight Allison.* She felt like she was on Walton's Mountain. A world apart from the silent and lonely bedtime at her house.

## 23

She headed for the recliner like a pigeon coming home to roost. "You didn't tell me I could go ahead and order the new air conditioning system for the shelter."

"Say again?"

"I hear the entrepreneurs are having another fund-raiser tomorrow."

"Damn! I was supposed to buy lemonade."

"Wait till your daughter finds out. You'll really be in the doghouse." When he bowed his head sheepishly, she couldn't resist adding, "Again."

"Say, the last time there was a lemonade sale, you were scraping your porch. Did you get it painted?" ·

"Funny you should ask. I was planning to do it tomorrow."

"The wood will be too wet tomorrow."

"I know." She snapped her fingers as they glided through the air. "Dagnabit."

He followed her lead. "Well, gosh darn. Such a disappointment for you. Did you get those boards replaced?"

"No, that hasn't gotten done yet, either. Although my friend keeps implying he intends to do it." Of their own volition, Carly's legs coiled under her. She didn't understand why, at the oblique mention of Eddie, she rolled into a ball like a pillbug.

"Your feet are cold! I should have been more considerate. I'll get you some socks."

"That's not necessary." But Charlie was already out of the room.

He returned with a pair of white sports socks. "Is there anything else you need? Are you hungry? Would you like something to drink? Coke? Tepid Beer? Instant coffee?"

"No, thank you. Unless...you don't happen to have any chamomile tea, do you?"

"No. But I might have some hot chocolate."

"Hot chocolate? Sounds delicious. I haven't had any in ages."

While he was in the kitchen, she slid on the socks. Wouldn't you know—new socks. She held both legs straight out in front of her and wiggled her toes against the cuddly softness. Despite the socks being an inch too long, her feet felt snug as a bug in rug. She almost giggled out loud. When she woke up this morning, she'd have wagered better odds of finishing the day with a winning lottery ticket in her hand than of being dressed in clothes belonging the dusky-eyed Councilman.

The strike of a match as he lit a gas burner cleaved a stillness that went beyond the absence of voices or a blaring television. Missing was the background hum of electric motors, cubes dropping from the ice-maker, the *swoosh* of the air from the air conditioner. And something else was missing. No rain.

He handed her a mug. "Hope hot chocolate with hazelnut is okay with you." He nudged the empty toe of the sock. "Perfect fit."

How could the simple touch of the tip of his big toe to the tip of her big toe though a thick layer of fuzzy cotton send an electric shock that made the hairs on her arm stand on end? She casually brought the mug to her lips while her heart defibrillated.

"Umm. Not exactly a summer drink, but it sure hits the spot tonight," she said as he took a sip from his mug and moved toward the couch. God, his butt was cute in those sweat pants.

She cupped a hand behind her ear. "By the way, I think Mother Nature finally turned off the spigot."

He cocked his head. After setting his mug on the end table, he went to the tall window and opened the drapes. As he slid open the bottom half of the window, the most magnificent scent swept over her.

"Oh, my gosh!" she breathed.

She set down her mug. As she scurried to the window, her socks flopped like the webbed feet of a duck. She knelt and pressed her nose against the screen.

Alarm filled Charlie's voice. "What? What's out there?" He dropped onto one knee beside to her.

She closed her eyes and filled her lungs with a protracted gulp. "Honeysuckle. Isn't it scrumptious?" When she didn't receive an answer, she opened her eyes and turned toward him. His face was inches from hers. The lamp's flame licked his features. Ohmygoodness.

"Don't look at me like I'm crazy," she told him. "Take a whiff and see for yourself."

He turned his face half toward the window but kept his eyes fixed on her. His knitted eyebrows expressed his concern at having opened his home to someone who was possibly unhinged. He took a sniff.

She laughed. "Your nose twitches like Rocky's."

"Like what?" His forehead crinkled.

"Rocky. Upstairs." Her finger jabbed at the ceiling. "Breath deep." She demonstrated by squashing her nose against the screen.

His chest rose and fell as he inhaled, but still he didn't turn toward the window. He stared at her like a hen waiting to see what the fox had up its sleeve. She could feel his breath glide along her cheeks.

"It does smell nice," he acknowledged.

"Nice? It smells heavenly." She clucked her tongue. "I always heard men have a lousy sense of smell. That's why perfume is designed for women, even though women wear it for men."

His laugh was rich and warm, like the cocoa, and Carly felt herself melt. She had a fiery longing to see if his mouth tasted like hazelnut chocolate. Oh, man, was she in trouble.

She rose, using the window sill for leverage—instead of his shoulder, as was her inclination—and commanded her feet back to the recliner. She wondered what in the world was wrong with her. She had the maturity of an eighth grader plucking petals off a daisy. Kiss me. Kiss me not.

Just as he moved back to the sofa, an unwelcome intrusion came from the kitchen. The refrigerator motor. Damn the bad luck, she cursed as she foresaw the end of the candlelight.

"Good. Electricity," he said but showed no inclination to turn on the lights. "The news will be on soon. We can watch ourselves on TV."

Carly groaned. "Don't remind me about this afternoon. I'd like to have one evening, just one evening, free from worries about the Zhirnov Springs Humane Society." She wrapped her hand around her forehead as if to ward off a headache.

"You certainly have a lot on your mind right now. The Advocates. An employee's death. A facility that's barely adequate."

"Not to mention our checkbook is running on fumes. Our old van, which we use all the time for everything, *was* on life support. Now the mechanic is ready to pull the plug. And I have no idea how we'll find the money for a new vehicle."

He pressed a finger to the furrow above his upper lip. His forehead crinkled. "You might talk to the folks at Jacobson Autoplex. The City just traded in five of its cargo vans, which aren't all that old. And Jacobson made good money off the deal. You may be able to talk him into donating one of the used vans to the Humane Society. The worst he can say is no."

"Do you know who I should talk to?"

"No, I don't. But I can find out from our purchasing lady."

"That would be great. Hey! This is nice having friends in high places!"

He guffawed. "High places. Yeah, right. You know what John Madden said about that? The higher up the flagpole you climb, the more your underwear is exposed."

Carly's laugh was brief before she turned glum. "I know that feeling. I used to be competent at my job. Ever since my promotion, I feel like I'm a bumbling idiot and everybody knows it."

"You've let the Advocates get your goat. You feel like their personal target because of your high visibility. According to the Chinese, the big tree catches the wind."

She gazed at the steam rising from her mug. "I'm not a big tree." She looked up. "You're the one who's so high up the flagpole your underwear shows."

As he pushed the sleeves of his sweatshirt up his forearms, she hungered for the strength of a man, both physically and emotionally. Someone to come home to at night and listen to her rant and rave and cry and then cuddle her against his chest. To hell with this "women rule" crap. She wanted the man across the room to scoop her into his arms and kiss away her fears. But of course, fears can't be kissed away. Not to mention, the man across the room wasn't making any moves to either scoop or kiss.

"Don't you get help from the Board of Directors?" he asked.

"Humph! Sometimes I question whether there's a lick of horse sense in the whole group. Most of them think a bake sale is the answer to our financial woes." She rolled her eyes. "Talk about a squirrelly bunch."

"Oh?"

"One Board member—an old goat by the name of Reinhardt—has the subtlety of a Hot Shot cattle prod. The treasurer understands numbers but not money. Of course, you met Sonny—the one who turns into a cyber geek after he gets done ridin' the range. And certainly you know Sophia Zhirnov. The bats in her belfry take their midnight dip in Chanel No. 5. And the list goes on." She glanced at her watch. "Show time."

He clicked on the remote.

"The top story tonight is, of course, the weather. Tropical storm winds and heavy rain have buffeted the entire viewing area. For more on this story, here's our Meagan Davis."

Miserable Meagan peered from under the hood of her slicker and described the scores of streets and highways that were under water.

Downed electrical wires added further danger. She closed with the classic line, "If you don't need to be on the road, police and emergency crews ask that you stay put."

The sixty-second story about the Advocates's protest was bumped to the end of the newscast. It opened with the newscaster's voiceover of a shot of Patsy on her platform. To Carly's surprise and delight, the camera picked up the contempt in Patsy's predatory eyes. There was the briefest flash of Carly giving the tour before the camera panned to the white crosses. Predictably, the bulk of the story focused on the hurricane evacuation efforts. The closing footage was of Charlie saying the City was in the process of reviewing its contract with Humane Society. As Carly listened to Charlie's steady cadence, she understood why he was popular with voters. And why his pillow talk would sound so good, too.

He rose, tapped off the TV, and turned on a brass floor lamp. Even though the light was soft, it seemed harsh after the golden shadows thrown by the oil lamp. When he returned to the couch, he laid his glasses on the end table and, using the palms of his hands, stretched his eyelids toward his temples. When he opened his eyes, she found herself sinking into the gray flannel warmth of her favorite pajamas.

She used a display of histrionics to bring her back to the here and now. Planting both hands on her hips, she said, "By the way, I have a bone to pick with you."

"Pardon me?"

"Cavorting with the enemy. The first thing I saw at that demonstration was Councilman VanCleave talking and joking with one of the Advocates."

"What can I say? That's what elected officials do. And I like people."

"Really-truly? You like people?"

"Really-truly. Not all of them, of course. But most people you meet are decent, if you dig deep enough. I like hearing their stories, their hopes."

She wondered if that was the motive behind his invitation this evening. He enjoyed talking to the common people on the street, and she was as common a person as ever walked the earth.

"So I guess you'll run for a second term on the City Council?"

"Probably. For a couple of reasons. One being that, for years, I was struck with a sort of civic amnesia, expecting the government to provide me with entitlements, forgetting that in order to keep getting things, you have to give something back."

"And the second reason?"

"It fills the gap that was left in my life when Alicia died. I can't devote all of my energy to Allison. If I did, I'd suffocate her, especially since she's, unfortunately, an only child. And real estate is nothing more than a paycheck to me. So for the time being, I'm finding fulfillment by giving something to the community."

"It sounds as if you'd prefer to have more than one child."

"Without a doubt. Brothers and sisters prepare you for the give and take you face in marriage, at work, as a member of society as a whole."

"I'm sorry you didn't have more children before…before…Alicia was taken from you."

A spot of color appeared on each of his cheeks. "She was two-months pregnant."

"Oh, Charlie, I'm so sorry."

He nodded as though he was grateful for the words of condolence but he'd heard the line a thousand times and it never eased the hurt.

Carly pushed herself from the recliner and ambled to the photographs on the wall. One was an 8" by 10" studio portrait of Charlie, a toddler, and a petite brunette. "You married a very pretty woman." Carly turned and winked at him. "Makes one wonder, doesn't it?"

"Wonder what?"

"Why she'd marry someone who walks around with his underwear exposed."

He looked thankful for a chance to grin. "Touché, Big Tree."

She turned back toward the wall and bit her lower lip. Why did his mouth have to have such nice laugh lines? Wouldn't it be fun to trace them with the tip of her tongue?

She continued to look at the pictures as she sidestepped to the book-shelves. Her eyes caught on a couple of boxes. Jigsaw puzzles. Interesting.

Something glimmered on the top shelf. "Trophies? For track?"

"High school."

"Apparently you did pretty well."

"Believe it or not, I was third in the state my senior year."

She stood on tiptoe. "I can't read the event."

"Mile."

"Do you still run?"

"I barely saunter. You know, a mile is really long."

She returned to what she now viewed as *her* recliner. June bugs thumped against the window as the final pit-a-pats of water dropped from the trees. The honeysuckle continued to dole out its fragrance. Charlie scooted down, put his feet on the edge of the coffee table, and stuffed a throw pillow between his head and the back of the couch. How she yearned to curl up against his drowsy warmth. Why didn't she do it? Why did she keep fleeing to the safety of the recliner? Afraid of rejection?

"I guess I should try to get home."

"I don't think so."

"Pardon?"

"You heard the news. The cops don't want you out there."

"But it's late. I'm keeping you up."

"I don't think you'll make it home. The water under the viaducts hasn't had a chance to drain off. You'll get part way home, your car will stall, then you'll call me to come pick you up."

"I doubt that. I don't even have your phone number."

"Why don't you forget about going home tonight? You can sleep in my bed."

Her heart launched into cartwheels, somersaults, and toe-touches.

He continued with, "I'll sleep on the couch."

"No. I can't. No." She shook her head like a rattle. "Un-un. *Nyet.*" She couldn't believe she was imitating Darrell.

"What choice do you have?"

"Well…I…I could try to get home."

"Why?"

"Well…because…I didn't come over here with the intention of spending the night."

"I know that. But give me a good reason why you should piss off the police just to get to your house tonight. Do you have a dog that needs walking?"

"No."

"Cats?"

"Yes, I have cats."

"So you need to get home and change their litter box?"

"Sarcasm does not become you."

"How many cats?"

"Two."

"Anything else?"

"In the way of pets? No."

"I guess you liked animals since you were a kid? Did you have some when you were growing up in Iowa?"

"Of course. We lived on a farm."

"When I think of Iowa, I think of corn."

"And pigs."

"Do you miss it?" He seemed genuinely interested.

"Iowa? The farm? Pigs?"

"All of it. Any of it."

She tucked her legs under her. The next time she looked at her watch, an hour-and-a-half had slipped by. They had talked about the things people talk about on a first date. Childhood. Favorite movies. Pastimes. Aspirations. At one point in the conversation, she mentioned she had been married for ten years and divorced for three, but she didn't elaborate. She was sure they could have talked till sunrise, but keeping true to her character, she stopped short of the gold, content with the silver or the bronze.

"It's time to call it a night. I'll make you a deal. I won't try to get home, since you insist it would be an asinine thing to do. I'll stay only if you'll let me sleep on the couch."

"You don't want the bed?"

*Not without you in it.* "No. It's the couch or nothing."

"Have it your way."

She gave the supercilious toss-of-the-head of an incorrigible brat. "I usually do." She grew serious again. "And you're really-truly sure I won't be an inconvenience?"

"Really. Truly." He put on his glasses, rose, and stretched his back. "I'll get you a blanket."

While he was gone, she closed the window. But first she took a final whiff of honeysuckle. She had a feeling that as long as she lived, the merest drift of honeysuckle would stir memories of this night.

She pulled the drape shut and lowered the wick on the oil lamp. Tendrils of smoke rose in curled ribbons before vanishing into nothingness. She lowered herself onto the couch. The leather cushion was still warm from Charlie. She planted an elbow on the sofa's arm, settled her cheek onto her fist, and reflected on the evening.

Why was he being so completely platonic? Perhaps she was nothing more than one of those common people he liked to talk with? Or was he worried that Allison might wander from her bedroom? Or was he being faithful to a girlfriend? Or to the memory of his wife?

Or was harebrained Carly-girl sending signals that kept him at bay? Like implicit references to a porch-repairing boyfriend. Why did she retreat behind her wariness? Was she afraid of falling in love again? And that the love would be unrequited? Was she scared she'd once again become a rug for the man in her life to walk on? That she'd lose the identity she'd worked so hard to build these past few months?

Why did she invariably tap the brake just when things were picking up speed?

She closed her eyes. Tomorrow. She'd wade through those questions tomorrow. Right now, she was too tired.

"Sleeping already?"

Her lids popped open. "Just testing out the couch. I can't believe you're making me sleep on this lumpy thing."

He opened his mouth to protest.

"Just kidding." She rose, stood before him and held her arms out.

He handed her the pillow and blanket and put his hands in the pockets of his sweatpants. "I might be gone by the time you get up. I have an early appointment to show a house."

"I'll probably be up and out of the house before you. I need to leave early to swing by the shelter and ease my mind that the electricity is back on." She scrunched her nose. "The freezer holds the dead animals, you know."

He grimaced.

"And I want to make sure the Operations Manager was able to find at least one additional employee willing to come into work to handle the extra animals. Plus I have a guy coming to my house at 9:00 to give me an estimate on a new roof."

She stood facing him, the mound of pillow and blanket pressed to her belly. His murky eyes dipped into hers. If he was going to make a move, he had to do it now. Her every sinew strained to appear at ease. The world got very still.

She waited a millennium, two millenniums. He never moved a muscle.

She let out the breath she'd been holding. "Well, thanks again." She smiled and lifted her eyebrows to brighten her expression. "Can't tell you how much I appreciate this." She indicated the bedding by swaying the bundle in her arms in an arch toward him, then letting it drop back. She felt as though she was using the pillow as a shield, a shield against an opponent who had no intention of advancing. She took a half-step backwards.

"Um, thanks, by the way," he said, "for pointing out the honeysuckle. I guess it's one of those stop-and-smell-the-roses things that I haven't done."

"You're welcome. And I can't thank you enough for your help at the shelter this evening."

"My pleasure."

"Goodnight, Exposed Underwear."

"Goodnight, Big Tree."

24

When Carly threw back the blanket at sunrise, Hailey was the sole ambulatory member of the household. She picked up her clothes from the hallway tile. They were still damp. Ugh, she moaned. Why didn't she have the foresight last evening to ask if she could use the clothes dryer? She'd have to wear the gray sweat suit home. It made an awesome combo with ankle-strap sandals with one-and-a-quarter-inch heels and soggy insoles.

As she pulled her hair through the emergency scrunchy she kept in her purse, she pictured Charlie starting his day. Did he spring out of bed or take an hour to wake up? Was he the type to eat eggs, sausage, OJ, the whole works? Or was he a cold-cereal-and-milk kind of guy? Or maybe a donut junkie? Did he drink his coffee with cream or sugar or neither? If cream, was it the real stuff from the cow or that flavored powder? Sugar or sweetener?

Snap out of it! Talk about irrelevant, addle-brained questions. For all their pleasant conversation, he gave no inclination that he wanted to spend another evening, let alone a night, with her. He in no way insinuated any sort of physical attraction. Not a single flirtatious innuendo. At the end of the evening, she didn't even receive the equivalent of "Glad you came over." All he offered was reassurance that she really-truly wasn't an inconvenience. Come to think of it, he didn't even ask her to stop by for lemonade today.

On the kitchen table, she jotted a note to Charlie and Allison thanking them for the couch, the card games, the hot chocolate, and the good companionship. She wrote that she was pleased to meet Claire and Rocky, was thrilled to see that Hailey was so happy, and hoped the girls' lemonade stand did a booming business. She looked at the stodgy, decorum-bound words and added that she'd return the sweat suit soon. She chewed the inside of her cheek before scribbling *Thanks for a fantastic evening!*

She stopped by the shelter. It survived the storm without any major damage–just a few downed tree branches and a mudflow that oozed across the parking lot like escapee lava from Darrell's lamp. Her sweat-suit-and-heeled-sandals outfit turned a few of the employees' heads, but no one mentioned the mismatch. She stopped by her office to check her phone messages and e-mails and to clean Mary Louise's cage.

While she filled the bird's water and food, Mary Louise flitted around the room singing, "I'm Looking Over a Four Leaf Clover." Regrettably, he knew only one line.

♫ *One leaf is sunshine, the second is rain* ♫

He sang the line again. Three times. Four times.

"Enough already!" Carly scolded the parrot.

Mary Louise stopped his investigation of her desk. With a foot atop the paperclip holder, he gave Carly a one-eyed glare.

"Why is it you never sing about rain? Like maybe "I Love a Rainy Night"? Ever heard of that one by Eddie Rabbitt?"

Mary Louise straightened his leg out behind him in a lazy stretch, bored stiff with the whole notion of singing about rain.

Carly sang it for him, snapping her fingers to give the bird the beat. "Well I love a rainy night. I love a rainy night."

Mary Louise soared across the room to the top of his cage. Using the combined forces of his beak and feet, he maneuvered down the bars to her shoulder.

She repeated the lines while the bird studied her mouth.

Mary Louise squealed with delighted laughter.

"Trust me, rainy nights can be pretty extraordinary. I know from experience. Very recent experience." She moved the bird to one of the orange chairs. "Stay over here. I have work to do."

As she spread newspaper on the bottom of the cage, her eye caught part of a personal advice feature. Much like Mary Louise, Carly cocked her head to eyeball a quote the columnist had adapted from Anthony de Mello.

> How many of the loves
> And dreams
> And fears
> Of yesteryears
> Retain their hold
> On me today?

Carly read the question again. Loves and dreams and fears—all bearing the name Eddie Chevalier. She tore off the page, folded it, and tucked it in the pocket of the sweat pants.

"Come on, Mister, back in the cage you go."

On the way to her car, she caught sight of some damage her earlier, cursory glance had missed. Juan Pablo was taping a piece of cardboard over the hole where the side panel window of the van had been. Every door in the rust bucket was hanging wide open. Her shoulders sagged. Great. Just great. The Humane Society still owed Walt for repairing the timing belt, and now this.

She detoured to the van. Juan Pablo looked up as her heeled sandals tapped across the pavement.

"Well. Well. Well." He leaned against the side of the van, crossed his arms and ankles, and gave her a once-over. "I was going to ask if you behaved yourself at the VanCleave hacienda last night, but I see I don't need to bother."

She shot him a shut-your-trap look. "I guess the inside is soaked?" she asked as she poked her head in the passenger door. She pressed on the seat cushion, and water oozed around her fingers.

"It's going to take days for it to dry out." Like a bloodhound who had picked up an interesting scent, Juan Pablo wasn't about to be sidetracked. "By the way, I must say I thought you looked great on the news last night. But it ain't nothing compared to your chic sophistication this morning. Or should I say, the morning after?"

"It's not what it looks like."

"Right."

Something behind his mocha eyes reminded her of a triple-X movie. "You have an unruly imagination. Just because I'm fashion-impaired this morning doesn't mean anything happened last night."

The muscles of his jaw mockingly worked a piece of gum.

"He has an eight-year-old daughter who I taught to stand on her head and she tutored me on the finer points of Crazy Eights."

"You little sex kitten." He tossed the roll of silver tape so it spun like a miniature Ferris wheel.

"I slept on the couch!"

"Come on. 'fess up, you naughty girl." He gave her shoulder a playful punch. She felt like she'd been sideswiped by a Bekins moving van.

"I'm not a bed-hopper."

Juan Pablo clucked like a hen. "Tell the truth now."

"I don't treat sex casually. Like some people do," she said pointedly.

"I'm sexually discriminating."

"Then I assume you understand why I slept on the couch while he slept in his bed."

"Can't say that I do."

She dismissed him with a wave. "You can believe whatever you want. The truth is, he never laid a hand on me. Or any other part of his anatomy."

Perplexity descended on Juan Pablo's face. He uncrossed his legs and put a hand on his narrow hip. He extended his other arm straight out to the side to angle his weight against the van. "You're serious?"

"Completely."

He looked genuinely baffled. "Why'd you do that?"

"Do what?"

"Opportunity knocked and you not only let it slide right past you, you elbowed it out of the way."

"It's easy to see why Ruby gets infuriated with you."

"Nothing happened?"

"Other than headstands and card games?"

"Other than headstands and card games."

"Really. Truly. Nothing."

As she drove from the parking lot, she glanced in the rearview mirror at the poor, old faithful van—held together with cardboard and metallic tape, its doors agape like it was gasping for its final breath. In a flash of inspiration, the words of two men came to her.

*Talk to the folks at Jacobson Autoplex.*

*You want to do all these good and wonderful things, but you just never get around to most of them.*

Why wait until next week? Today was as good a day as any to grab the bull by the horns. Sure, Charlie was supposed to let her know the name of the City's contact person at Jacobson, but she could ferret out that information for herself. She'd show her worth to this organization.

At home, her answering machine was blinking.

"Hello, ma'am. This is Ralph over at Exciting Roofing. We've got calls about damaged roofs coming in right and left. I was hoping we could reschedule your estimate."

Carly went outside and looked at her roof. She never thought she'd be happy to see wind and hail damage. But there it was—not a catastrophe but definitely patches of missing shingles plus some damaged flashing. A new roof was on the way, and all she'd have to pay was her deductible. Luck this good never fell into her lap. She called her insurance agent, who promised the adjuster would get with her this afternoon.

She calculated that if she hustled her bustle, she could get to Jacobson Autoplex this morning. And then, well, goodness gracious, her note said she'd bring the sweat suit back *soon.* Plus she really should show support for the lemonade fund-raiser. Two perfectly good reasons to visit Jackson Street. Charlie should be finished with his client by noon. That way, he could be home for lunch with Allison and help set up the lemonade stand. Carly smiled. Assuming he remembered to buy the lemonade.

She took the newspaper clipping from the pocket of the sweatpants and stuck it under a magnet on the refrigerator. She slipped into high gear as she washed and dried the sweat suit, took a shower, wolfed down some yogurt, and tended to the cats and her appearance.

As Carly turned into the megaplex, her resolve crumpled. It had four different showrooms, one for each make of car. Across eight acres of sticky blacktop, vehicles were crammed together like kernels on an ear of corn. Strewn between light poles were little flags, silk screened with the Jacobson logo and frayed from last night's storm. Lasers of sunlight glared off the acres of chrome like thousands of tiny torches.

She circled the megaplex twice before she found a parking place. She squeezed her eyes tight and tried to collect her thoughts. She had seen vans with "City of Zhirnov Springs" on their doors hundreds of times. What kind were they? White. But what make?

She studied the names on the four signs spaced what appeared to be a mile apart. The vans definitely weren't Hummers, so three possibilities remained. She may as well start at the closest showroom, a mere city block from where she was parked.

A fresh-from-high-school girl sat inside a kiosk in the showroom. The length of her miniskirt exceeded the width of her belt by mere centimeters. Carly did her best to explain why she was here while the sweet young thing answered the phone, forwarded calls, and paged salesmen.

"So you think they traded the vans in here?" The girl's fingers served as a fulcrum as her pen oscillated like a frenzied teeter-totter.

"I know they traded the vans in *here*. I'm just not sure which part of the dealership."

"I guess I can call around. Why don't you take a seat over there and have some coffee."

I don't suppose you have any tea, Carly asked silently and cynically as she crossed the showroom and lowered herself onto a chrome and black vinyl chair. On the end table was today's Megalopolis newspaper. She found the Metro section.

**Protestors Bark at Zhirnov Springs Pound**
**Humane Society Bites Back**

Carly's quick scan of the article didn't reveal any obvious bias on the reporter's part. The facts appeared relatively accurate. Alan and the City Manager were both quoted as saying the animal control program met acceptable standards but was hampered by budget constraints. The sole photo was of Fernando unloading the Bay Pointe van.

Carly looked up to see Sweet Young Thing's cardinal red fingernails gesturing to her. Apparently the girl was tethered to the kiosk. Carly tucked the Metro section in the side pocket of her purse.

"You want our GMC dealership." The girl smacked her wad of gum.

"And where is that?"

The girl's eyes, which looked like they were smeared with tar rather than mascara, gestured over her shoulder. "Down there."

Carly thanked her and went outside. The late morning sun ricocheted with hot brutality off the endless sparkling windshields and high-gloss clear coat finishes. She shielded her eyes as they followed the lines of colorful but tattered pendants. There was GMC. All the way at the other end. Of course.

She debated which would be less painful—to drive and hunt for a place to park or to walk in the blistering heat. She shoved her sunglasses on her nose, hitched her purse higher on her shoulder, and began the hike.

She went through the same spiel as she had with Sweet Young Thing, this time with a young salesman. "You'll want to talk to the person in charge of our fleet sales. Wait here just a second."

Carly sat down on another chrome and black vinyl chair and reapplied her lipstick. Her face was a glaze of perspiration. Sweat streamed from her every pore, drenching her underwear and soaking through to her new blouse. She hated asking for handouts. Not only was she a moocher and a leech, she was ruining good clothes in the process. On what would probably turn out to be a wild-goose chase.

She fixed her gaze on the interlocked fingers in her lap and repeated Charlie's words. *The worst he can say is no. The worst he can say is no. The worst he can say is no.*

She shivered as goose bumps formed on her hot skin. She looked up at the air conditioner vent blasting directly on her.

Her mouth was as dry as a horny toad's scales. Her tongue swished around what little saliva was available. She looked about for a soft drink machine.

"If you'll come with me, I'll show you to the office."

As she followed the salesman up the stairs to the inner sanctum, she wondered if she was old enough to be his mother.

She inhaled deeply, stepped into the office, and smiled at the person behind the desk.

Like the pause button on the DVD player had been hit, Carly and Jocelyn stared at each other in mind-stunned disbelief.

**25**

When Carly took her next breath a full minute-and-a-half later, her voice quivered. "Hello, I'm Carly Shannon." She mentally thunked her head. "I guess you know that." She slid her business card across the desk. "I'm here on behalf of the Zhirnov Springs Humane Society."

"Have a seat." Jocelyn's face was still pretty, her makeup doing a good, but not perfect, job of hiding the fine lines around her full mouth and midnight blue eyes. Streaks of bottled blonde framed her high cheekbones. From what Carly could see behind the desk, Jocelyn's body could still be used as a mannequin for camisoles.

The pleasant expression on Carly's face felt as taut as a stretched rubber band. "I guess I should have given that young man my card so he could have passed it along to you. You could have avoided that shocked look of horror."

"The look on your face was pretty priceless, too." Jocelyn's feigned smile almost looked authentic.

"I really didn't expect to see you. I expected the fleet salesman."

Jocelyn raised her hands alongside each shoulder, palms facing Carly. "One and the same. I don't usually work on Saturdays, but I came in to catch up on some paperwork."

Carly hadn't realized how trigger-happy she was to blast Jocelyn with three-and-a-half years of pent-up accusations and insults. "Working six days a week? I heard you spend a lot of time at the office."

Jocelyn's lush mouth tightened. "Been talking to your ex-husband?"

Carly gave a half-shrug. "Yeah, been talking to my ex-*husband*. I guess you two never got married." The *ha, ha* in her voice was unmistakable.

"No, we didn't. But if you've been talking to Eduard, then you'd know that." Barbed wire was less prickly than Jocelyn's voice.

Eduard? Carly had forgotten that Jocelyn addressed him by that portentous name with its foreign spelling. "We discussed a lot of things. He mentioned that you stayed pretty busy."

"Right. I have a life of my own."

Carly's eyes narrowed. That was a definite slam about how she kowtowed to Eddie during their marriage. Well, she could punch back.

"Yes, I can see that." Carly's gaze methodically swept the pocket-sized office, its ecru walls, industrial gray carpet, and window with a panoramic view of metal and fiberglass.

Jocelyn's eyes skewered her. "I have a career and an active personal life."

"As I said, so I hear."

"Oh, yeah? Well, I heard some things, too."

"Oh, yeah? I can imagine how accurate they were." Warning lights flashed inside Carly. Such hotheadedness was completely at odds with her passive character. But at a more immediate level, an irrepressible need demanded *Let her have it!*

"Accurate enough that your ex-husband was ready to bail out of his marriage long before he met me." Jocelyn wasted no time peeling the scab off Carly's sore.

"And you believed him. He handed you the same spiel used by every married man who's looking for some blonde to screw. And you fell for it hook, line, and sinker."

"You're the one who started this conversation about hearsay."

Carly ground her teeth. "Look, why don't I just talk to someone else? It was stupid of me to just barge in without calling first. Then you and I wouldn't have been forced into this conversation."

"There is no one else to talk to. I'm the person who handles fleet sales." Jocelyn puffed up like a rooster getting ready to crow. "You said you're here on behalf of the Humane Society? How many vehicles are you interested in purchasing? Or are you interested in leasing?"

"One."

"One?"

"Just one."

"Then perhaps you *do* need to talk to someone else."

"No. I need to talk to you." Realizing she sounded as tactless as pasty-faced Reinhardt, Carly scaled back the rancor in her voice. "I don't want to talk to you any more than you want to talk to me. But it's part of my job and part of your job. So let's get on with it."

"Which *one* vehicle are you interested in?"

"You know, you could treat your customers with a little more courtesy."

"Somehow, I'm having trouble viewing you as a genuine customer."

"Well, I *am* a genuine customer." Carly thrust her chin out to make up for her lack of conviction. A non-paying customer was still a customer. "I'm a customer that would appreciate some respect."

"Then maybe you could show me a little respect instead of tossing about catty comments."

"Not catty. Just honest. It's not like we don't have a history."

"Oh, yeah. We have a history, all right."

"Yeah. Quite a history. You stole my husband."

"I didn't steal anything. I merely picked up a few things that weren't being used."

Was the bitch referring to sex? Eddie was the one who was at the office or the health club all the time. If sex bottomed out at the Chevalier house, it was because Eddie was never there.

Carly jerked forward and propped her elbow on the desk. She pointed a finger at Jocelyn. "I guess marriage vows don't mean anything to you? Stupid question. Of course they don't. How long did you shack up with my husband?"

"He wasn't your husband. You always seemed to have trouble with that concept."

"What's that supposed to mean?"

"You wouldn't leave him alone, even when Eduard was living with me. You called him all the time, wanting him to come over to your place."

"We were in the middle of a divorce. There were things we had to discuss. Papers that needed signing. Ten years of sheets that needed splitting."

"Even after the divorce, you clung to him like a tick, sucking the life out of him."

"I don't have to put up with this!" Carly flew to her feet, the back of her knees toppling her chair backwards. She almost flipped her middle finger at Jocelyn but somehow found the self-control to merely storm out of the room. As her foot crossed the threshold, her mind snagged on a picture of the old faithful van, its tailpipe belching blue smoke. The next image was of the Board of Directors, flanking that endless, hard-shined table, their expectant eyes converging on her. More importantly, mixed into the blend of faces were the hundreds of animals that needed to be transported to the vet for their surgeries.

Carly stopped in mid-stride. Yes, she did need to put up with this. She also needed to swallow her pride. Besides, this situation was so stupid, it was almost comical. Neither woman would win this pissing contest. In fact, they had both already lost. They were the women Eddie left behind.

Holding the doorframe for support, she turned and looked at Jocelyn.

She fought to steady her voice. "Look. Let's not get into a cat-fight. We're too old for it. And Mr. Chevalier isn't worth skirmishing over. So let's drop the hissing and spitting and clawing."

Jocelyn shifted her weight. She waited a moment before answering. "You're right." She folded her hands on top of her desk. "Why don't we start over?"

"Okay." Carly wondered how a person accomplished starting over? Perhaps with a neutral topic. "You know, it's funny how a person has preconceived notions. When I came in here, I assumed you'd be a man. In fact, I didn't even realize you worked here." With desperate determination, Carly moved back toward her chair.

"I've been here a long time."

"Really?"

"I grew up here. Jacobson is my maiden name. I broke away from my family when they couldn't dissuade me from getting married at the tender age of nineteen to a stud who rode the rodeo circuit."

"You *were* young. I at least waited until I was twenty to make the leap." Carly righted the overturned chair and sat down.

Jocelyn gave a pinched smile. "I was young and rebellious, but I divorced him two years later, went to college, and crawled back into the fold. Been here ever since."

Jocelyn's phone rang. She excused herself and swiveled her chair so her back was to Carly.

When she turned back, she apologized for the interruption. "It was the nursing home calling about my grandfather."

"Anything serious?"

"Oh, no. They just have to let the family know every time one of their residents falls down."

"So he's okay?"

"He'll never be okay, but this tumble didn't cause any harm."

"Eddie mentioned your grandparents had some health problems."

"Yes, that's true. My grandmother passed away last winter."

"I'm sorry."

"It's been a rough couple of years. Their health failed, and they needed constant medical attention. My mother's an only child. My brother is living somewhere in South America with his head up his ass." Jocelyn gave a dismissive wave of her hand. "Of course, Dad's busy with the dealership. So Grandma and Grandpa's care fell to Mom and me."

"So your grandfather is in a nursing home here in Megalopolis?"

"Yes. Grandma did a good job of taking care of him while she could.

He has macular degeneration and was almost blind when she had her stroke. Fortunately, we were able to find a nursing home that could take both of them. Since Grandma died, Grandpa is determined to send himself to the grave, regardless of what Mom and I do."

"Gosh, it must be difficult for you." Dumbfounded by her archenemy's candidness, Carly felt some of her bottled-up bitterness leak away. Jocelyn's story was a far cry from what Eddie described as "spending a lot of time taking care of her grandparents."

"As I said, it's been a rough couple of years. In more ways than one." Jocelyn nibbled her lower lip. "Would you care for some coffee?"

"No, I'm not a coffee drinker."

"How about hot tea? I keep a pot of hot water handy. I'm afraid I'm addicted."

"You don't happen to have any chamomile, do you?"

"I might."

Jocelyn swiveled her chair to face the credenza behind her and flicked her fingers through the teabags lined up in a white ceramic holder. When she spun back, she was holding a steaming Styrofoam cup.

Carly accepted it gap-mouthed. What was going on here? No one ever had chamomile tea. "I'm surprised at a native Texas drinking hot tea."

"I spent four years in Yankee territory."

"College?"

"Vassar."

Carly missed a beat. "I guess we should get down to business. As I said, I'm the Executive Director of the Zhirnov Springs Humane Society. Actually, I'm just the interim Director." She wondered why she felt compelled to add "interim." Because Jocelyn made her feel insecure with that Vassar comment, that's why. "We're a non-profit organization that relies on donations to achieve our mission."

Jocelyn's forehead wrinkled. "Didn't I hear something about you on the news last night?"

"Yes, you did." Carly pulled the Metro section from her purse and held up Fernando's picture toward Jocelyn. "The truth is, we're struggling to do as much for the community as our limited budget will allow." She described the condition of their van and its many uses. "So, bottom line, I understand the City of Zhirnov Springs just traded in five of its vans for new ones. I came here to ask you to donate one of them to the Humane Society. We'd acknowledge your contribution on our Web site and in our newsletter. And you'd be welcome to put 'Donated by Jacobson Auto' on the vehicle." Winded, Carly brought the Styrofoam cup to her lips.

Jocelyn remained quiet during Carly's pitch and for some time after. "I'd like to help you. I'm an animal lover myself. After Eduard moved out, the house was always empty. When I wasn't at work, I was with my grandparents. I didn't think it was fair for Neal, our little Border collie, to be alone all the time so I asked Eduard to take him. I really miss that little rascal. Far more than I miss Eduard." She looked askance. "I'm sorry. That was uncalled for."

"It's okay. I've had similar thoughts myself."

They both smiled, not just with their mouths but with their eyes.

After years of hating Jocelyn's guts, despising every morsel of her voluptuous body, loathing her very name, and imagining her to be the world's nastiest vixen, here Carly was chatting away with her like...well, maybe not like friends, but at least like business acquaintances. She was floored to find out that beneath Jocelyn's Diane von Furstenberg blouse, Lancôme nail polish, and N.V. Perricone moisturizer, she was just a basic person. A decent, basic person.

"I might be able to help you. Last night's hail wreaked havoc on our inventory. Probably including those vans. If you could live with a few dimples and pockmarks...."

"No problem."

"I'll have to clear this donation with the appropriate managers. Can I reach you at work next week?"

"Yes." This was going so smoothly, Carly considered pushing her luck. "I was wondering, when your body shop puts 'Donated by Jacobson' on the van, might you also consider painting the Humane Society logo as well?" She pointed to the business card on Jocelyn's desk. "On both side panels plus the rear doors? Before our fund-raiser gala next Saturday?"

"You're not at all timid about asking for things."

"Not when it comes to asking for things I believe in." Carly said the words with such conviction, even she believed them.

Jocelyn opened her mouth but required two tries to get out any sound. "Carly, I hope you believe me that it was never my intention to hurt you. Love is blind and love is selfish. I was both. And I'm sorry. I know that doesn't make up for how you suffered, but I wanted you to know that."

Carly looked down at her lap while her thoughts collided with one another. Eventually, she forced herself to meet Jocelyn eye-to-eye. "No, it doesn't make up for the hurt. But it helps to hear you say you're sorry." She gathered her purse and stood. "Thank you for seeing me this morning. I hope to hear from you Monday."

"You will. Goodbye."

"Goodbye." Carly knew she should initiate a handshake, but accepting the extended olive branch had stretched her magnanimity to its limit.

Carly glided above the sizzling pavement as if gravity were a thing of the past. Everything was going indescribably, unbelievably, incredibly well. Yes, indeed. She handled that surprise encounter with remarkable finesse.

Not only was a new roof on its way and possibly a new vehicle for the Humane Society, but she buried the hatchet with The Other Woman. She was seized by the compulsion to sling her arm around a light pole and launch a Fred Astair whorl while simultaneously bursting into a sunshine song. Instead, she indulged herself with an atta-girl thumbs-up, then glanced around to make sure no one saw it.

But besides the elation and cockiness, she also felt chagrined. That's what she got for harboring hate. Jocelyn was just a person, like any other. Not a bad person. Just a person who got caught up in her emotions and the charming gorgeousness of Eduard Chevalier. Yes, what Jocelyn did was wrong, but at least she had the gumption to own up to her moral turpitude. Carly wondered if the situation were reversed, would she have the courage to do the same.

She slid into the car and glanced at the neatly folded sweat suit in the back seat. She definitely needed to return the clothes. And see how the charity fund-raiser was going. And tell Charlie the good news about the van.

She censured herself for getting swept up in the excitement of the moment. Jocelyn said she would look into donating a van. She didn't make any promises. Carly also reminded herself that Charlie kept last evening strictly platonic. Could be he wasn't as interested in her as she was in him. Being just friends would be enough, she tried to delude herself, while her thoughts meandered to how great those gray sweats would go with his charcoal eyes.

She made tracks back to Zhirnov Springs, Jackson Street in particular, in need of a lemonade fix.

**26**

Councilman VanCleave apparently remembered to buy the lemonade this morning because a sign advertising ice cold drinks tempted like a seductress beside the steamy asphalt. Carly pulled up to the curb in front of Claire's house as two men from Zhirnov Springs Public Works carried their lemonade back to the fallen tree limbs they were shoving into the cavernous mouth of a giant shredder.

"How's business?"

"Great!" Allison said.

"It's sooooo hot!" Claire said.

"You'll make a killing." Carly wiped the perspiration from her brow. "I know I could use some lemonade."

"On the rocks or straight up?" Allison asked.

Carly raised an eyebrow. Interesting lingo for an eight-year-old.

"That's what Sonia likes to say."

"Sonia?" Carly asked.

"My friend."

Sonia must be a very worldly third-grader. "I'll have it on the rocks."

Carly leaned over the table. "Just between you and me, what time did you two go to sleep last night?"

She made small talk with the girls while she sipped her lemonade and sent covert glances down the street toward the VanCleave driveway. It was empty. Was the SUV in the garage?

"So, is your Dad home? I want to return his sweat suit." She felt the need to explain, "I had to wear it home. My clothes were still wet."

Allison shook her head. "No, he's not home yet." Carly wilted. "We had breakfast with Sonia. Then he brought me home before they went over to her house to talk some more."

Evidently Sonia was a little older than third grade. "You went to breakfast? Where did you go?"

"Amaya's."

"Un-huh. And then he went over to Sonia's? I thought he said something about showing a house this morning."

Allison's forehead scrunched up. "Showing a house?" She hoisted a shoulder. "Not that I know of. Dad's been reminding me all week we were taking Sonia to breakfast for her birthday."

"Any idea when he'll be home?"

"Him and Sonia," Allison rolled her eyes, "who knows when he'll get home. But you can leave the sweat suit with me."

Carly tried to push past the vertigo that suddenly tilted her world. "Oh. Oh. Okay. Good idea."

As she retrieved the sweat suit from the car, Carly's chest tightened with anger. She had half a mind to toss the garment in the Public Works shredder. Instead, she calmly placed it on the table. "So, does Sonia like her lemonade on the rocks or straight up?"

Allison giggled. "I don't know. I'll have to ask her."

"I like mine straight up," Claire said.

"I like mine on the rocks. Dad likes his—"

"How much do I owe you?" Carly no longer cared what Dad liked.

She conquered her fierce urge to peel away from the curb. However, as she drove past the VanCleave residence, the middle finger she had refrained from bestowing on Jocelyn shot up like a proud soldier. Showing a house this morning, my foot!

Carly figured Sonia must be his girlfriend. It was the most logical explanation, right? Right. Why hadn't he simply told her that he had a breakfast date? Why the big secret? *Him and Sonia, who knows when he'll get home.* Allison's little tidbit of information certainly explained why he kept his distance last night.

Sonia. What kind of name was Sonia? Carly had never known anyone by the name of Sonia. In a space of forty minutes, some cosmic sleight-of-hand shifted Carly's scorn from Jocelyn to a faceless woman named Sonia.

Wait a minute. Carly retraced last evening. Allison mentioned the name Sonia. In what context? The gerbil. Allison got Rocky from Sonia when he was a baby a year ago. That means Charlie's been dating this woman at least that long. Carly snorted. Had he even waited for the grass to grow over Alicia's grave before he started making the rounds? Hey, no point in letting the other side of the bed grow cold.

Carly's hand whacked the steering wheel so hard her head jolted back. She brushed aside the strand of hair that fell over her eyes.

"You know, it's time for a change," she told herself out loud. "It's time for a change in a lot of ways."

She whipped into the parking lot of the Clip N Go.

"Cut it off," she told the stylist. "Cut it all off."

She liked it. The ultra-short wash-&-wear look was more appropriate for an Executive Director than were ponytail scrunchies, bungee bands, and jaw clips. The hairdresser used some softening conditioner that transformed the short locks from the corkscrews of an Airedale to the feathers of a Saluki. Naturally, Carly bought a jar.

She paced the floor while she waited for the insurance adjuster. She needed to divert her annoyance. Otherwise, she'd console herself with a feast of Nestlé chocolate chips straight out of the bag. She called Annalisa and got her answering machine. Rats!

After writing a draft of her short speech for the gala, she logged onto her office e-mail. One of the messages was from Eddie asking if he should keep next Saturday open for "that art thing."

It was 5:30 when the insurance adjuster left. She kicked off her shoes and fell face first on the bed. She had managed to keep Charlie VanCleave out of her mind most of the afternoon, but now thoughts of him smothered her like an Iowa snowdrift.

So he had a girlfriend. That was hardly surprising. He was a good catch. But why hadn't he told her he was dating someone? Of course, she hadn't told him whether or not she was seeing anyone. In fact, wasn't she guilty of alluding to a bogus boyfriend?

Maybe what hurt the most was that she had so misjudged Charlie. He seemed like a genuinely nice guy. Instead, he had lied to her.

But why did he lie? Why had he concocted that story about going to work? Did he know she was attracted to him and wanted to keep her dangling in case the thing with Sonia didn't work out? But they'd been seeing each other at least a year, so that theory didn't hold water. Nor did the fact he was still wearing his wedding ring after dating someone that long.

Was she jumping to a false conclusion? Maybe Sonia wasn't a girl-friend. Maybe she was just the "friend" that Allison called her. But that was neither here nor there. Facts were facts—Charlie's intent to deceive her was unmistakable. And therefore inexcusable. She remembered only too well the pain of uncovering Eddie's tall tales of being at work or the gym when he was really with Jocelyn. The thought of once again opening her heart to someone selling a pack of lies—no thanks.

Charlie VanCleave had been the first man who had truly been able to push aside her thoughts of Eddie. With Charlie, she had been at the verge of looking away from the closed door and seeing the opening one. But it wasn't to be. Not if he was duplicitous.

A commotion whirled under the bed. Yuri was tyrannizing dust bunnies. Carly rolled onto her side and reached an arm over the edge of the mattress. She sweet-talked the cat into joining her on the bed.

"Hey, fella, you're too old to be acting like a kitten. And you're too old to put up with a new man in our lives. So let's forget about Charlie VanCleave, shall we? He obviously has some integrity problems. But what about ol' Eddie Chevalier? Why do you like him so much? Don't you realize how badly he treated us? The better question is, why can't I make a clean break from him?"

She rolled onto her back and put Yuri on her chest. The slow rumble of the cat's motor helped downshift her own agitated emotions.

When it came right down to it, she questioned whether she even wanted to see Eddie again. Did she want to expose herself to his disparaging remarks about her shortcomings? And his stinging bits of humor, like the way he poked fun at her jigsaw puzzle?

Did she really want to participate in his endless array of hobbies? He had expected Jocelyn to abandon her responsibilities in order to dedicate herself full time to trailing along in his shadow. Which was exactly what he had expected Carly to do. And exactly what Carly did do. She became Carly's Catering Service—We Accommodate Your Every Wish, Need, and Expectation (Realistic or Otherwise).

Sure, Eddie was still knock-your-socks-and-your-clothes-off good-looking, but he no longer wore it so well. Or maybe she saw through his shenanigans now. How he'd flash that killer smile. How he'd turn those dimples on and off at will. How he'd move with the languid grace of a cheetah until he was standing just a little too close for comfort.

What about his latest e-mail? Why was he so intent on following up their conversation about the gala? He certainly wasn't that persistent in fixing the boards on the porch. *A hundred-and-fifty bucks a ticket?* he had asked. It was exactly the type of clientele his new law practice could use.

"Your former father," she told Yuri, "is a gold digger."

The low slant of the sun dimmed the bedroom. She moved Yuri aside and turned on the small milk-glass lamp beside her bed. Her cheek rested on the cool pillow.

She had been toying with inviting either Charlie or Eddie to the gala. It was now clear she could ask neither. She'd e-mail Sophia that she would attend the gala alone. The event was still a week away. Maybe Sophia could find someone who wanted the ticket.

At the far end of the house, the refrigerator compressor kicked on. The sound took her back to Charlie's house. She flattened the pillow over her head to block out the images. It had been an enchanting evening, but the party was over.

The hum of the refrigerator brought the newspaper clipping to mind. She went to the kitchen and removed the scrap of paper from under the magnet.

> How many of the loves
> And dreams
> And fears
> Of yesteryears
> Retain their hold
> On me today?

For far too long, she's lived with the repetition of worn-out memories. It was a stale story even she was tired of. Clinging like a security blanket to the hope of a happily-ever-after with Eddie was akin to keeping three-year-old coffee. It was time to throw it away.

Her mind turned the pages of a pretend but vividly stark photo album. Eddie casting a line into the lake. The hollow of Eddie's hand holding a tiny fur ball with the whopping name of Comrade Yuri Andreyevich Zhivago. The billows of Eddie's robe as he walked across the stage to accept his law diploma. Some of the images were of happy events; others weren't. But the pictures themselves were neither good nor bad. They simply *were*.

Eddie might have hurt her, but she's the one who chose to lick her wounds with such crazed ardor they couldn't heal. But her mistakes went further back in time than that. Since the day she met Eddie, she shored up her self-worth with his strength and his joie de vivre. That, far more than a stolen evening with Junior Swenson, had produced disastrous consequences not just for her marriage, but for her self-esteem.

She had turned off the bitterness machine with Jocelyn. Now it was time to make peace with Eddie.

Conciliation with an ex-spouse wasn't a solitary process. It involved two people. In the darkening kitchen, she eyeballed the phone. She'd rather be staked to a fire ant mound than make that call.

She stopped gnawing on the knuckle of her thumb and picked up the dead weight of the receiver.

She couldn't do it. She hung up.

She had to do it. Her finger settled on the first digit of his number. She pressed it, then willed her finger to move to the next six.

His phone rang once. Twice. Saturday night—she hoped he wasn't home. By tomorrow, she will have abandoned this silly idea.

"Hello."

"Hello, Eddie. It's Carly. Do you have a minute?"

"Yeah, sure. In fact, I was going to call you first thing Monday morning."

"Oh?"

"Yeah. But you go first."

Her hands became slick with sweat at the same time her mouth went dry. "I wanted to thank you for offering to go to the gala with me. And I wanted to let you know that it won't be necessary."

"Oh. You're taking someone else?"

The temptation to say "Yes" was almost overpowering, but lying would defeat the whole purpose of her call. "No. I plan to go alone."

"Okay." He sounded unclear as to why she would do such a thing. "But I'd be happy to go with you."

"There's no need. It's part of my job, so most of the evening will be spent working." She was being both honest and considerate of his feelings.

"Okay." He seemed confused but not brokenhearted.

"Eddie?"

"Yeah?"

"I also wanted to apologize for anything and everything I might have done that contributed to the collapse of our marriage."

"Huh?"

God, Eddie, please don't make me repeat this too many times. "I'm truly sorry for anything I did that damaged our relationship, whether they were things I intentionally did or things I don't even realize I did."

"Why are you bringing this up now?"

"Because I never told you before."

The line went dead for several moments. "You been drinking?"

"No drinking. Just thinking," she said, happy the poetic lyrics gave her reason to lighten her tone.

Another pause. Another "Okay." Another pause. "What's this about?"

"It's not about anything except that I've always unjustly blamed you. Look, I don't mean for this to be an earth-shaking conversation. I simply wanted to tell you that I'm sorry for any of my shortfalls or misbehavior or unrealistic expectations that contributed to the failure of our marriage."

"I'm sorry, too, that things didn't work out."

"You said you were going to call me Monday?"

"Right. You'll never guess what happened this morning."

"What?"

"A client came to see me about her deceased mother's will. The mother had spent her final days at the Legacy Care Center. Apparently one of your employees took dogs there to visit. The visits meant so much to the old woman, she included the Humane Society in her will."

"You're kidding!"

"To the tune of $40,000."

"Not really!"

"Really. She put one stipulation on the money. It has to be put in an account where it can earn income. The Humane Society is free to use whatever income is generated, but the principle can't be touched."

"Holy cow! I can't believe it!"

"Believe it. You'll receive the check as soon as the will is probated."

"Eddie, thanks so much!"

"Don't thank me. I had nothing to do with it."

"Well, okay. Thanks, ummm, for talking to me."

When they said good-bye, her voice was filled with finality; his was crammed with question marks.

She covered her eyes with clenched fists. That call had been so hard to make. But it felt so good having done it.

And the news about the $40,000! She crossed her arms, grabbed hold of her shoulders, and squeezed. Finally there was seed money to start an endowment fund.

Thank you, Penny. It will be your legacy.

The sun had turned an inviting amber. She picked up the newspaper clipping and headed to the front porch swing. She brushed the broken twigs and rain-plastered leaves from the slats.

With one bare foot curled under her, she used the other one to set the swing in motion. The day was cooling down, and the heat radiating off the sun-warmed planks felt good on the ball of her foot. And wouldn't you know, floating from the neighbor's yard was the heady fragrance of honeysuckle.

She rested her temple against the swing's chain. Her heart was as heavy as if she had gone through two deaths—Penny's and the final throes of her marriage.

After years of living in suspended disequilibrium, she was at last free of Eddie. She might always love him, but she was no longer in love with him. Nor was she in lust with him. While holding onto the old passions with the tenacious grip of a terrier, she had run through the whole spectrum—shock, hurt, anger, grief, bitterness, insecurity, loneliness. Today when she dipped into the caldron of emotions associated with Eduard Chevalier, she finally came up empty-handed.

So now she had neither Eddie nor Charlie. And she didn't really have a job. She couldn't go back to her old position when Hugh returned. She could never again be "one of the staff." She'd have to move on to something else somewhere else.

Carly looked at the hand she had been dealt—no husband, no boyfriend, no kids, no career. But tucked in between all the loser cards was her trump card. Herself. In the end, she reasoned, wasn't that all anyone had? Spouses, lovers, family, friends—at some time or other, they wander away, die, or let you down. When all is said and done, there's only one person you can rely on.

Dad-blame it!—as techno-cowboy Sonny would say—she'd find a way to forge a life for herself that rose above today's crumpled illusions. No longer would her future be anchored in the past. For the first time in her life, she'd actually chart a course and follow it.

This evening, before the unruliness of daily life interrupted her, she'd phone her parents to decide on a date to visit. Then she'd book a flight. Her parent's subtle journey toward old age, brought to the forefront by her father's cataract surgery, hung like a bludgeon over her head, reminding her that she had better return some of their love before it was too late.

A lightening bug winked from among the branches of the fig tree. Amethyst shadows fell on the old-fashioned daylilies, oxallis, and Mexican petunias. The cuckoo called out the hour.

She pried her leg from under her and picked up the newspaper clipping from the slats. As she walked to the door, she glanced at the backside of the page. There it was, the new ending for her gala speech.

28

Diamonds flashed.

Silk stockings shimmered.

Eyeshadowed lids fluttered like iridescent butterflies.

Necklaces draped the pendulous breasts of women who had long ago forgotten the natural color of their soufflé hair.

Carly sipped her diet cola as she walked through a mingling crowd that smelled of powder, perfume, and booze. She eavesdropped on the rousing repartee of "Love that gorgeous dress!" and "You look fantastic!" She didn't recognize most of the people at the gala. However, those women she did know all told her they absolutely adored her hair.

Unabashed singing rose above the chatter. Mary Louise loved nothing more than being the epicenter of attention, meaning he was in his glory tonight. Egged on by his admirer's accolades, he went hog wild with his entire repertoire of sunshine songs.

Carly figured A.A. was struggling to keep her sanity at her booksigning while being bombarded with the recurring medley of tunes. The same went for the owner of a local bookstore, who set up a table to sell A.A.'s new book as well as an anthology of art books. Ten percent of the sales would be donated to the Humane Society.

Carly wasn't the only one with a new hairdo. Darrell's scalp was as bald as a plucked Pocahontas turkey. Plus his wispy goatee was a fragment of its former self, pruned to a narrow frond centered below his lower lip. And—Carly blinked her disbelieving eyes—he was wearing a tuxedo.

Thanks to logistical arrangements, there was no conflict between Mary Louise's "You Are My Sunshine," and Darrell's "God Save the Tsar." Mary Louise was relegated to the foyer due to health department regulations about commingling animals and food. Darrell, meanwhile, plucked his guitar in the banquet room atop a stool. He shared the small stage with the shrouded sketch of A.A.'s future mural.

The glimmering, scented crowd began to migrate to their seats. Carly found Sophia's table-for-ten at the front of the banquet room directly below the on-stage podium. Darrell put his guitar in its case and slipped onto the burgundy chair next to her.

She laid a hand on his arm. "Great job! I'd tell you that you're good enough to play professionally, but I don't want you to leave the Humane Society."

Darrell blushed to where the roots of his hair should be.

On Carly's other side were Alan and Hugh with their wives. Hugh's eyelids still sagged like a Basset hound's, but at least the cadaverous hollows of his cheeks had filled in. His wife required help walking and her speech was slow and difficult to understand, but her recovery was progressing steadily.

Across the round table was a couple Carly didn't know. Sophia took her seat, leaving three chairs tilted forward waiting for occupants.

Just as Alan rose to assume his role as master of ceremonies, an ankle-length teal caftan signaled the arrival of A.A. from her booksigning. Her long braid was coiled into a chignon.

Directly behind A.A. was Ruby. Carly frowned. It wasn't like Ruby not to mention that she'd be at the gala. While A.A. maneuvered through the labyrinth of tables with the elegance of Mikhail Baryshnikov, Ruby moved with the grace of a Russian tank. Despite her oxen-like bearing, Ruby looked pretty in her satiny pants suit. Her face wore a hint of blush, a swipe of mascara, and a touch of lip-gloss.

A.A. took one of the vacant chairs at Sophia's table and—Carly's mouth fell open—Ruby took the adjacent seat. The *immediately adjacent* seat. And moved the seat *closer* to A.A. Carly watched as they lowered their hands beneath the table. Shoulders separated by no more than the width of Darrell's new goatee, they had to be holding hands beneath the table. Carly contemplated dropping her napkin so she could peek under table. Instead, she told herself to grow up.

Alan welcomed the attendees and asked his fellow Board members to stand so he could introduce them. Right in the middle of pasty-faced Reinhardt's introduction, Charlie VanCleave slid into the vacant chair next to Sophia.

Carly stole a peek at him. He looked terrific in a tux, which was hardly surprising. With steadied indifference, she looked back at Alan. Well, well, well. Isn't this the evening for surprises? First Darrell wears a tuxedo. Then Ruby finally takes Juan Pablo's advice. Then Councilman VanCleave shows up.

Out of the corner of her eye, Carly saw Charlie whisper in Sophia's ear, perhaps an apology for being late. Sophia smiled and patted his hand that lay next to hers on the table. Everyone was playing their roles. Sophia was greasing the skids with the politician, and the politician was looking for votes among the well-heeled.

Carly looked around the room to find Sonny Palmer, whom Alan was introducing. Sonny turned one direction, then the other, as he gave the crowd a howdy wave. Yokes spread like wings across the front and back of his rumpled western suit jacket. Carly contemplated the lengths one had to go to in order to wrinkle polyester.

Charlie caught her eye and smiled. As she returned the gesture, she wondered if he thought chrome-dome Darrell was her date.

Alan moved along with the introductions. "Next, I'd like to ask Mr. Hugh Sherman, the Executive Director for the Zhirnov Springs Humane Society, to come to the podium."

Hugh stepped up to the microphone and cleared his throat.

"This is a poignant evening for me as I look out at the faces of the many friends and colleagues I have known over the past eleven years at the Zhirnov Springs Humane Society. It's been an incredibly meaningful period of my life. However, my personal life has changed, and I've had to adjust my priorities. It was with mixed emotions that I submitted my resignation this week."

A rumble coursed through the audience. Alan presented Hugh with a plaque and an oratory of kind words. But Carly heard little of it. Dazed by Hugh's announcement, she stood with the rest of the audience in a standing ovation.

"Next," Alan continued, "I'd like you to meet the person who does more behind-the-scenes work than any of us, Ms. Carly Shannon, who has been filling Hugh Sherman's shoes while he's been on leave. Carly will tell us about some recent major contributions to the Humane Society."

Carly stumbled up to the podium, unable to calm her tidal waves of astonishment and confusion over Hugh's announcement.

She nodded at her soon-to-be ex-boss. "First, I'd like to second everything Alan Drake said about you, Hugh. You've been more than a terrific boss. You've been a great mentor. Thank you.

"I'd like to continue the introductions by asking two of our Humane Society employees to stand up. Ms. Ruby Wesolowski is our Operations Manager."

Ruby's eyes almost popped out of her head in surprise. She rose and did a quick about-face.

"Also with us tonight is Mr. Darrell Darnell. Although his official title is Animal Caretaker, tonight his role is our virtuoso for the classical guitar."

♪ *One leaf is sunshine, the second is rain.* ♪

This time, it was Carly's eyes that bulged. She shot a *Help me!* look at Ruby. Laughter rippled through the room as Ruby careened between the tables and into the foyer to cover the birdcage.

"Mr. Darnell isn't the only musician with us tonight. The vocalist is our shelter mascot, Mary Louise, who can't stand playing second fiddle."

Flustered by Hugh's disclosure and Mary Louise's shameless performance, Carly scanned her notes while waiting for the audience's titter to die down.

"There are a couple of businesses who deserve special mention tonight. First, you may have noticed the van parked outside the main door. The vehicle was donated by Jacobson Autoplex. We can't thank them enough for their very generous and very much appreciated contribution. Our previous van was just about to give up the ghost. A heartfelt thanks goes to Walt Zimmerman of Walt's Service and Repair. Over the years, Walt went far beyond the call of duty to use his many talents to keep the old van running as long as possible. On the back of your programs are the business sponsors who contributed either cash or donations-in-kind for tonight's gala. Please return their kindness by patronizing their businesses."

Carly looked down at her notes and took in a long, slow breath.

"It requires staff, volunteers, businesses, and patrons such as yourselves to keep the doors of any humane society open. From the bottom of my heart, I thank each of you who contributed either time or money or adopted an animal to give it a second chance at life.

"There are advantages to cleaning cat cages for a living. You get to read the newspaper while you're on-the-clock." She held up a copy of the *Zhirnov Springs Courier* and received a smattering of chuckles.

"I recently came upon something Paul Harvey wrote several years ago." She cleared her throat.

> Civilized nations do not sanction cruelty to animals; they just look the other way and let it happen. Cruelty to animals remains a blind spot for most Americans. We'd see and object to it on television, but we allow it in real life. Because in real life, the dying is usually sufficiently distant so that we can't hear the crying.

"Thank you for hearing and answering those cries."

As she nodded to Alan that she was finished, the dining room rang with applause.

"Far out!" Darrell said as she slid into her seat, a dribble of pickled purple cabbage clinging to his new, abbreviated goatee.

The banquet continued with Sophia and A.A. unveiling the miniature representation of the mural of animals and people that would be painted on the west wall of the shelter. After announcing the successful bidder for the oil painting, Sophia entered her closing statements.

"Tragically, I see the number of animals needing our help rise every year. I see our cruelty investigator answering more and more calls. I witness our staff pull yet another litter of kittens from a dumpster. I watch this organization labor to do as much as possible on a budget that is grossly inadequate. Sometimes I look at the endless tasks before us and I wonder where we will find the fortitude to keep going. Those of you who know me, know that I can't tell a basketball from a beach ball, but my nephew shared a quote with me from Michael Jordan. And I'd like to share it with you."

Sophia adjusted her turquoise glasses.

> I've missed more than 9,000 shots in my career. I've lost more than 300 games. Twenty-six times I've been trusted to take the game-winning shot and missed. I've failed over and over and over again in my life… And that is why I succeed.

She scanned the audience. "We may not be able to right every wrong, but we will to do all that we can. We will continue to reunite lost pets with their owners. We will continue educating our government officials on their role in creating a humane community. We will continue finding homes for the excess dogs and cats that our society has allowed to be born. And those for which we can't find homes, our staff will put them to sleep with compassion and tears. We won't be able to solve this horrendous problem in our lifetimes, but to that mother cat and kittens that we brought in from the rainstorm, we made a difference. To that starving horse that is now grazing in a green pasture, we made a difference. To that family that adopted a friend for life, we made a difference."

Carly joined the audience in applause. Over the past few months, she learned not only to overlook Sophia's excesses, but to enjoy them. The tremendous respect she had gained for the woman doubled tonight.

She folded her hands atop the white linen napkin in her lap and thought about the little blonde girl at the Pet Expo and her cat she talked her mother into spaying.

Yes, Carly-girl, she silently told herself. You certainly won't cure all of society's ills, but even you have made a difference.

She was both humbled and proud to be part of an organization that was accomplishing so much good. She knew that she had found her life's work. Forever, she would give her best to animal welfare. And she would always hold herself responsible for ensuring that what happened to Penny Downing never happened again.

As the waiters doled out the blueberry cheesecake, Ruby rose. Carly followed her into the restroom.

"What was it you said to me a couple of weeks ago? '*Maybe* I'll go to New York for my vacation this year.'" Carly winked at the Operations Manager. She had never before seen Ruby blush. "You look very happy."

"I am. I feel like I'm starting my life over."

"I know the feeling."

Carly gave the staunch Operations Manager a hug. It was a little like putting her arms around a boxer's heavy bag, but Ruby reciprocated with an earnest, if rigid, squeeze.

"Are you going to tell Juan Pablo?" Carly asked.

"I'm sure the sorry-ass will find out on his own some way or other."

As Carly left the restroom, she spotted Alan. She clutched at the new resolve she found that sultry Saturday evening a week ago. She gritted her teeth and tapped his shoulder.

"Can I speak with you a moment?" she asked.

"Of course."

She motioned him to the edge of the foyer. "Needless to say, I was quite surprised by Hugh's announcement tonight."

"Carly, I'm sorry I wasn't able to tell you about Hugh before tonight. But he wanted to make the announcement himself. It was important to him."

"I…" she struggled to push out the words, "I want you to know that I would like to be considered as his replacement on a permanent basis."

He put a hand on her shoulder. "Trust me. The Board has looked very favorably on your performance over the past six months. I suspect they'll want to advertise for the position, but you stand an excellent chance. I think the Board has more confidence in you than you have in yourself."

"But I figured when Penny…."

"I explained to the Board that you and I had been in the process of trying to help her. No one said they hold you personally responsible."

"So you'll put a good word in for me with the other Board members?"

"Of course."

"Thanks. You know what I said about Hugh being a great mentor? The same goes for you."

Carly walked to Mary Louise's cage and slipped off the cover for an after-dinner serenade. When she turned around, she saw Charlie talking with a man and woman she didn't know.

Carly's chest tightened. She hadn't heard from him since the night of the storm, a full week ago. No phone calls, no e-mails.

She asked herself what if circumstances were different. What if she wasn't trying to overcome her teenage crush on him? How would she act? She'd walk up and thank him for the invaluable lead on the new van. She prodded herself into being a big girl and going over to him. Unless she let him, he couldn't hurt her. Or make her angry. Or tug at her at her emotions.

Carly moved her legs in his direction. She stopped a few yards to one side of him. His raised forefinger indicated he'd be with her in a minute.

She bided her time by glancing around the room at the 11" by 17" black and white photographs mounted on easels. The photos were Ruby's idea, and Carly let her run with it. Like all black and white pictures, they were largely gray—gray images of small, great things.

Monica rubbing cheeks with one of the kid goats.

Father Donahoe blessing the animals.

Bullzy and Sophia in their Mutt Strut outfits beside the City Springs.

Darrell bathing a cat.

Juan Pablo with an emaciated mare and her foal.

Penny and Hailey at the Legacy Care Center.

Penny. Penny. Carly fought the familiar tingle in the back of her nose.

She turned back toward Charlie, who was still in earnest listening mode. She shifted from foot to foot, clenching and unclenching her hands as she stood alone in a beehive of hobnobbing. Three times she started to walk away. Only by sheer force of will was she able to keep her feet firmly planted. Finally another couple walked up to the threesome, and Charlie extricated himself.

"Hi! I wasn't expecting you to be here." Her mouth felt like it was full of Mary Louise's feathers.

"Sophia called me at the last minute and said she had an extra ticket."

"Oh, really?" Carly averted her eyes. Golly gee, where in the world had Sophia gotten an extra ticket?

"I was hoping to see you here," he said.

Against her will, her heart leaped like a fish breaking the surface of the water and soaring through the sunlight.

"I wanted to return your flashlight. You left it last weekend. It's in my car."

"My flashlight?" The fish belly flopped back into the water with a dull *thwnk*. "Thanks. I didn't realize I had left it."

"Also, I wanted to let you know that the first draft of the City's budget has an increase in the Humane Society's contract."

"Hey, that's great news!"

"Now's when you need to meet with the City Manager to go over contract revisions while there's still time to make adjustments."

"Thanks for the suggestion. I'll follow up on it." The thought sprinted through her mind that she should request extra money to hire a full-time humane educator to visit classrooms. The City should be responsive. Wasn't "Failure to provide humane education to school children" one of the Advocates's top ten complaints?

Sophia glided up in a gold lamé gown followed by a vaporous cloud of Chanel No. 5. "It's a masterpiece of a gala, don't you agree?" She slipped an arm through Charlie's. "Thank you, by the way, for the Malcolm Jordan quote."

Charlie laughed. "It's *Michael* Jordan."

Something didn't compute properly for Carly. "I'm confused. You said you got the quote from your nephew."

"I'm tickled pink that someone actually listened to me! It was a small fib to make the talk go smoother. Charlie's not technically my nephew, but he *is* a cousin four or five times removed."

"Oh." Carly shot him a thanks-for-telling-me look.

He gave the tip of his nose a guilty brush with the joint of his bent index finger. He diverted the conversation by lowering his head and his voice toward Sophia. "Just between us three, how much did the painting sell for?"

The gala coordinator fingered the ropes of pearls around her neck as she whispered, "Fifty-five hundred and thirty dollars."

"No kidding!" Carly and Charlie both howled.

As the artist's godmother, Sophia looked a tad miffed that they were both so shocked. "A.A.'s oils are known around the world. That painting is worth every penny."

"You're right, Sonia. Every penny and more," Charlie agreed.

"Hold on a minute." Carly knitted her eyebrows and thrust her neck toward Charlie. "What did you just call her?"

"Oh, that." He looked at Sophia. "Do you want to explain?"

"To make a short story long, Charlie's parents were very good friends with my husband and me. As I said, we are cousins of some sort. Because Leo and I had only one child and she died as an infant, we grew very close to Charlie and his siblings. So that's why I view Charlie as a nephew." Sophia rested her steel blue head on his shoulder.

"Remember Rocky?" Charlie asked Carly.

"The gerbil?"

"Did Allison tell you his real name? Rocket J. Squirrel. Do you know why?"

"No, but I assume you'll tell me."

Sophia took over the story. "You'd put two and two together if we gave you a minute, but let me give you a clue. Bullwinkle J. Moose."

"Rocket J. Squirrel? Bullwinkle J. Moose?" The light came on. "Bullzy!"

Sophia removed her arm from Charlie's and put a hand flat against each of her rouged cheeks. "Hokey smoke! She got it!"

"Sophia got Bullzy about the same time she gave Allison the gerbil," Charlie said. "Which was also about the time Allison happened to catch an old rerun of *Rocky and His Friends.*"

"So Allison named both Rocky and Bullzy." But Carly's question still hadn't been unanswered. "But you called her 'Sonia.'"

Sophia explained, "Russians are fond of giving people what's known as diminutive names. They're like nicknames used only by close friends and family members. Certainly you've seen *Dr. Zhivago*?"

Carly swallowed. "Yes. Several times."

"Lara is the diminutive of Larisa. Lara calls her daughter Katya, which is the diminutive of Ekaterina."

Carly tapped her finger against her temple. "So the diminutive of Sophia is, obviously, Sonia." She shut her eyes and gave a single nod of her head. "Sonia." She slid her eyelids apart, tipped her head back, and soundlessly mouthed "Sonia" at the chandelier.

"Right. Sonia," Charlie said, baffled by her obsessive repetitions.

Lady Stetson breezed past, wearing her weight in costume jewelry. She hoisted a wineglass at Carly. "Love your little black dress! And your hair!"

"Your hair does look nice," Charlie said.

Heat crept up Carly's neck and bore straight toward her cheeks. She stammered out a thank-you, wishing she could shake loose of the sweet-sixteen effect Charlie had on her.

The foyer filled with an obnoxious but on-target impersonation of Stevie Wonder.

♫ *You are the sunshine of my life* ♫

"I guess I'd better take that overbearing bird back to the shelter."

"You're leaving?" he asked.

Carly looked around the room. "My cheeks are getting a charley horse from so much smiling. Plus I've had enough empty flattery for one night."

"I'll help you carry the cage to the car. And return your flashlight."

"Not the car. The *van*," she corrected him. "The used-but-new-to-me *van*." She turned to Sophia. "Charlie was the one who put me on the trail that led to Jacobson's."

"He's handy to have around." Sophia stroked his arm like she was petting a horse's neck. "That's why I've kept him by my side for thirty-plus years. By the way," she looked up at Charlie, "have you heard anything on that lake property?"

"Not yet. I'll give the realtor a call on Monday."

*I have an early appointment to show a house.* "I don't mean to be nosey, but you're buying some lake property?" Carly asked.

"Yes, Charlie's finally found a little getaway cottage for me. I plan to take up waterskiing."

"Waterskiing?" At her age? Carly couldn't help but question. Maybe she's hooked up with Eddie. Hey, nothing would surprise her tonight.

Sophia's faded eyes came alive with a young woman's fervor. "Not really, but maybe sailboating, if Bullzy likes it. I know people think I'm a loony old bat, but when some folks get my age, they're content with gray. Gray hair. Gray thoughts. A grim, gray existence. I don't want my life to be gray. I want it filled with color and vibrancy until the day I die."

Carly reached out and squeezed Sophia's hand. "I am so glad I got to know you over the past six months."

Sophia smiled warmly, then her face lit up. "Now that Hugh's not coming back, we need to feminize your office. At least paint the walls. Perhaps a blush?" A brainstorm hit her. "No! A pastel green, to signify new life, vitality, hope. Perhaps celery with a touch of cream so it's not overpowering." Sophia paused and would have wrinkled her forehead had it not been Botoxed. "But that would clash with your pumpkin chairs. I have to say—I never understood why you like those chairs."

Carly tried to put her mouth in gear, but it just wouldn't go.

Sophia wandered off to talk to some of her wealthy friends. Carly and Charlie walked to Mary Louise's cage, her head spinning like Sophia's color chart. The hues were all blurring together. Ruby and A.A. were lovers. Sophia was Sonia. And not only was Hugh not returning to the Humane Society, but Alan and Sonia-Sophia thought Carly had a chance at getting his job. What an un-be-leev-a-bul evening.

After she picked up the cloth cover for the birdcage, she turned and looked Charlie full square in the eyes. "You told me you had a contact at the Humane Society, but why didn't you tell me it was Sophia?"

"I confess. I'm guilty of misleading you. Twice you mentioned that you thought she was flaky. I guess I just didn't want to admit to you that she and I are closer than most family members."

"It's true. She's as odd as sleet in July, but I didn't mean she's flaky. She's probably done more for the Humane Society than any other Board member. In fact, I kinda view her as a role model." She shook out the blanket. "Please don't misunderstand me. I never meant that I thought Sophia was—"

Mary Louise yodeled ♫ *Well I love a rainy night. I love a rainy night.* ♫

"Mary Louise!" Carly shrieked louder than the bird.

Mary Louise jerked back his head and scrutinized the hysterical woman. He shook out his feathers and started over. ♫ *Well I love a rainy night. I love a rainy night.* ♫

"Enough!" She flung the cover over the cage. Her cheeks radiated heat like a furnace. She turned to Charlie. "He can really be an obnoxious bird. If you grab that side of the cage, I'll carry this side."

His gray eyes were full of mirth. "I like that song. Mary Louise is right. Rainy nights can be fun."

She turned her head so he couldn't see her rolling eyes. Wasn't that exactly what she had told the parrot?

"Did you say Mary Louise is a *he*?" Charlie asked.

Anxious to leave the topic of rainy nights, Carly explained why the parrot had a gender identity problem. Mary Louise, who had been having a field day with his fans in the foyer, muttered his discontent the whole time he was being carried into the warm June evening.

They walked up to a white van parked by the Country Club's main door.

"I hope you didn't view what I said earlier as 'empty flattery.' You do look very nice tonight," Charlie said as they slid the cage into the back of the van, followed by a hinged sandwich sign lettered with, "Donated by Jacobson Autoplex."

She closed the door. "You do, too. Except your underwear is exposed."

Panic crossed his face for a split moment before half of his mouth curled in a lopsided grin. He closed the other door and extended his arm to lean on the Zhirnov Springs Humane Society logo.

"I don't suppose you want to walk in those heels to the far end of the parking lot to retrieve your flashlight."

"That's right. Tardy people don't find parking places close to the door."

"Some of us have jobs that involve work, not just partying at galas."

"I'm glad Sophia had an extra ticket for you. Hope you weren't too bored."

"Not at all. Over the past few months, I've learned to appreciate why Sonia, er Sophia, is so dedicated to this organization." He looked toward the moonbeams shimmering off the swimming pool. "The truth is," his eyes reluctantly came back to hers, "the truth is, I came tonight to see if you brought a date."

Carly let her gaped mouth speak for her.

"A couple of things you've said led me to think you were seeing someone."

"As in a man?"

"As in a man."

"No, I'm not seeing a man." She thought of Ruby and A.A. "Or a woman, for that matter." She gave a wry smile and looked down as the toe of her shoe pushed loose pebbles around the pavement. "The ironic thing is, a couple of things Allison said made me think that you might be seeing someone. Someone named Sonia."

His mouth hung open until he threw his head back and laughed at the stars. When his eyes returned to her, he said, "With all of today's phones, cell phones, e-mail, wireless Internet, you and I are pretty abysmal communicators, aren't we?"

Take a chance, she goaded herself. Nothing ventured, nothing gained. "If you and I are such abysmal communicators, why do we get along so well?"

Charlie stopped leaning on the van and looked up at the sky again. He pulled his lips into his mouth and inhaled. When his mossy eyes looked back down, he gave a nervous laugh but a beautiful smile. "Look, I'm not very good…. This wasn't so difficult when I was seventeen."

Her world turned topsy-turvy. "Neither was running a mile."

"Point well made." His mouth worked to get the next words out. "You see, you're the first woman who's been in my house since Alicia died. I mean, besides Sophia or family or a neighbor."

Carly's legs felt as sturdy as gummy bears. Take it easy, she warned herself. Take it slow and easy. Wherever this road might be going, you don't have to travel it in overdrive.

"Allison has been twisting my arm to take her and Claire to San Antonio. We're planning on the zoo, followed by dinner on the Riverwalk. We're hoping, I'm hoping, you'll make it a foursome."

Postcard images floated through her mind. Strolling with him through the shadows of the reptile house. Standing shoulder-to-shoulder as they watched the monkeys' antics. Followed by dinner at a dimly lit Mexican cafe beside the San Antonio River.

"I could use some adult company. It would be just a day-trip," he said as if his request needed clarification. "Perhaps next Sunday."

More images. Allison and Claire asleep in the back seat on the return drive. Quiet conversation in the dark front seat.

"I'd really-truly love to." She paused just long enough for the corners of his lips to curve upward. "But," she swiveled back and forth like a first grader trying to decide between a giant hot fudge sundae and plateful of freshly baked chocolate chip cookies, "that means I'll have to put off painting that porch *yet again*."

"You haven't painted it yet?" He tsk-tsked her.

"Those boards never got replaced. My friend, who I thought would help me, has moved on to other things. I guess he and I have both moved on."

# Epilogue

Leaning on her cane, Nola Bethke moved one step at a time from the dining room to the common area of the Legacy Care Assisted Living Center. She used her arms to lower herself into an overstuffed chair near the fireplace where she could warm her bones. The little calico stretched from where she had been napping on the Christmas tree skirt and leapt onto Mrs. Bethke's lap. Her gnarled hands stroked the ball of fur while she waited for Carly and her nice friend Charlie to arrive. She closed her eyes and allowed herself to remember a glider beneath a pecan tree and little Persimmon, just a hair bigger than a breadbox, lying under it.

## About the author & Hailey

Dr. Jane Caryl Mahlow was a teenager when she first volunteered for a humane society. She holds a Doctor of Veterinary Medicine and a Master's degree in Veterinary Public Health.

Home for Dr. Mahlow in a 100-year-old Texas farmhouse with an ever-expanding assortment of ducks, geese, chickens, goats, cattle, cats, and dogs, one of whom is Hailey. Just like the fictional Hailey of *Hiss, Whine & Start Over*, she was a shelter dog passed over by potential adopters because she was too big, too furry, too old, and too un-purebred. Always a softie for the underdog, Dr. Mahlow adopted her and brought her home during a hailstorm.

*Hiss, Whine & Start Over* was penned with two purposes in mind, both expressions of the heart. First, the book was written in honor of animal care and control employees and volunteers in order that their story be told. Second, perhaps the tale will instill in the public an understanding of its obligation to curtail pet overpopulation and the mistreatment of the animals mankind has domesticated.

Please visit the book's website for:
◊   information on Dr. Mahlow's motivational presentations on animal sheltering and pet overpopulation.
◊   details on how your book order can qualify for a volume discount or result in a donation to the animal welfare organization of your choice.
◊   links to Darrell's T-shirts —"No-Balls" & "Texas. It's their state too."
◊   discussion questions for reading groups.
◊   an update on Dr. Mahlow's current novel-in-progress.

**www.hisswhine.com**